Turning August

Unsung Heroes of the German Resistance

Shelia Watson

Tidal Creek Press
A Division of Tidal Creek Productions LLC
Charleston, South Carolina

TIDAL CREEK PRESS
A Division of Tidal Creek Productions LLC
PO Box 80983
Charleston, SC 29416
www.TidalCreekProductions.com
www.TidalCreekPress.com

First Edition
ISBN: 978-0-578-63545-3 (print)
ISBN: 978-0-578-63546-0 (ebook)

Second Edition
ISBN: 978-0-9766373-8-7 (print)
ISBN: 978-0-9766373-9-4 (ebook)

For information about the author and other published works by the author, visit:
www.TidalCreekProductions.com
www.TidalCreekPress.com

Acknowledgment

This is a work of historical fiction. The background and the events surrounding the story, however, are real.

Some of the characters are fictitious or composites of those who were there; others are real people whose actions and words have been widely documented. In both cases, I have presented them as I have come to know them through a dedicated study of the times in which they lived. It is my privilege to let them speak again in this story.

As many authors do with works of historical fiction, I have taken some literary license with a few elements of the story—specific timing of various events, for instance—but in the end, the core truth of this story remains:

> *The light shines in the darkness, and the*
> *darkness can never extinguish it.*
> *(John 1:5, NLT)*

Dedication

To the brilliant lights of my life:
Alexis
Bishop
Elliott
Nathan
Luke
Ravi
Kairi

I pray that your lives are
fruitful, joy-filled, and spirited—
and ever free from the struggles
the Resistance encountered.

And to Tony,
my constant beacon of all that is good.

Part 1

*We must be ready to allow ourselves to
be interrupted by God.*
                    ~ Dietrich Bonhoeffer

Chapter One

THE SERENE GERMANY COUNTRYSIDE HELD SECRETS that could deceive almost anyone, and for many years, they did. For quite some time after the catalyst events of the 1930s, the secrets were held tight enough for massive betrayal.

In June of 1937, the deception was still in place for most of the population. A golden hue stretched out across the pristine backdrop, targeting fragments of the landscape—a field here, a river there, houses and buildings and bridges—all drawn together in a portrait of tranquility.

Farther along, cars and machinery dotted the rural areas. The occasional horse and wagon trod a dirt road. In the more populated areas, streets and sidewalks were paved. Smoke meandered from brick chimneys atop the factories: a mark of industry, a testament to trade and commerce.

The summer breeze was idyllic, the air heavy with the promise of plenty, all the time in the world to breathe in warmth and ease. It was Sunday, a day to relax, to enjoy the bounty of the season, to live free and give thanks.

It was all a sham.

The Nazi banners marred the building fascia. The

swastika fluttered across the morning sky and chilled the air. Harmony, if felt at all, carried an undercurrent of dread.

Cruelty was in abundance, though for a brief moment it subsisted in the crevices, kept alive by the dark minds who were rising to prominence.

Nineteen years ago, World War I ended.

Sixteen years ago, Hitler became leader of the National Socialist Party.

Four years ago, Hitler became Chancellor and a year later Fuhrer of Germany.

Two years ago, the Nuremberg Race Laws stripped German Jews of their rights.

One year ago, the Gestapo was placed above the law.

Today, a pastor would preach for the last time in the Third Reich.

For many, his arrest would be the last straw.

The toll of carillon bells ushered in any who were willing to listen. The sermon echoed beyond the ancient stone.

And the Resistance found its footing.

~ ~ ~

St. Ann's Church in Dahlem, a suburb of Berlin, was packed. Men, women, and children crowded together as a unit. Row after row of neighbors huddled for enlightenment and comfort.

In the pulpit, Pastor Martin Niemoller held their attention. A gaunt, slight man at first appearance, his clerical vestments added weight and strength, but the stole around his neck—an ancient symbol of being yoked with Christ—reminded him that any strength he felt was not his own. With Hitler and his gang of thugs in charge, he found himself needing the reminder more and more.

The church door creaked open and closed with a bang. Heads swiveled around and saw the boots, uniform, insignia. The congregants tensed up, averted their eyes, and turned to the front.

The Gestapo agent stood in the aisle, rigid and arrogant. He ignored the pews and stared at the man in the pulpit.

Niemoller's hands started to shake. *I'm forty-five. I'm too old for this.* Then the absurdity of thinking that there was a proper age for persecution washed over him. He steadied his hands and continued.

"We have no more thought of using our own powers to escape the arm of authorities than had the Apostles of old," he said. He locked eyes with the Gestapo agent and mustered a stronger voice. "No more are we ready to keep silent at man's behest when God commands us to speak."

The agent glared at him, drew up to full height, and waited for the next words.

Niemoller took a deep breath. It was a moment of judgment, not from the agent before him, but his own conscience. *Take up your cross and follow.* He knew the command well. He stole a glance back at the altar, girded himself, and turned back to his fate.

"For it is—and must remain—the case," he said, his words slow and emphatic, "that we must obey God rather than man."

The agent whirled around, flung open the doors, and rushed out.

For a moment Niemoller stood still and imagined the activity outside the church. *First a phone call to headquarters. The conversation would be brief: a report of my sermon and the command to seize me. They'll be back, no question of that. Dear God, let me get through the Eucharist without gunfire.*

He looked around at the congregation. Their eyes were wide, terrified. He flashed a smile of comfort and peace he didn't feel. He continued the service. By the time the organ rang out the closing hymn, he breathed a sigh of relief that the crisis was over.

A few days later, judgment found its way to him.

During a meeting at his home with a few friends and colleagues, a brigade of black sedans screeched to a halt at his front door, and a group of Gestapo agents swarmed in the door. One of them—the agent who'd been at the church—stepped forward.

"We are here to search the premises." It wasn't a request. Everyone present was under house arrest, including his wife.

The search took almost eight hours, and when it was over, everyone was free to go except Niemoller. He was to report to Gestapo headquarters, as they agent said, "a personal prisoner of the Fuhrer."

As the agent led him to the car, Niemoller managed a brief smile. After weeks of apprehension at how he would handle this moment when it came, he was surprised at how calm he felt. Peace had caught up with him. He turned to the agent.

"I forgive you," he whispered.

The agent smirked and shoved him into the car.

Chapter Two

AUGUST WICHMANN WAS FINALLY IN HIGH SPIRITS. After weeks of enduring hostilities from his sister, ranging from bitter silences to despondent tears to shouting matches, they had reached a kind of détente: He would host a party for some of her friends, and she would hold her wrath long enough to make the day enjoyable.

He doubted that she could—she never held back anger or opinions, especially toward him—but he was glad she was making the effort.

Helga asking him to host was mere decorum; he knew that. It was simply part of the compromise. She didn't need his help, and the house was as much hers as his.

They lived together in the house where they had grown up and continued to stay after their parents died ten years ago.

Back then, with no other family to turn to, the eighteen-year-old August had shouldered his fourteen-year-old sister's upbringing. He had provided her basic needs and saw to her education, but he could never instill in her the same philosophies that enabled his relaxed nature. Though he encouraged her to have a distinct personality and form her own opinions—and he loved the singular woman she had become—it was also a source of friction between them.

August was action-oriented. When he encountered a problem, he took steps to correct it, and he did so with a practical approach, at least for the things he felt strongly about. He had to be passionate about the issue, or he didn't waste the effort. He had a patient, calm, logical thought process, and he was economical with his time and energy. That gave rise to a live-and-let-live attitude that some people mistook for indifference.

Helga was August's opposite in almost every way: short, feisty, and fiercely passionate about righting the wrongs she saw in the world. These days, she perceived quite a few of them. Her judgments were rarely without substance—she had learned from August to at least research a topic before denouncing it—but unlike him, she rarely kept those opinions to herself.

August's best friend, Kurt, had agreed to help him host the party. The two had gone through school and completed their degrees at the same time—even spending a semester at Cambridge together—and it was only natural that Kurt and Helga would hit it off, which they did immediately and had been inseparable ever since.

It was an endless delight for August that Kurt would soon become his brother-in-law—that is, if his sister's bent toward fretting and worrying didn't do them both in.

It almost did, a week before when August and Kurt were building a wooden swing in the back yard. Or rather, August was building, with Kurt reading the directions and handing him various tools and fasteners. Kurt was a recent graduate of the medical college at Munich University and was student-teaching while he waited for his residency to start. He was thin and lanky, and his skills leaned toward memorizing parts of the anatomy and the manual dexterity to apply sutures.

August spent most of his time inside a classroom, so he relished any time he could spend outdoors. In his late twenties, his tall, athletic build drew a sharp contrast with his vocation. Not that being a professor meant he had to look a certain way. He was simply aware that no one would ever look at him and guess that his passion was studying languages and cultures.

He pounded the hammer, his muscles rippling across his back and shoulders. Kurt held a handful of nails, doling them out to August.

"So, tell me," Kurt said, "what's the big secret?"

"What secret?" August reached for a nail.

"The man who came to see you at the university last week."

August twisted around. "What do you know about that?"

"The provost told me," Kurt said. "Apparently the military stopped by?"

"Yes," August laughed. "They want—"

Helga flung open the door and bounded out onto the step. August saw the tears streaking down her cheeks, her breath coming hard and fast. He threw down the hammer and dashed over.

"What's happened?"

Helga's eyes were red and swollen. "Pastor Niemoller." Fresh tears rolled down.

"What about him?"

"He was arrested," she said. "By the Gestapo. Brutal, horrible, conniving—"

"What did he do?" August asked.

Helga bristled. "What makes you think he did anything?"

"Because people don't just get arrested for no reason. He must have violated some law or—"

As it always did, his calm logic infuriated her. "I can't believe how naïve you can be sometimes," she yelled. "The Gestapo doesn't need a reason or a law to arrest someone! They don't even obey the law themselves!"

August gave Kurt a half smile and raised an eyebrow. A look passed between them: *There she goes again.*

Kurt barely concealed a grin in return. They were used to her rants. Most of them centered on the latest political news, some involved the plight of neighbors, and all were dismissed by the two men as little more than a wild expression of her passionate nature. It was a condescending, eye-rolling assessment. *There she goes again.*

"Fine, Helga, fine. Someone you know gets arres—"

"It's not just *someone*." Helga stepped down into the yard and began to pace. Her rant required more area than the step. She looked from August to Kurt, flinging her arm with each emphasized word. "It's Pastor Niemoller. Father's friend. He's a good and decent man, and he doesn't deserve to be treated like this."

"Okay, an old family friend does or does not do something, and he gets into trouble," said August. He leaned back against the house, folded his arms over his chest. A lazy grin punctuated the moment. "What do you want me to do about it?"

"How can you be so callous? He and father served together in the Great War. Doesn't loyalty mean anything to you?"

"As a matter of fact, it does," August sprang to life. "To me in particular." The patronizing stance disappeared. He was energized. Helga and Kurt looked at him in surprise.

"What are you talking about?" Helga asked.

"I had a visitor last week at the college," August said. "From the military. They want my help."

"The military needs your help?" Helga said with a short laugh. Her eyes, still red and shining from the tears, couldn't quite form the menacing look she meant to give him. Her face gave off a mask of fury, which was closer to her true feelings. "What possible help could an untenured professor of linguistics provide? Translations!?" She spat out the word.

August still wasn't taking the bait.

"Sure. It's a valuable skill for the SS," August said.

"Oh, the SS?" Her voice was high and shrill. "Not just military but the SS??" She looked at Kurt for support.

Kurt stared at August, not sure what to say.

"So, yes, loyalty does mean something to me," August said. "I think serving in the military is a loyal thing to—"

"Good God!" She stomped to the door, turned back, and lowered her brow at him, dredging up the most threatening look she could muster. "Do this, and I will disown you!" She slammed the door behind her.

August turned to Kurt and shrugged. Helga had been threatening disownment since they were children.

She hadn't disowned him in the week since their argument, but she might as well have. When he came into a room, she left. If he asked her a question, she tuned the other way. At first, he was concerned, but as the days went on, it vexed him.

That was why when she came to him about the party, he agreed right away. And when she asked him to run to the market for food and drinks, he went immediately, relieved to be reconnected with her.

Now, sauntering home from the market, he whistled a snappy tune. From his vantage point, Munich was the most enchanting city in Germany, maybe in the world, and early summer was the perfect time to enjoy it. He looked forward to an afternoon of fun and games—and a sister whose emotions he didn't have to tiptoe around.

When he got home, the guests had already arrived, and he was puzzled—*Did I misunderstand the time?*—until he spotted Helga fluttering around, tossing quick nervous smiles to the guests. It was not like her to be flustered, especially in her own home, and that fact alone stirred up his suspicions. When he gave her a pointed look, she turned to one of the women and complimented her dress. He was right; something was up.

Introductions were a flurry of smiling nods and out-stretched hands as he made his way through the living room and into the kitchen. August thought the gathering was rather small considering the fuss Helga had made to have it.

She had invited two young men and two young women, and in the midst of the introductions, he discovered that only one of them was Helga's friend, two others were recent applicants to the medical college, and one was still in secondary school.

He wondered if the party was Helga's revenge for the row they'd had about his joining the SS. The thought made no logical sense, but just the same August kept his guard up against his sister. He knew Kurt would never concoct a plan to prove him wrong the way Helga would.

As he unpacked the food, August studied the dynamics of the group. That wasn't a matter of suspicion; it was simply second nature for him to watch how people interacted, to observe the subtle power plays that happened any time two or more were gathered. Such powers of observation were integral to his being, no less than an arm or an eye. Any time he was in a group, he scanned the room to determine who was playing which role, who would come out on top, who was being played.

Like now. In the time it took him to heat the coals to grill the bratwurst, he had made a few deductions. They were all about the same age—late teens, early twenties. One of the young men was the clear leader of the group, almost to the point of hero worship for the others. August stifled a smirk, wondering what heroics could be accomplished at such a young age.

The oldest of the group was Brigitte Bauer, who had completed a degree in nursing in Frankfurt and had come to Munich to continue her medical training. Kurt was mentoring her during her initiation into the university.

She and Helga had met several weeks ago, and August could tell they were becoming close friends. They whispered, laughed, and joked together, both in a breezy, impassioned manner.

In fact, were it not for their looks—Helga's straight blonde locks and light green eyes, and Brigitte's wild brown curls and deep blue eyes—August thought they could be each other's doppelganger.

The others in the party were Brigitte's friends: Sophie Scholl; Sophie's brother, Hans; and Hans' friend, Christoph Probst.

Hans and Christoph were recent applicants to the medical college. Sophie was still in secondary school and planned to attend college in a few years.

In between the introductions, August busied himself with the grill, musing over why Helga had told him it was a party for her friends. He left the bratwursts sizzling and the potatoes frying and went into the kitchen.

He leaned against the counter, placing himself eye-level with her.

"So, it's an ambush, is it?" It wasn't a question. It was an accusation. "Strength in numbers, that's your plan."

Helga gave him a sweet smile and opened the ice box. "I'll get the sauerkraut."

Chapter Three

GENERAL LUDWIG BECK SWIRLED HIS GLASS OF BRANDY and looked out the window. Though he did have the occasional glass of wine, he wasn't much of a drinker by nature, and his choice of beverage today was a portent of current troubles. He suffered from chronic indigestion and insomnia, likely due to the rigors of command, and when things were not going well, his health was the first casualty.

Things were not going well.

Now in his second year as Chief of General Staff, his concerns about the regime were wearing on him, rounding his shoulders and creasing his forehead.

Thus far, his military career had been outstanding, but being the exceptional thinker and writer that he was—some called him the Sage of the General Staff—he could see disaster ahead for the country.

His intellect was matched by his determination. Whenever he encountered difficulties, he applied thoughtful—usually brilliant—examination to the situation, then found a solution with his usual blend of diplomacy and authority.

It was generally known that once Beck had made up his mind, he would not be moved. "Here I stand, I can do no other, God help me" may have been spoken by the German theologian Martin Luther, but it could have been Beck's personal motto.

Captain Ludwig Gehre sat across from Beck and fixated on the swirling glass. He'd been called to this secret meeting, but so far nothing had been discussed beyond Beck's announcement that he had come to a decision. He hoped Beck was there to announce an imminent *coup d'etat*. Gehre had been waiting for such a moment, and he was wound tight like a spring, ready to jump into action—so ready, in fact, that he was tempted to ask Beck to stop swirling the glass and get to the point. Only his military training stopped him, as it was hardly proper for a captain to stand in judgment on a general, especially this one.

Their host, Admiral Wilhelm Canaris, was irritated at Beck stalling, but he hid it well. That was not a matter of hospitality; it was his standard conduct. As a veteran of the Great War, with a bulk of that time spent with intelligence and now as head of the Abwehr, it was second nature for him to hide a reaction. He rarely showed his feelings about anything to anyone, not even his wife or daughters.

Canaris was in his fifties, grey-haired, with a small stature, and those elements alone often caused others to overlook or underestimate him. As the spymaster, that was fine with him—the less conspicuous he was, the better he liked it—but those who did underestimate him often regretted it later. He carried deep secrets, and his sharp intelligent eyes missed nothing.

Seated next to Canaris was Hans Oster, Canaris' deputy and most trusted advisor. In his late forties, he was a calm, loyal, and determined man. His hatred of the Third Reich was so fierce he was known to participate in almost any effort to destroy the regime. He was careful to keep his seditious activities secret and managed his role of Abwehr officer with efficiency. Nevertheless, his forced duplicity had limits: He stubbornly refused to wear a military uniform, no matter what the occasion.

Canaris decided they'd had enough of a stage wait. It was his home, and he could call the meeting to order.

"Don't keep us in suspense," Canaris said. "What have you decided?"

Beck took a long drink and an even longer deep breath. He turned to face them. When he did speak, his voice was measured and determined. "I am going to resign."

The others stared in shock. Gehre's jaw dropped. Even Canaris didn't see this coming.

"You can't resign," Canaris said. "Not now. We need you on the inside." He paused, mustering his argument. "Why do you think I stay in this position? It's certainly not for glory or honor."

It was Beck's turn to be shocked. This was as close as he'd ever been to hearing Canaris reveal his thoughts. But Canaris' admission was not enough to convince him.

"It's the only course of action that makes sense, Willi. I look into the future, and do you know what I see?" Beck turned back to the window and looked into the distance, painting their prospects as they appeared to him. "Devastation. Ruin. Oppression. All because we are dancing to the tune of a tyrant with unchecked powers."

Gehre leaned forward. "Which is why we need you to remain in your position. To push back."

Beck returned to his seat. "I have tried to engage England. I sent Goerdeler to England as an envoy to try to avert an all-out war. But now—" He threw his hand up in exasperation. "England will capitulate to Hitler's demands for land. Chamberlain is already wavering, and it won't take much to push him over."

Oster started to respond, but Beck pressed on. "And those troops we sent to Spain to help Franco with his civil war? You know Hitler will want repayment for that favor. Spain will be forced to back us in war. Even with their help, any war we begin to wage now would be unwinnable."

"Don't worry about Franco," said Canaris. "I'll talk to him."

Beck shrugged. "I'm sure you heard about Stalin executing most of his generals in the Red Army."

"Yes."

"But do you know who engineered that feat? Heydrich."

"You have proof?" Canaris caught the odd look Beck gave him and soothed him with an apology. "I believe you. I just want documented evidence we can use later."

"Of course, of course," Beck said. "I'll get you the proof. There should be quite a bit to document. More each day."

"Like Pastor Niemoller," Oster interjected. "They took him into custody as a personal prisoner of the Fuhrer. He was accused of 'abuse of the pulpit.' The worldwide church won't take kindly to that."

Beck looked at him sharply. "When did this happen?"

"Last week," Oster said. "A group of us were there when the Gestapo came. We were talking about how dangerous it was becoming for him. We didn't know the danger was that imminent."

"Niemoller." Canaris' voice was melancholy. "He commanded a U-boat during the war. One of the best commanders in the fleet." He frowned and fell silent.

Beck leaned back in the seat and resumed swirling his glass. "A small sampling of what Hitler's capable of. And there's much more he's aiming for. He won't stop until he's bankrupted the country and gotten us all killed."

"All the more reason to stay where you are," said Canaris. "You're in a better position to fight it from within."

Beck sighed and mulled over his answer.

"Very well, Willi," he said. "I'll stay. At least for now."

For the second time in the discussion, Gehre was shocked. He thought Beck was immovable. Gehre was reminded of a story he heard a few years ago. During the Great War, Beck was at the western front when he received word that his wife of two years had died. He had been a talented musician, but when he returned home for the funeral, he put away his violin and never played it again. If the topic of his playing came up, he refused to discuss it.

Gehre was impressed with Canaris. Persuading Beck against an action he had already chosen took considerable acuity.

Beck had a caveat, though. "If I stay, I'll ask the other generals to resign *en masse*. Then Hitler will have no way to move the army into place."

Canaris disagreed with Beck's assessment—Hitler had innumerable ways of getting things done, few of them lawful or ethical—but he didn't say so. He'd won the battle of getting Beck to stay; he'd live to fight another day the battle of keeping Beck from an irrevocable action.

Beck downed the remainder of his drink, stood, and looked down at Canaris.

"I doubt they'll hold Niemoller for long," he said.

"After all, what could a pastor say that would be worth incarceration?"

Canaris shook his head. "It's not about Niemoller," he said, his voice quiet but firm. "Hitler has just proven he can take the church hostage."

"The church? That's hardly a concern," Beck said. "Now if it were politics or the military—"

"Politics is downstream from culture, but religion is upstream from it," Canaris said. He stood and looked Beck in the eye. "If he controls the pulpit, he wins the pews." Canaris let that sink in before he continued. "And if he has popular support, then nothing can stop him."

Dismay spread across Beck's face. He knew Canaris was right. "You're such a cynic, Willi," he said.

Canaris smiled. "I have to be. I'm a spy."

Chapter Four

DESPITE HELGA'S CAREFULLY PLANNED AMBUSH, August was determined to have a pleasant afternoon. The guests tried to start conversations about his joining the SS—and it was obvious that Helga had put them up to it—but he fended them off with amusing anecdotes as he finished cooking the meat.

By the time all the food was on the side table in the backyard, he had decided to turn the discussion into a classroom lecture. He thought that assuming the role of professor might be the only way he would survive the afternoon.

He sat on the swing, the one he and Kurt had finished the week before. The others arranged their chairs in a semi-circle around him, balancing their plates on their knees.

"It's a simple military assignment," he said. "Nothing more than a logical request for my skills, and they asked that I fulfill it in an honorable way: with a uniform on. What do you assume the hazards are?"

"Oh, the hazards will be minimal," Hans rang out, "as long as you allow them to indoctrinate you."

"Indoctrinate?" August frowned.

Christoph leaned forward. "That might be too strong

of a label. Let's just say they like to mold people. They do have a strong propaganda machine."

August laughed. "I work with words. I think I'm immune to propaganda."

"Not any longer," Sophie said.

"Why do you say that?"

"Because they convinced you to join."

August gave her a benevolent nod. "Excellent logic."

"Oh, for God's sake, August," Helga cried out, "this isn't a debate with your students over suppositions." She swept her arm around the backyard to include all of them. "They know what they're talking about. They've *lived* it."

"Fine. I'd like to hear." August pointed his fork toward Hans. "Tell us about your experiences."

Hans had just taken a bite, so he had a moment to mull over his argument. When he spoke, it was in a calm, matter-of-fact tone. "A few years ago, I was part of the Hitler Youth."

"Like most of the boys his age," Sophie interrupted.

Hans nodded to her. "Sophie was in the League of German Girls. We were both very active. And we loved it. At least I did. At first."

Sophie spoke up again. "He even carried the banner for our town at the Nuremberg Nazi Party rally last year."

Hans nodded. "I talked my branch into creating our own banner. I thought it would be nice to incorporate our town's symbols into it. I thought it was a harmless thing to do, but apparently it was forbidden, and no one ever said why. They stripped me of my rank of youth leader. For doing nothing more than wanting to create a unique banner."

August gathered up a forkful of potatoes. "I understand how disappointing that must have been for you."

It was a bit too condescending for Sophie. She drew herself up and bristled at him. "Disappointing?? Do you know what they asked us to do? We were required to report any subversive activities we witnessed in our homes to the authorities."

"The word subversive has many connotations. It's usually—"

"—Anything against the National Socialist party. That's the connotation. Essentially, we are called on to turn in our parents if we thought they were anything but completely loyal to the regime."

In her agitation, she overturned her plate, sending her food to the ground in front of her. She ignored it and leveled a gaze at him, her eyes shining with unshed tears.

"Does any of this seem logical and honorable to you?" Her voice was quiet, but the tone was hard.

August saw that he had offended her. He hadn't meant to, but because she was the youngest there, he had simply engaged her as he would any young person in class. He would need to make amends.

He stooped to pick up her fallen plate. "You're right. Those are not logical and honorable actions," he said, quiet and sincere. "I'll get you another plate."

The conversation continued while he went to the table and made another plate for Sophie. Hans brought up the recent mandate that every nineteen-year-old German, male or female, was required to spend six months on a construction project or a farm in the National Labor Service.

"But this could be advantageous for some people, couldn't it?" August called to them from the side table. "It would help them learn a trade or—"

"—No, this is how they plan to keep us under their control!" Christoph scoffed. "They start with the Hitler Youth and then drag us into this."

August brought Sophie's plate to her and returned to the swing. He looked at each of them in turn.

"How do you plan to respond?"

"I got my notice a few weeks ago," Hans said. "I'm in road building. The new autobaun system."

August raised his eyebrows, impressed. "That should be interesting."

Hans shrugged. "Maybe. But after that I'll be conscripted into the Army. I plan to volunteer for the cavalry. Horses are so much easier to deal with than the Wehrmacht. After that … well, assuming there is an after—"

"—Hans!" Sophie admonished through a mouthful of bratwurst.

He grinned. "Sorry. After that, I will be allowed to complete my education." He flashed a smile at August. "When the military and the regime are finished with me, I'll finally be able to pursue medicine."

"I'll be eligible for conscription next year," Christoph said. "Not something I'm looking forward to."

August looked at Brigitte. "What about you?"

"I have a special exemption," she said. "A few years ago, the SS killed my father."

August stared at her, wondering if he'd misunderstood. "What?"

"It was a mistake," she said, her voice low and clear. "He was innocent. Turns out they were after someone else. They sent an apology that included my exception from the projects." She stared him down: a challenge.

"I am truly sorry to hear that," he said.

"See? That's what you're signing up for!" Helga said.

August leaned back and kicked one foot, starting

the swing. He kept his eyes on the ground as he moved back and forth in a lazy arc.

"I will not be part of that," he said. "The military has a genuine use for my skill with languages, that's all."

"So do your students," Brigitte shot back. "At very least, your military career will deprive them of your skills."

The others chimed in with similar sentiments, each one delivered more brusque and caustic than the last.

Kurt stood up. It was time to rescue his friend.

"Enough talk about the military," he announced. "It's a beautiful day. Let's play a sport. August is skilled in archery too, did you know that? He's even been able to teach me a few things. Come, everyone."

August gave him a quick grin. He knew what Kurt was up to, and he appreciated the effort to lighten the mood.

"Haven't you always wanted to learn archery?" Kurt asked Hans and Christoph. They nodded.

They all moved to the other side of the yard where a target was tacked to a wall.

Helga sidled up to Kurt. "Why did you interrupt? We were making progress."

He leaned over and whispered, "He's had enough badgering. They won't be able to convince him any more than you have."

She sighed and went to put the food away.

"Here's a quick lesson." August picked up the bow and arrow and assumed the neutral stance, lining his body up to the target, leveling his gaze at the bullseye. "You want to get it in your sight," he called out, keeping his eyes fixed. He was firmly in teaching mode. "Know exactly what you're aiming for. And make sure your feet are steady. Like this."

He turned to see if they were paying attention.

They were not. They were watching Brigitte as she watched August, her arms folded and her head cocked to one side.

"Is this another role?" she asked, a teasing half-smile on her lips. "Athletic marksman giving advice to young novices?"

He returned the half-smile. "What do you mean?"

"Oh, I've heard about you and your role-playing."

Kurt rushed to interject. "I told her about your classes—"

"—how you label different groups of people," Brigitte continued.

"I don't label them," he said. "I observe them. How they do things and move around and then I—"

"—draw the more obvious conclusions," she broke in, "at which point, you present caricatures."

"That's not what I told her," Kurt said. "I said you were a popular professor because of how you get into a role to match a given language. And also because you encourage that kind of role-playing in your classes." He realized he was jabbering and stopped.

August shook his head. "I encourage my students to watch the actions and learn the movements of people in other cultures," he said. "Because they're not just learning how to speak the language. They're adopting a culture."

Brigitte raised an eyebrow. "So you become Gorgio from Italy or Miles from England or Steven from the United States to enlighten your students. Correct?"

"Something like that."

"My goodness," she laughed. "How many people are inside of you, August Wichmann? Which one am I talking to now?"

"Can't you tell?" Helga called from across the yard. "He's playing the role of new SS officer trying to convince those who know better that what he's doing is worthy."

August narrowed his eyes at her but said nothing.

"Come now, professor," Kurt said, aiming for humor. "Show us how well you can shoot an arrow in Japanese or Swedish."

Brigitte picked up on Kurt's attempt. She put her hand on her hip and tossed August a wink. "Why evah would you want to go shootin' a li'l ole circle on a board that's not movin'?" she said in a heavy southern American accent. "Y'all know that nobody'll be standin' still when they see the SS comin'."

He laughed. "That's a mighty fine way you got of talkin' there, little lady," he said in a heavy Texan drawl.

She picked up one of the arrows. "Well, now, this thing you callin' archery is all well and good." She was speaking in an Irish accent now. "But what'd you think'll happen with all this posin' and pointin' with sticks? Guns and bullets you'll be needing to know about now. And plenty of it, from what I been hearin'."

They all laughed, including August. Then he grew serious. He studied her face, his eyes roaming down, then back up, holding for a moment at her lips.

"I'll never need to use a gun."

He turned back to the target and steadied himself in the neutral stance. In one swift movement, he nocked the arrow, raised the bow, drew back, and released the arrow with ease. It sped across the yard and hit the bull-seye.

They all clapped.

August turned back to her. "*C'est bon?*"

"*Oui, c'est tres bon!*"

"*Merci, mademoiselle. Et vous! Vous parlez fran-*

cais. Tres bien."

"Someone stop him before he takes you on a tour across the globe," Helga said, moving across the yard. She positioned herself before him, one hand on her hip, the other motioning to the others. "Did you hear anything at all?"

He turned to her. "I did. And I understood. The SS will not need my skills in archery. Point made."

"That's not what I mean."

"Did you hear Brigitte?" Kurt cut in, desperate to head off the argument he knew was coming. "She's skilled with languages too. As good as August."

"Yes, but she's not stupid enough to trade that skill for an SS uniform," Helga spat out.

At that point, August's calm, logical demeanor broke. "Why does the idea of this bother you so much?" he asked. "It's only a uniform! Doctors and nurses wear them—" He waved his hand toward Kurt and Brigitte. "—as a sign of their profession."

"It's not the same thing!" Helga yelled.

"Being in uniform is not a disgrace!" he yelled back. "In fact, it's patriotic. I'll be wearing a symbol of our country. There is nothing wrong with that! Maybe what happened with Brigitte's father was an isolated incident. Not everyone in the military is like that. How can you not see that?"

"And how can you be so good at self-deception? It's dangerous!"

Wanting nothing more than to drop the argument, he aimed for humor. "If I'm injured, Brigitte will patch me back together." He winked at Brigitte.

Brigitte didn't wink back. The guests looked at each other and inched away, murmuring "thank you" and "have to be going" to Kurt as they went through the side gate to the front yard.

August watched them leave, shaking his head, hands on his hips. He was frustrated with how things had turned out. He turned to go into the house—and Brigitte was standing there, studying him, her eyes like sapphires piercing into him.

"One question, Professor. The military is one thing, but why the SS?"

August spread his hands wide. "They came to the university with a special request for my help. Why shouldn't I use my skills for—"

"—Forget it" Helga's voice was shrill. She glared at him, then turned and stomped into the house

August looked at Brigitte. He opened his mouth to make an apology, but none came. She shook her head, stepped closer to him, and put her hands flat against his chest. She moved them across his chest to his shoulders.

August held his breath. Being this close to her, feeling the warmth of her body next to his and her hands spreading across his chest was enthralling—but the reaction was more than physical, far more. It was as if his soul had awoken from a long slumber. He wrapped his arms around her and moved his fingers through her brown curls.

But she pulled back out of the embrace. He looked down at her and frowned, confused.

She kept her eyes on his chest and shoulders, and he realized she wasn't embracing him. She was measuring him.

"You will look quite imposing in the uniform," she said, her voice quiet and sad. "What division?"

"Security Service," he said.

"*Sicherheitsdienst?* What they call the SD?"

He nodded.

She dropped her hands. "That's a particular form of hell. And you're willingly descending into it." She shook her head at him. "That's what grieves your sister."

He took a moment to measure his words. "The last thing I want to do is cause her any grief."

She flashed her eyes at him, the blue sapphires now cold. "Are you role-playing *Adagia* now?"

"What?"

"Didn't you read Erasmus? *'The clothes make the man.'*"

She turned and went through the gate.

August stared after her, waiting for her to turn around. But she didn't look back.

Chapter Five

DIETRICH BONHOEFFER WAS LEADING A GROUP discussion on the Ten Commandments at Finkenwalde Seminary when an aide popped his head in and said he had a visitor.

Bonhoeffer went into the hallway to find his brother-in-law, Hans von Dohnanyi, pacing the floor.

He greeted Bonhoeffer without preamble. "They're holding Martin," Dohnanyi said.

Bonhoeffer had been among those in the meeting at Niemoller's home. All those who watched him get arrested were hoping that he would be released soon.

"I'm gathering evidence on the incident. Here's what I have so far." He handed Bonhoeffer a folder and looked around furtively, a reflex from working with the Abwehr. Dohnanyi was a lawyer by trade, but it was his bearing—intense, bright, and fiercely dedicated to building a case against the Nazis—that made him a crucial part of the Resistance. Part of his job—not his position in the *Reichsgericht*, the German Imperial Court of Justice, but rather his real job, his mission with the Resistance—was documenting evidence of the crimes of the Third Reich.

"You'll have to read it now," he told Bonhoeffer. "I'm due back in Berlin, and I can't leave it."

Bonhoeffer, a theologian who wore a deep calm and a shrewd mind, was known for his tranquil manner, which is why he received the news with hardly a ripple. For a moment he stood still and stared at the folder.

"So it begins," Bonhoeffer said. "For the church, at least."

Bonhoeffer flipped through the folder and handed it back to Dohnanyi. "I appreciate your coming to tell me."

"I bring word from your parents too," Dohnanyi said.

"Let me guess," Bonhoeffer smiled. "They're worried."

"They're *concerned*," Dohnanyi corrected. "Your father told me to remind you of the invitation to teach at Union Seminary."

Bonhoeffer smiled. He was right. They were worried. "He wants me to return to America?"

"Just give it some thought." Dohnanyi said. "I have to go."

Bonhoeffer watched him walk out. "So it begins," he whispered, but he shook his head. He knew it wasn't exactly true.

Niemoller's arrest wasn't the beginning. Perhaps it all began when they worked together to form the Confessing Church—their response to the failure of the churches in Germany to stand against the Nazi attempts to usurp Christianity and replace it with leader worship.

Or maybe it began four years ago, when they established the Pastors' Emergency League, opposing the Aryan Clause that excluded Jews from ministry.

For him personally, the beginning may have been when he watched his ninety-year-old grandmother in a display of civil disobedience. Soon after becoming chancellor, Hitler had scheduled a boycott of Jewish businesses. Bonhoeffer's grandmother had no intention of participating. Stepping past the picket lines, his family's matriarch held her chin high and ignored the guards as she went into the shop to purchase some fruit. None of the guards would dare interfere with an old woman in her pursuit of groceries. Bonhoeffer smiled at the memory.

He gazed down the hallway toward the door, where the bright rays of the summer sun broke through and beckoned. For a moment, he yearned to burst through the doors, out into the warmth, and stroll across the grounds, working at the question that haunted him: *Where did it begin for me, this restless need to protest the injustices?*

When he was fourteen, he announced his decision to become a theologian. The announcement surprised his father. A prominent psychiatrist, Karl Bonhoeffer assumed his son's bright incisive mind would lead him into an academic field. His mother was pleased at the news. As the daughter of a chaplain of the court of Kaiser William II, she knew well the life her son was seeking.

After seminary, he embarked on an ecclesiastical life that included internships in Barcelona and London, a trip to America to learn about religious practices in the "new world," and lecturing in theology at Berlin University even before his ordination.

By the time he was ordained in 1931, at only twenty-five years old, he had already established a wide network of colleagues throughout the world.

He had also established more than a few enemies. His radio broadcast on "the leadership principle"—a sharp criticism of the Nazi regime—was cut off the air in mid-sentence. A few years later, the Nazis declared him a "pacifist and enemy of the state" and terminated his authorization to teach at Berlin University. A year after that, he resigned as youth secretary at the ecumenical World Alliance in protest of that organization's failure to speak out against the plight of the Jews in Western Europe.

No, he thought, *this isn't where it begins. It began long ago. Now it merely continues, as it should.* He stepped back into the classroom, wondering where and when it would end.

He called his students together and told them the news. They were distressed, not only because of the threat to Niemoller personally, but because it brought the danger closer to home: Finkenwalde was an underground institution, in constant threat of discovery and closure by the Nazis.

They clustered around him, eager for details, the lively and stimulating discussion on the Ten Commandments cast aside for the moment. A mild clamoring started, and the questions rang out: *What do they mean by "abuse of the pulpit"? How could they do this? What was in his sermon that caught their attention? What will they do to him?*

And then one last question: *Will we be arrested too?* Silence fell over the room. They turned to Bonhoeffer and steeled themselves for the answer.

He looked around at each of them, wanting desperately to give them an optimistic view, a sense of courage. But he would never deceive them, not even with false hope.

"I don't know what will happen," he said, the most honest answer he could offer.

"We're operating illegally," one of them said.

"And the Gestapo is bound to find out sooner or later," said another.

The clamoring began again, this time with an undertone of fear. Bonhoeffer took charge.

"Christ calls us to tread this path." His voice rang out strong and certain. "We will continue on this path until he moves us onto another."

They were calmed, at least for the moment.

"What can we do for Pastor Niemoller?" one of them asked.

They looked around at one another, considering options.

"Why don't we go to his home church and lend support to his parishioners?" Bonhoeffer suggested.

They all agreed.

"And now let us pray for his safety and for his congregation."

Their heads bowed automatically.

A month after Niemoller's arrest, Bonhoeffer and the Finkenwalde students traveled to Niemoller's church. The doors had been boarded up and the property was guarded by several Gestapo agents. Nevertheless, the seminarians gathered with the parishioners on the lawn and held a worship service. For two hours they sang hymns and preached, ignoring the jackboots and guns in their midst.

After the summer session was finished, Bonhoeffer went with a friend on holiday to the Bavarian Alps. While he was there, he received word that the Gestapo had seized Finkenwalde Seminary, sealed shut the doors, and arrested twenty-seven of his students.

He returned to his parents' home in Berlin, where he spent a large part of his time on his knees in prayer, searching for the next path.

Chapter Six

AFTER WHAT HAD HAPPENED TO BRIGITTE'S FATHER, it was ironic that her arrest was a case of mistaken identity. When a group of SS agents pushed their way into the Scholl house and rounded up Sophie and her siblings, they simply assumed Brigitte was one of them.

They were seized by a unit of the *Sicherheitsdienst*, the Security Service commonly referred to as the SD (the same "particular form of hell," in fact, that she had accused August Wichmann of willingly descending into). But the mistake of taking the wrong person would never be acknowledged. The SD were above mistakes. And above reproach.

She had spent the earlier part of that day at the Scholl home, ostensibly helping Sophie with a school paper, but in reality sharing ideas about how to rid the country of the National Socialist regime. Hans was expected back at any moment—he had been away with the Cavalry Unit—and the absence of his drive and energy was profound. Nevertheless, it had been a gratifying morning, full of wit and schemes and determination. Brigitte shared Sophie's trenchant, insightful style of expression, and the two held the household spellbound with their plans and intentions.

The lively fun was all swept away in an instant with a sharp knock on the door. Sophie opened and, without introduction or invitation, four agents swarmed in, guns drawn. Sophie darted across the room to her mother.

"What is the meaning of this?" Robert Scholl demanded. Magda Scholl held on to her daughter.

The agents ignored them. Two agents grabbed Sophie's brother and sister, Werner and Inge, and pushed them outside.

Brigitte felt a hand grip her shoulder. She tensed up and her mouth went dry. She stole a glance at Sophie, who was clinging to her mother, eyes wide and wet. The agent spun Brigitte around and pushed her out the door and down the walkway. He pushed the gate open, but the spring was tight, and it snapped back on his hand.

"*Sheisse!*" the agent yelled. Blood rolled down his hands and dripped off his fingertips. He held his hand out, away from his uniform.

Without thinking, Brigitte reached into her dress pocket, drew out a handkerchief, and held it out to him.

"You'll want to clean the wound," she said. "That spring is rusty."

The agent stared at her in shock. He took the handkerchief and gave her a short nod. He opened the car door and, instead of pushing her, allowed her to climb in and get seated.

"No! Stop!" Sophie's voice rose louder, becoming a screeching wail. "Noooo!" Brigitte looked up and saw an agent pull Sophie away from her parents, drag her to the car, and push her in.

Robert ran into the street after them.

"You cannot do this!" he yelled. "You can't burst into homes and just take people away like this!"

The agents ignored him and drove away. Each car

held two agents, with Werner and Inge in one and Brigitte and Sophie in the other.

Brigitte noticed that there were no door handles on the inside of the back doors. The agent with the hand wound drove; the other faced the back seat, his weapon drawn. No doubt about it: They were captives. But they didn't know why yet.

Sophie caught Brigitte's eye, then turned her head and scratched her ear so she could hide part of her face while she mouthed, "Hans?" Brigitte knew no more than Sophie did, but she realized her friend was desperate to know where her brother was, whether he was incriminated, whether he was safe. Brigitte gave a furtive shrug of her shoulders and saw Sophie's eyes grow wide with fear.

When the agents pushed the four of them in the door and up to the desk, Hans was already there. He turned to them with a smile, his lip battered and bleeding, left eye purple and swollen.

"Hans!" Sophie shrieked. "Your face! Oh my God! What happened? What did—"

Hans shook his head to silence her. He turned to the agents. "You'll have to forgive them," Hans said. "You know how it is with little girls. They get so excited over everything." He nodded toward Sophie and Brigitte. "My little sister and her little friend do this all the time."

At first Brigitte bristled. *Little girls?* But Hans stared at her, his eyes dark and serious and filled with warning. The meaning was clear: *Don't protest.*

One of the agents looked Brigitte and Sophie up and down. "Which is the little friend?"

Brigitte stepped forward, gripping her hands together to keep from shaking.

"Name," the agent spat out.

"B-brigitte B-bauer," she whispered.

The agent wrote it down. "Age."

Her mind raced. She knew Hans was trying to portray her and Sophie as young so their interrogations would be easier. Could she pass for younger? She had to give an answer, and they had the means to check her story. But how important was truth and what were the consequences of a lie? *Not a lie,* she told herself. *I'm pretending.* The agent tapped his pen on the paper, waiting.

She went for the lie. "Sixteen."

The agent wrote it down, then turned to the other agents. Brigitte stole a look at Hans. He returned a furtive smile.

The agents conferred among themselves, their voices a low rumble. Round and round they went, the discussion becoming more heated, with a few words rising here and there—"...find out what they know..." and "...only little girls..."

Just then, fist pounded on the table and a voice rang out: "Let them go! They're young. What menace could they be to the state?"

Brigitte looked at the speaker. It was the agent with the wounded hand. He still held Brigitte's handkerchief.

Brigitte and Sophie were ushered out. No fanfare, no apologies, and no chance to talk to the others. As they were led away, Brigitte looked back, but the agent was blocking her view. And then they were out the door. Free.

Sophie looked around. "What can we—"

"Sophie! Brigitte!" Robert bounded up the steps and threw his arms around both of them. Then he stood back and looked at them. "Are you hurt?"

They shook their heads.

"But Inge and Werner are still inside," Sophie said.

"Hans too. He's injured, Father. We have to help him." She pulled his arm and led him toward the door, but he stopped her.

"I'll take care of this. You and Brigitte go wait with your mother."

They made their way to the car, where Magda greeted them with hugs and tears. They filled her in on what had happened in the station and kept an eye out for Robert to come back.

When he did, they were shocked. They had expected Sophie's sister and brothers to come back with him, but he was alone.

His face was red with anger. Without a word, he got into the car and drove away.

Magda started to cry. "Where are my children? We can't just leave them here."

For several moments, Robert remained silent. When he spoke, his voice was unnaturally high and strained. "They must remain and be interrogated."

"But—?" Magda nodded toward Sophie and Brigitte.

"The agents said they are too young and pose no threat," Robert said.

Sophie threw herself back against the seat and crossed her arms. "I'm not too young to be a threat to them."

"Nevertheless, you were released," he said. "And I am grateful."

"Why were they arrested?" Magda asked.

"They found out that Hans had taken part in activities that were not part of the Hitler Youth program," he said. "That's why they arrested him. And then they assumed his sisters and brothers were guilty of the same so-called crime, and they arrested his family."

Brigitte asked. "So taking part in something other

than the Hitler Youth is such a serious crime?"

Robert looked at her in the rear-view mirror. "I am sorry you were caught up in this, Brigitte. But yes, they have arrested people for less."

Brigitte leaned back against the seat and turned to Sophie. She saw anger and determination in her friend's eyes. Sophie leaned over to her.

"They tried to silence me," Sophie whispered in her ear. "But I will only get louder."

Brigitte grabbed her hand and squeezed. "So will I."

Part 2

*Extraordinary times demand
extraordinary actions.*
~ General Ludwig Beck

Chapter Seven

PARIS HAD MOURNED LONG ENOUGH OVER HER FATE. Having been taken in by the fanciful notion that she could stand up to the neighborhood bully—with the Allies behind her and the Maginot Line at her front—the French had faced the Wehrmacht without flinching.

But then the German forces had broken through the Ardennes with deadly efficiency, skirted the Maginot Line, and pushed back the French and British to the sea. There, weary and spent, the Allies had fled the massacre, many of them crushed at the Dunkirk bottleneck.

With French forces depleted, the Germans swaggered into an undefended Paris on June 14, 1940, mere days after launching Case Red. Soon after that, an armistice was signed between the two countries. The fall of France was complete.

By December of 1941, the nightmare continued, but the spirit of the people refused to surrender. Conceding defeat would have crushed them, so they opted for denial. In a direct rebuff of the occupation, Paris smiled in the face of the brute and adorned herself for pleasure.

One man could see past the veil. August Wichmann—in his early thirties, a more somber and serious man than he'd been in the days of hitting bullseyes with ease—strolled toward a café. His look was different here: a cravat around an upturned collar, hair slicked back and parted on the side.

He knew the casual smiles that passed him were merely cosmetic, as fake as his clothes and hair. The ersatz details didn't faze him, but he did take note. Minutiae like that were important. He scanned the surroundings, ignored the beauty, and searched for threats. Enemies were often camouflaged. That fact he knew well.

He spotted an image ahead, just out of reach—a short woman, blonde hair, a toddler at her side. Something about her gait charged him. He passed the café, his stroll hastened to a clipped walk. He gained on her, reached out, and grabbed a shoulder.

"Helga?" He spun her around—and the face was not familiar.

The toddler was a stranger.

The woman was startled. *"Pardon, monsieur?"*

He exhaled and spread his hands, palms up. "I'm sorry. *Je suis desole.*"

The woman nodded and walked away.

He retraced his steps to the café. *Remember, you're Jean Louis Mardot,* he thought. *A patriot, a rebel. You're here to help.*

He knew the name August Wichmann would never inspire trust. And trust was vital to him.

He started to dart in, but something down the block caught his eye. A black car, swastika flags on the fenders. He eyed the darkened windows and let out a groan. *Not now.* With a sigh, he entered the café.

He breezed through, scanned the patrons. Nothing unusual. He spied Janette, a cute petite brunette, behind the bar. He moved up to her, slipped his arms around her waist, leaned in.

"You disappeared again last night," he said, his voice low and seductive. "All these secret meetings. Why do I put up with it?"

"Because I look good in your robe," she giggled, but didn't turn around. "And better without it. That's what you always say, isn't it?"

"That doesn't answer where you were," he said.

"You didn't ask that question," she said, still turned away from his gaze. "You only wondered why you put up with it." She leaned back and pressed herself against him. "And you know the answer to that."

He grinned. She was such a delight to him, so eager and full of life. He bent down, kissed her neck, then released her and made his way to the back.

Just before the back door, he turned left, paced a short hallway, and inched down a tiny stairwell into the basement. He slipped in and eased the door shut.

He turned to face a group of twenty men and women seated around the room, their faces white with anguish. Most of them sported a yellow star on their sleeves—a new law, passed a few months ago. Rumors had started almost immediately that there were ways to circumvent the directive. August had heard the rumors. It was his task to find out if they were true.

They looked up, hopeful. They'd been waiting for him.

A soft rumble of *bonjour* in various inflections greeted him. "Sorry I'm late. Unavoidable delays." He made his way to a table.

One of the men stood and took position as leader in front of them. "I'm glad you're here," the leader said. "We could use a voice of reason."

Another man jumped up, his mustache bristling.

"Reason? With the Gestapo?"

"Quiet, please," the leader said. "Let's not rouse *les gendarmerie*. The new edict is—"

"You want to talk about the edict?" a woman in the front said, her round face flushed. She ripped the yellow star from her sleeve. "There! That is what I think of it! I am French, not a star on my arm!"

The mustached man turned to her. "That violates the law. German law! If they find out..." He trailed off, looked at them with wide eyes. "Well, you know what they do to lawbreakers."

The woman jumped up her flushed face now taut. "Stop it! You with your horror stories! No one wants to hear them."

A general clamoring began.

August stood up and smiled at them. "Wait, wait. We're here about the star and who has to wear it, *oui*?"

His gentle easy manner always managed to calm them. The clamoring subsided.

"Jean is right," the leader said. "Let's get back to the issue."

The woman stood her ground. "But to be singled out like we're criminals, just for being Jews!"

"Fake papers. That's how to avoid this," a quiet voice said.

All conversation stopped. Everyone turned to see a woman in the back, her shoulders rounded and frail, her eyes wary. She peered around at them. "I know where to get them."

August leaned in. "Where?"

The door flew open and hit the wall with a *whump*. Two Gestapo agents burst in, weapons drawn. One pushed the people into a corner. The other spotted August and pointed to him.

"There he is!"

The men and women shook, white-faced. The second agent stomped over, cuffed him, and pushed him up the stairs and through the café. August stole a glance at Janette. She backed away, eyes wide.

The agents took him outside and shoved him forward. He turned on them in anger—but the French persona was gone. No need to pretend here. They knew who he was.

"*Das War Dumm!* You idiots!" He struggled with the cuffs.

Out of the corner of his eye, he noticed a woman stop and stare at him. He went quiet, then stole a quick glance. She was petite, with curly brown hair. His eyes met hers: dark blue and sultry, a piercing sapphire gaze, a flash of recognition. *She knows who I am. She'll give me away.* His heart started pounding.

He lowered his head, rushed to the car, and got in. The two agents followed. After they closed the doors, he turned on them.

"Did you really have to come here? I had them talking!"

It wasn't the first time the Gestapo had mangled one of his assignments. His methods of gaining information were simple: assume a persona and gain their trust. Then they would talk. But trust took time and patience—something the Gestapo regarded with derision and scorn. They had caught up with him more than once simply to relay a message or check on his whereabouts. He stopped letting them know where he was. Or who he was supposed to be.

"Yes, we had to come here. You're not an easy man to find," the first agent said.

August rolled his eyes and looked out the window.

That's by design, jackass. I don't want them to think I associate with you. The words almost came out. But he merely continued struggling with the cuffs. "I'm compromised!" August yelled. "How do I regain their trust when I return?"

"You won't be returning."

"Why not?"

"Heydrich wants to see you," said the second agent. "Probably a new assignment. He's moving things around after what happened in America."

"What happened?"

"Japan attacked them at dawn. Some place in the Pacific called Pearl Harbor. Caught them completely by surprise. Destroyed the entire fleet."

August stared at him, stunned. "So they're in the war now."

"Looks like it. Oh, and you've been promoted to obersturmfuhrer."

All frustration melted away. A promotion. August smiled, and his shoulders squared with satisfaction. *Finally, a step forward. Maybe it can lead to what I really want.* He stopped struggling and relaxed.

"Mind getting these cuffs off me?"

"You'd better get changed," said the agent as he unlocked the cuffs. "You look like a Frenchman. And you know how Heydrich hates the French."

It was a joke, but August didn't laugh. As the driver lurched forward, he looked back. The woman was still standing on the sidewalk, staring at him. He turned back around, searching his memory for those eyes.

Chapter Eight

CANARIS WAS MAKING HIS WAY TOWARD THE STABLES when the messenger arrived. Every day he went for a morning ride with his neighbor, Reinhold Heydrich, not because he enjoyed his company—in fact, he despised him—but because it was an avenue for gathering information.

It had been two years since Heydrich had been appointed to the Reich Main Security Office, a department that overlapped and often undermined the Abwehr.

With Heydrich in charge, the constant power struggle was a thorn in Canaris' side. If it weren't for the adage about keeping one's enemies close, Canaris would've had nothing to do with him.

The actual gathering of information was effortless. Heydrich was an incessant braggart, and most of the time, Canaris only had to listen. In the course of proving his importance to the Fuhrer and the regime, Heydrich eventually would reveal everything he knew.

Their morning rides were common knowledge, so the messenger knew where to find Canaris. He glanced around, assessed that they were alone, and handed over a small note. He stood back while Canaris scanned the paper and waited in case a reply was necessary.

It was from Generalisimo Francisco Franco, the un-disputed leader of Spain since the end of that country's civil war two years ago.

The memorandum had been decoded, but the message was still cryptic, which of course was by design:

> *Interesting thing about birds: Ducks swim,*
> *but eagles do not. Eagles fly higher than ducks,*
> *even to mountaintops. Ducks make better meals,*
> *but eagles are not eaten. Are they good pets?*

Canaris nodded at the messenger, dismissing him. A brief flash of disappointment crossed the messenger's face—he'd have given anything to know the meaning of the note—but he saluted Canaris and left.

Canaris folded the note and stuffed it into his pocket. He and Franco had been on good terms for years. They had similar ideologies about cultural matters, and their sentiments on politics were almost identical, including a reluctance to trust anyone. Hence the cryptic message. They were both extremely intelligent, which also accounted for the mysterious wording. Franco knew that Canaris loved to solve puzzles. Canaris bent his thought on this one.

Eagle. That would be America, of course. *Ducks swim, but eagles do not.* He frowned, thinking hard. He recalled Franco calling Germany a "sitting duck" if America got into the war. And a large part of America's fleet had been destroyed at Pearl Harbor—he'd gotten confirmation about that just last night—but she still had her air power. *Eagles fly ... even to mountaintops.* Probably a reference to Gibraltar.

And the question about *being good pets:* he knew exactly what that meant. *Franco's been contacted, prob-*

ably by the OSS, and he isn't sure whether to trust them.

Trust was a precarious gift to grant, rewarding when used properly, devastating when guessed wrong. Canaris readied his horse to ride and thought about his visit with Franco a year ago.

He'd had to wait a half hour to see Franco, but he didn't mind. He passed up the seat offered by the aide and stood at the window, looking out at the city.

He loved Madrid—the sights, the sounds, the food, the people. In his secret dream, he saw himself living here, alone, with only his trusted dogs for company. And there would be no warplanes or tanks or soldiers to mar the scenery.

He was ushered into Franco's office. Franco rose to greet him.

"It is good to see you again, old friend," said Franco. "Too long, too long. Come. Sit. Tell me about this official business you mentioned in your wire."

Canaris glanced back at the guards posted on either side of the door. Franco took the hint and nodded at them. They exited quietly.

"My business is both official and personal," Canaris said. He opened the giant doors beside the desk and stepped out onto a portico. Franco followed him.

"And secret as well, it would seem," Franco laughed. "My friend, you have no need to worry. They sweep my office every morning. No hidden microphones. Total privacy, I guarantee it. And our conversations always stay between us. Yes?"

Canaris nodded, satisfied. "Officially, I'm here to negotiate access to Gibraltar."

"I suspected that was the prize you were seeking."

"Hitler seeks it, not I."

Franco shrugged. "He seeks, you negotiate. The

agenda is the same, is it not?"

Canaris gave him a speculative look. They were both aware of the game they were playing, but it wasn't time yet for either to yield.

Suddenly there were shouts from the street. They both turned to the commotion. From nowhere, several military agents surrounded two men. Canaris nodded to the scene below.

"I can send some of my agents here to assist in operations," he said, "should you ever have a need."

Franco gave him a long look. His eyes turned chilly. "Germany has been generous with assistance, but I am reluctant to accept more of your generosity. Such favors come at a cost."

Canaris smiled. They were on the same page.

"I understand," he said. "The assistance is not Germany to Spain, but friend to friend."

Franco smiled back at him. "In which case, I suspect you already have agents here that you might contact at a moment's notice."

Canaris looked back down at the street. "Perhaps I do."

Franco opened the door and motioned Canaris back into the office. "For the moment, let us speak generalisimo to admiral."

"Very well."

They eased into the chairs and eyed each other across the desk. Canaris was perfectly composed, though inside he was wary.

Franco leaned back in his chair, trying to achieve the same composure as his guest.

"I am grateful for the German soldiers who were sent to fight with us," Franco said. He stopped, his mind stepping through a minefield of words, searching for the route that would get him through without exploding the conversation. "I assumed Hitler would accept the same in return, our soldiers sent to help in your battles."

"That would be logical," said Canaris, "but he wants Gibraltar."

"That is hardly equitable."

"I agree."

Franco dithered. He felt certain he could trust Canaris, but could he trust the head of the Nazi's Abwehr? He decided to lay out the dilemma and watch for a reaction.

"Here is my position," he said. "Why would I give up part of our land, with no guarantee of ever getting it back? And yet, how would history judge my actions if I were to go back on an agreement?"

They each had taken a step forward. It was time for Canaris to quicken the pace.

"Not as harshly as they might judge your granting Hitler control of the Mediterranean," he said. "Because that gives him a gateway to the Atlantic. And unrestricted access to Great Britain." He took a deep breath and forged on. "Which makes his defeat more problematic."

Franco was shocked at the direct admission. He searched Canaris' eyes. Was this a trap? But he saw truth in the man's eyes. He relaxed and dropped the charade at last.

"There are plans in place for such a defeat?"

"Yes."

"Can you share them?"

"No."

Franco frowned and looked around the room, deliberating. Canaris could see the man's dilemma, his point of indecision: keeping his word would grant even more muscle to an already brutal dictator; not keeping his word would throw a gauntlet. Spain's resources were depleted from its civil war. He could hardly engage in a fight at this point. Canaris had an idea that he hoped would tip the scale.

"Offer it to him," Canaris said, "but set the terms too high."

Franco studied him, wheels turning. Canaris waited patiently, barely breathing.

"Agreed," Franco said. "I will not go back on my word." He grinned. "But Gibraltar will not come cheap."

It was back to friend-to-friend. Canaris broke into a warm smile. "Trust never does."

He leaned back and relaxed. *Done deal*.

~ ~ ~

Trust. From inside the stables Canaris eyed a figure across the yard and thought the word "trust" would never apply in his case. Reinhard Heydrich, late thirties, tall and thin, strolled toward the stables. Someone had once described him as "a strutting peacock with no reins of modesty." Canaris thought it was a gross insult to the peacock.

He watched Heydrich walk toward the stable with one of his assistants, the two of them immersed in conversation. The exchange grew heated, and one phrase— "No! I should be the only one who sees this document!" —rose up and made its way to Canaris.

The assistant handed over a packet and walked away. Heydrich put down his riding crop and gloves, opened the packet, and started to read, so engrossed that he left the gear behind. He read all the way to the stables, then stuffed it in his pocket.

"You're smiling," said Canaris. "Must be good news."

Heydrich removed his coat and hung it on a peg. The document rose up out of the pocket.

"Are you going to pick my brain again today?" Heydrich asked.

"Is that what you think I do?"

"Isn't it? Head of the spy network, always picking for news."

"From someone so important?"

Heydrich missed the sarcasm and took it as a compliment.

"I get things done," he said. "That's how you advance in the Third Reich."

"A far cry from service in the Navy," Canaris smiled. He knew this would goad Heydrich into drivel. Which it did.

Heydrich whirled around, his face red, his eyes hard coals. "Yes. And that slanderous evaluation was expunged."

Canaris feigned ignorance. "Which evaluation? I don't recall."

"Some imbecile reported me 'deemed unfit to be an officer.'" Heydrich spat out. "Where is that imbecile now?"

"Nowhere important, I'm sure."

Heydrich leaned in toward Canaris. "Would someone 'unfit' be able to get rid of the Brown Shirts?"

The incident was known by many names—*The Night of Long Knives, the Rohm Purge, Operation Hummingbird*—but to Canaris, they were a mark of decay in the character of his country. The series of extrajudicial executions resulted in a consolidation of authority under the SS and, consequently, a rapid rise to power for Heydrich.

Canaris raised an eyebrow. "Is this the same someone who burned Abwehr headquarters to destroy any evidence of these activities?"

"No evidence pointed to me," Heydrich said. "And you got a new office out of it."

Canaris turned away and busied himself with his horse. *"Seig Heil,"* Canaris said with a touch of sarcasm. "You're certainly someone now."

Again, Heydrich took a compliment that wasn't there. "Yes I am. Hitler trusts me with getting rid of the Jews."

Canaris knew that Heydrich never could resist giving everything away with all his boasting. For a moment he was tempted to deride him, but he let the temptation pass. He turned back and raised an eyebrow in mock curiosity.

"What do you mean?"

Heydrich stared at him, aware that he had talked too much. It was a face-off. Canaris had years of training and knew when to call a bluff. And he could keep his focus on a mark longer than the mark could endure it. Heydrich blinked first.

"I meant getting rid of the problem," he murmured.

Canaris let it go. He pointed to Heydrich's hands. "Where are your crop and gloves?"

Heydrich stomped out. Canaris waited a moment, then got the documents from Heydrich's coat, pulled out a tiny camera from his pocket, and started clicking away. He heard footsteps just outside, hurried to replace the document, and went back to his horse. Heydrich strode in and mounted his horse. He ignored Canaris and rode out without a word. Canaris relished the silence.

Chapter Nine

THOUGH GERMANY WAS AT WAR, THE PARK IN THE center of Berlin was filled with people enjoying a carefree afternoon.

Bonhoeffer paced the park's perimeter with Dohnanyi. The air was crisp and clean, and the laughter of young voices rang out from the playground, but the two men weren't there for the ambiance.

They were spies—double agents, in fact—and they were there to meet a contact.

Bonhoeffer's venture into the spy network was a path he could not have foreseen. After Finkenwalde had been shut down, he tried to remain quiet and inconspicuous for a while, but his natural inclination toward protest rose up. His sermons and writings were filled with disapproval of the Nazi party, and by 1938 he was forbidden to live or work in Berlin.

At that point, Bonhoeffer contacted Dohnanyi and asked whether he could assist the Resistance network. Dohnanyi introduced him to Admiral Canaris and his deputy, Hans Oster. Together they considered how Bonhoeffer's contacts with clergy throughout the world could be leveraged for the group. He made several trips abroad to strengthen those relationships.

In November, anti-Semitism was unleashed in the form of *Kristallnacht*, when the SS looted, vandalized, or burned Jewish businesses and synagogues. The systematic violence merely served to whet the Nazis' appetite for annihilation, so they pulled the defenseless Jews from their homes and offices and beat them. When the Nazis tried to ascribe the actions to God's retaliation on the Jews for the death of Christ, Bonhoeffer fled back to Berlin to discredit the outlandish claims.

He reached out to his fellow clerics in the Protestant churches and begged them to join with him in rising up against the claims.

"Was our church not founded on the concept of protest?" he asked them, aiming for reason and logic that would appeal to the other Lutheran pastors. "Would Christ have you avert your eyes from the horrors taking place, or would he have you do something to stop them?"

But the clergy, even when they couldn't fault his arguments, were too complacent or apathetic or fearful to take part. He was alone. It was a depressing, disheartening thought.

But then he pulled himself together with a serious heart-to-heart: *Did John the Baptist weep and moan at being the lone voice in the wilderness? Christ did not ask you to take a stand only if others joined in. He demands obedience. Now what is there left to do? Obey.*

And so he did. He protested, even when his protests drew ever more attention from the Nazis. His family and friends grew alarmed. Recognizing the danger he was drawing to himself and those around him, he helped get his twin sister Sabine and her Jewish husband to safety in England.

His family urged him to flee as well, reminding him that he had friends in New York, where he could preach and live in safety. Eventually he saw the logic of their arguments and took a position at Union Seminary. He set sail for New York in June of 1939. His plan was to stay there at least a year.

He regretted the decision almost immediately. He wrote to a friend saying he'd made a mistake in coming to America and worried that he would have no right to participate in the reconstruction of Christian life in Germany after the war if he didn't share in the trials.

He returned to Germany in early July.

His return seemed to open a wellspring in him. He found out that Martin Niemoller had been released with a fine, but then was immediately arrested again and sent back to the concentration camp for what the Gestapo called "re-education." Bonhoeffer tried to visit his friend but was denied.

He grew more outspoken in his stand against the Nazis, and his sermons against the tyranny were sharper than ever. Earlier in the year, the Gestapo banned him from any public speaking. A few months later, he was forbidden to publish.

"I expect a letter any day telling me not to pick up a pen," he joked to Dohnanyi.

He had joined the Abwehr primarily to avoid conscription into the army. Working with the cell of Resistance workers that included Dohnanyi, Admiral Canaris, Captain Gehre, General Beck, and several others, he felt that at least there as a purpose.

On this particular day, Bonhoeffer and Dohnanyi were waiting for information Beck had requested. The clandestine nature of the meeting didn't stop Bonhoeffer from enjoying the walk. He looked around the park.

"Children at play, Hans. It's the same no matter where you are," he said. "This could be Central Park in New York. Such happy faces, such happy little lives. They're not bound by geography or ideology."

The children on the swings waved to him. He smiled and waved back.

"I think that might be the first time you mentioned America since you came back," Dohnanyi said.

"It's hard not to think about America these days," Bonhoeffer said.

"Do you wish you'd stayed?"

"No. It was important for me to come back." He walked a few paces, deep in thought. "But even if I hadn't felt the need to come home, I don't think I could have stayed for long."

"Why do you say that?"

"They were so..." he paused, searching for the right word, "Complacent. So dismissive. It wearied me. I tried to talk to them about what was happening here, but it all seemed so far away to them. 'Another European war' is all it was to them."

"War is now closer to them," Dohnanyi frowned.

"Yes," said Bonhoeffer. "It's no longer a foreign war when you're attacked."

"As England has learned," Dohnanyi said.

Bonhoeffer nodded and thought back to the day he visited Bishop Bell of Chichester on his way to America.

~ ~ ~

Sandbags had been piled outside most of the buildings in London. Signs pointed the way to bomb shelters. The occasional pedestrian strolled by carrying a small bag with a gas mask.

"You seem to be preparing well," Bonhoeffer called over his shoulder, still taking in the view.

"Most are on their toes, but some think the worst is over," Bell said. He was seated at his desk, turning a paperweight over and over in his hands, a nervous habit that cropped up whenever he was troubled and thinking around the edges of problems.

"I wish I could share their enthusiasm," said Bonhoeffer. He watched two young boys bounce a ball down the street, a scruffy dog keeping pace beside them. He smiled at their youthful innocence, remembering a moment long ago with Walter, his older brother.

Walter had been killed in France during the Great War. He had been only eighteen, and Bonhoeffer had never stopped aching to see him again.

The children moved out of Bonhoeffer's view. He closed his eyes and said a silent prayer that the German bombs would miss them.

He turned away from the window and made his way back to a chair.

"Where was Niemoller sent?" Bell asked.

"After Sachsenhausen, they sent him to Dachau. They're sending all of the insurgent clergy there."

"What an outrage!" Bell said, rising in anger. "I'll do what I can, I can promise you that. Publish a few letters, speak out when I have the chance. It needs to come to light."

"Thank you, Bishop," Bonhoeffer said. "There's little we can do from the inside, but there's an opportunity abroad. I hope that while I'm in America I open some eyes and ears to the injustice."

Bishop Bell was as good as his word. He sent letters to the editor and spoke about the pastor's plight as often as he could, even from the pulpit.

But despite all of the bishop's efforts, awareness had not gotten Niemoller released.

~ ~ ~

As he paced beside Dohnanyi, Bonhoeffer considered the bitter reality that had he stayed until Pearl Harbor was attacked, Americans would have come out in droves to hear him speak out about the war. It was a fateful mistiming of events.

Dohnanyi spotted a man across the park and made eye contact with him. The man gave a slight nod and headed their way, giving the impression of meandering, but still managing to aim straight for them.

The man strolled by, sat at a nearby bench, and opened a newspaper. He flipped through a few pages. After a few moments, he got up and left the newspaper on the bench. Dohnanyi waited until the man left, then he retrieved the newspaper and a folder hidden under it. He pocketed both.

"We can go now," he said.

Bonhoeffer laughed. "I never thought I'd be in the spy network. Ordination vows don't cover this scenario."

"Ah, but you're not just a spy in the Abwehr. You're working with the Resistance. And the Resistance is working to overthrow the madness. There's honor in that, Dietrich."

"I know. And I'm saved from having to join the army and face the prospect of killing in Hitler's name. I've weighed that against any deception I'm involved in." He looked skyward. "I've made peace with it."

"Good. Because tomorrow when we meet with Canaris—"

A high-pitched noise blasted out from the loudspeakers set up on poles around the park. They heard a few bars of music, then by a moment of static, followed by a brief silence.

Then a voice from the loudspeaker rang out, energetic and strong:

"Citizens of Germany! We have taken Kiev! Germany has achieved victory!"

The people cheered wildly and hugged each other. Someone started a patriotic song. Arms rose up in the Nazi salute.

A group of Hitler Youth marched by and raised their arms to salute, their faces beaming.

"I remember talking with a gentleman in New York about the burdens of society," Bonhoeffer said, watching them. "I told him that the true test of a moral society is the kind of world it leaves to its children." He turned to Dohnanyi, his eyes filled with grief. "We have so much work to do."

Dohnanyi put his hand on Bonhoeffer's shoulder. They gazed across the park and watched the celebration in silence.

Chapter Ten

AUGUST TURNED FROM SIDE TO SIDE IN FRONT OF THE floor-length mirror and appraised his uniform. The new insignia seemed to add a degree of gravity. He stiffened his shoulders.

A memory surfaced: himself as a young boy, about five years old, talking nonstop to his parents as they strolled the sidewalk, pestering them with questions while his baby sister lay bundled in a carriage. Their indulgent, proud smiles urged him on. They fielded question after question, marveling at his precociousness. He turned to his mother.

"Mother, why did you choose father?" he asked. "Why didn't you choose a king? You're beautiful enough."

His father laughed. "I'm not sure whether to be insulted or praise him for how well he judges women."

Young August kept his wide eyes on his mother. She looked down at him and beamed.

"I could never resist a man in uniform," she said behind a quiet chuckle, exchanging a secret look of pleasure with her husband.

At that tender age, he misunderstood the tone in her voice and the look the adults exchanged, and he heard only her words.

"When I grow up, I'll wear a uniform too," he said.

She looked at him fondly. "And you will be dashing in it, my darling."

The boy walked on, pleased with his plans.

Now in front of the mirror, he smiled at the memory. He tried to imagine what his parents would think of his promotion.

He checked his watch, paced, looked at the phone, checked his watch again. He hated waiting. Especially when there was no action to take.

He sat on the chair, took a deep breath, and forced himself to relax. He tried to analyze his nervousness. When he was on assignment, he felt nervous only when he thought his identity might be compromised. Because he took such pains to prepare for the roles, those moments were rare.

Where was this anxiety coming from? He tried to reason it out. Today would be a celebration. There was nothing to fear.

Easy, easy. You're home. You can drop the mask. You don't have to pretend to be anyone else.

It took a lot out of him to keep up the pretense. Although languages—and adopting a persona to go with it—came easily to him, it was still a matter of having to be "on" all the time. He could never let his guard down, not even with people he grew close to. Like Janette. There was a risk with growing close. He always had to hold something back. Not only his true identity, of course, but other things as well: the need to share hopes and dreams and fears.

He took a deep breath and let out an audible sigh. Would he ever again be in a relationship where he could trust and be trusted?

The look on Janette's face when he was led out of

the café gave him the answer. There was no way he could reach her to reassure her that he was okay. That was the other thing he hated about the job. Separations became permanent. Like death.

Thoughts of death brought back the image of the day when he answered the door to a military officer holding his hat in his hands and wearing a sad, pitying look. He brought news of his father's death at sea, and when his mother clutched her chest and collapsed on the floor, the man sprang into action and called for an ambulance. They rushed her to the hospital, but she never recovered.

Two days after the funeral, Helga, then fourteen years old, began to have nightmares in which she searched and searched but could never find some elusive prize. She awoke drenched and shaking, sometimes screaming.

August thought her dreams were likely a reaction to loss or perhaps a stern refusal to accept the irrevocability of death. But there was no action he could take to make it right for her. All he could do was bring warm milk and tell her stories—playing all the characters with accents and mannerisms—until she fell asleep again. And that was what he did.

He retrieved a pouch from a secret pocket in his boot. Inside were two photos and a letter. One showed August and Helga side by side, his arm draped over her shoulder. He gazed at the photo. How young they were. It seemed a lifetime ago. It was taken the summer after their parents had died, just before he entered university.

The other photo was more recent. It showed Helga and Kurt holding a toddler between them. Gunther, his nephew. August smiled at the chubby arms and legs, the happy little face.

He unfolded the letter, heavily creased and dog-eared. Her last letter. When Helga and Kurt fled Germany, her fury at August went far beyond her usual threat to disown him. She had banished him from her life.

He brushed it off at first, but when he tracked them down and visited, she refused to see him. Kurt tried to intervene and play the role of peacemaker, but Helga refused to budge. After months of his attempts—and, he was certain, a great deal of urging from Kurt—she sent the letter. He treasured it.

Dear August. You're relentless. Yes, come and visit! You know I could never stay angry with you for long. As for Kurt, he too is—

August scanned down the page.

—because after mother and father died, we had only each other. But when you decided to—

Agitated, he turned to the next page.

—and I regret that all this has happened. To let something like that come between us. You—

The phone rang. An indistinct professional voice gave him a curt greeting. "The Obergruppenfuhrer will meet with you this afternoon."

"Thank you."

He hung up, carefully refolded the letter, and slipped it and the photos back into the pocket.

He had visited Helga as often as he could. Winning his way back into her good graces became a hard-fought campaign. He sent her flowers and letters and little gifts that he knew would melt her heart, and gradually her anger dissipated. They were close again. The relationship had healed.

Then three months ago he made a trip to their house only to find it empty. The only thing he found was a pendant he had given her years ago, a miniature hand mirror on a chain. It had special meaning, and he knew it was something she cherished. The fact that it had been left behind was an alarming sign.

Every day he grew more desperate to find them, recalling every conversation, wondering whether he had offended her again. But that made no sense. Her happiness at seeing him again had been real. They had simply vanished, and he had no idea where or why.

As he stared at his reflection, a thought that had been circling the back of his mind came forward. I need to impress Heydrich. He was desperate for this promotion, not for the status or prestige it may give him, but because it would give him latitude to ask for favors.

And when the thought was articulated, August realized the source of his nervousness: He was planning to use Heydrich's influence to find his sister. It was a risky move. But he brushed away his nervousness by reminding himself that he had never been afraid to die.

His only fear was never seeing Helga again.

Chapter Eleven

FOUR YEARS AFTER THE ENCOUNTER WITH THE GESTAPO, Brigitte was still confined, though not by bars. Her inability to find work as a nurse drew limits around her life that she found hard to bear and harder to understand.

Her searches had followed the same pattern with the same inevitable outcome: a convivial interview that led to an enthusiastic offer of employment, and soon after, a curt withdrawal of the offer.

The experiences left her baffled. If she were not right for the job, why did they make the offers? How could they be enthusiastic one minute and dismissive the next? She fixated on scenarios, trying to solve the puzzle. After several positions fell through, all in the same manner, she drummed up the courage to ask why.

She called the places where she had applied and asked to speak to the administrators. At one place, the administrator was available until she gave her name, then he was not in and not expected in for several days.

At another, she gave a false name and said she was calling from the university. When the person came on the line, she admitted who she was and why she was calling. The line went dead. Other places refused to put her call through.

One afternoon she waited outside one of the hospitals in Berlin until she spotted the man who had interviewed her.

She followed him to his car, her heels beating a rapid tap-tap-tap-tap on the pavement.

"Herr Bluth?"

"Yes?" The administrator turned, smiling, but his smile faded when he saw who it was. "What do you want?"

"I want to know what is happening," she said. He ignored her and kept walking.

"Please talk to me. I need to know what's happening. My credentials are good. You said you were fortunate to hire me."

He looked around to see if anyone was watching. "Please, sir! I just need a moment of your time."

He called over his shoulder, "Things don't work out sometimes. Good luck in your search." He continued to his car.

"No, this has happened several times. I just—"

"I have no answers for you." He reached his car and turned to face her. "Please don't come here or call again."

She watched him drive away.

Over the next few days, she went to the other hospitals and waited. None of them would talk to her. A few threatened to have her arrested. At one place, the administrator screamed at her, drawing a crowd of onlookers. After being rebuked for several minutes, Brigitte stumbled down the street in tears.

Half a block away, a pair of strong arms steered her into the doorway of a fashion boutique. She looked up to a white coat and a kind smile.

"I'm Dr. Gerhard," he said. "I hope you will forgive my following you. My job is healing, and sometimes that healing includes the wreck and ruin inflicted by Herr Faber."

His voice was calm and soothing, full of compassion. Fresh tears flowed over her lids and trekked down her face. He handed her his handkerchief.

"Thank you, doctor."

"I saw what happened," he said. "Alas, I cannot influence whether you are hired. I can, however, offer you work."

She looked up, surprised and hopeful.

"Probably not what you are looking for," he rushed on, "but a bit of work that will give you something to do until you find the place lucky enough to hire you."

So Brigitte became a maid for the Gerhard family. The work was easy—cleaning and dusting the already immaculate house on Schafer Strasse—and it gave her the means to pay for rent and food.

Dr. Gerhard's wife went out of her way to encourage her. Frau Gerhard gave Brigitte clothes, always with the excuse that she needed to clear out her wardrobe, but Brigitte knew it was her way of being generous without making Brigitte feel like a charity case.

Dr. Gerhard came home from work early one day, sat her down, and said he had solved the mystery.

"It seems you are the victim of a system that keeps track of wrongs, even perceived wrongs that have no basis in truth," he said.

"I don't understand," she said.

He looked at her over the rim of his glasses. "Your arrest four years ago."

Her jaw dropped. *That* was why no one would hire her? "But I was released without being charged!" she sputtered. "I wasn't even supposed to be arrested. They mistook me for someone else. Maybe if I—"

"—No, my dear." Dr. Gerhard's voice was calm but firm. "Do not try to fight the system."

"Then they win?"

"Only for a little while," he patted her hand. "The tide will turn. Believe me, it will turn. In the meantime, there is work to do."

She took the hint and stood up. He laughed and motioned for her to sit back down. "Not dusting and cleaning. No, no, you are far too talented for that to be long-term. I am talking about the real work."

"I don't underst—"

"You'll learn more. Soon. Trust me."

Chapter Twelve

IAN JASPER WAS HANGING ON EVERY SINGLE WORD of Walt Wembley's tale, mouth agape and eyes wide, so much that he tripped over the curb when they arrived at one of the outpost offices of British Military Intelligence.

Walt caught him in time—no losing his audience if he could help it—and they camouflaged the incident with a quick laugh before Walt soldiered on with his story. Ian resumed an attentive stare, glad no one was around to see his near blunder.

Inside the office, James Reville had been watching from the window and saw the stumble and Walt's catch. He rolled his eyes at the gawd-help-us who was at this moment climbing the stairs into the building with Walt and wondered what the Germans would think if they realized these two were part of their intelligence network. *Perhaps they'd get so busy laughing their bums off they'd forget about fighting. As good a way to win a war as any, I suppose.*

James picked up the newspaper from his desk and did his best to focus while he waited, but he could hear the voices down the hall and knew Walt was in storytelling mode. He had two favorites: the day Rudolph Hess landed in England and the day he got word that his brother-in-law had been killed at Dunkirk only to find out later it was another man with the same name and how when he showed up at the house, it caused his sister to faint in the doorway.

James had heard both stories enough to have memorized them. He tried to guess which one this was. He had his money on the yarn about Hess.

The two toddled up to his desk, still talking, neither paying attention to James.

"So he picks him up and who do you think it is? Bloody Rudolph Hess!"

"You don't say!" said Ian.

Oh, but he does say, thought James, *over and over*.

"Sure enough, that's who it was," said Walt. "Captain almost pissed himself."

James tossed the newspaper aside and cleared his throat, hoping to stop the story before Walt got into red herrings and the blitz.

The two men looked at him in surprise.

"Hallo!" said Walt. "Well, look who it is! Jamie Reville!"

"James," he corrected. He looked at Ian. "I take it you're Jasper."

"Ian Jasper," Ian said, holding out his hand.

"From Bletchley Park," said Walt. "How about that? A math whiz in our midst."

"I know, Walt. We requested him." James turned to Ian. "Ready for a trip to France?"

He nodded and tilted his head toward Walt. "Foreign Office gave me their names and some key phrases I'll need when I go."

"Right. Now you're going to be coming back with some Germans. We've contacted one of our men over there and he'll meet up with you."

"So I'll be getting the codes off these Germans, I take it."

"Exactly."

"Why are you having to send him for the codes?" Walt asked. "Why can't you just get 'em when the Germans get here?"

James gave an exasperated sigh. How did this guy even get into the Foreign Office? "Because we need the codes right now and we need someone from the Park to verify and it might take a while for our guy to get there to bring these men back. If you must know."

"I heard they're being sent over straight from Canaris," Walt said. "Looks like he'd figure out a way to get 'em here. Hess managed to get here without us—"

"Look, all I know is the information we get through the channels," said James.

"Yeah, but what if these guys are red herrings?" Walt asked. "Like Hess. I still think he's one. Gerries blitzing us day and night, here he drops in on us. Just the thing to take our thoughts off defending ourselves."

"Not arguing this point with you again, Walt," said James, dismissing him. He plopped into his chair, opened a desk drawer and began flipping through folders.

Walt sat on the edge of the desk, earning a dirty look from James. Walt's eyes landed on the newspaper. He leaned over to read it.

"What's this? 'Support for German Clergy is Critical.' Says who?"

"That's Bishop Bell's letter to the editor," said James.

"So this Bell wants us to support German clergy, does he?" Walt laughed and turned to rib Ian. "And on a critical mission at that."

"It's an opinion piece, Walt," James rolled his eyes.

"Is that right? Well, my opinion is that he's guilty of treason," Walt said with a guffaw. "Supporting Germans of any stripe is a bit against policy these days, what?"

"Oh, I don't know, not all Germans are bad," Ian said thoughtfully. "Good and bad in all people. Across a whole country, there's bound to be some good."

Walt didn't like it when people tried to weigh in with logic. He stared Ian down. "You serious?"

"What do you mean?"

"You really think you could find a good Kraut?"

"Well ... sure."

"That'll do, Walt," James pulled out a folder, spread it out, and nudged Walt off the corner of the desk.

"Our mission is to kill Krauts, right?" Walt said, itching for a debate. "If they were any good, they wouldn't be working for Hitler. Which is why I say kill them all. Best course of action there. Be done with it."

"Which is why you and your idiotic course of action are not called on for field duty," James said hotly. "Some Germans want to help and they're informing to us."

Ian looked from one to the other. From the look on James' face, he was worried that a full-fledged fight would break out with blood drawn. He thought of something to break the tension.

"So what about that ruckus in America?" He elbowed Walt to get his attention.

"Pearl Harbor you mean?"

"Yeah. They say whole fleet's dead in the water."

"Not the whole fleet," James said, schoolmaster style. "Some of their ships were lost, some are still afloat. And they still have a large air force."

"At least Roosevelt got war declared right quicklike," said Ian.

"The doughboys'll be joining us any day," Walt bleated. "And it's about bloody time. Let the Yanks deal with the likes of Rudolph—"

"Give it a rest, Walt," said James, rolling his eyes again. He handed a folder to Ian. "Here's the address of the safe house in France where the SOE are waiting. Good luck."

He snatched the newspaper from Walt's hands and turned his back on them.

Chapter Thirteen

THE GERHARDS HELD A VARIETY OF GATHERINGS —including dinner parties, cocktail parties, salons— where Brigitte met many people.

They called it the Schafer Circle, and at first, she thought she would be working at the parties as a maid, but Dr. Gerhard told her he wanted her there as a guest.

"Not so much for you to meet the right people, but so they can meet you," he said.

The gatherings were lively and thought-provoking. Many of the attendees were high-ranking government officials, some from an aristocratic background, and she was grateful to be included. Dr. Gerhard introduced her as a colleague and left it at that. No one questioned her past. No one asked where she worked or what she did.

Brigitte noticed that Dr. Gerhard carefully orchestrated the topics. There was never an overt complaint or insult about the Nazi regime, but the discussions were kept high-level, centered around issues such as improving work conditions in factories or the importance of restoring cordial relations with other countries after the war.

Occasionally a group of three or four would go into the study or library—for more pointed debates, Brigitte assumed—but it was so subtle that their absences were rarely noticed.

As time went on, Brigitte came to know many people at the gatherings: some new faces, a few well known.

At one gathering, a man struck up a conversation by asking if she knew how to lie well.

"I beg your pardon?" she asked.

"Tell me a lie and I can point out the changes in your face and body," he said.

She laughed and told him she had ten brothers and eleven sisters.

"Ah! Not true. You rubbed the side of your nose," he said.

"But what if my nose itches? I won't be able to scratch it until I'm telling a lie. Otherwise I'll confuse the interrogator."

"Very insightful," he said. "Now tell me what kind of work you do."

"I'm—" she hesitated, then rushed on, "—a colleague of Dr. Gerhard."

He studied her face and gave her a quick smile. "So you are."

Then he told her about the various signals one could look for when spotting deception: tightened lips, little or no eye contact, elbows tucked in close to the body.

He regaled her with stories of people who tried to lie but gave themselves away in comical ways. She listened in rapt attention, suddenly self-conscious about what her face and body were doing. The stories became more outlandish, and her laughter drew a crowd.

He paused to take a sip of wine, and she rushed into the pause. "Who are you?"

He raised his eyebrows at her. "Ah, but after this discussion will you believe anything I say?"

"Probably not," she laughed, "but I want to know anyway."

He frowned, thinking hard, then said, "My name is ... uh ... Hans Gisevius. I am ... let's see, what am I? ... I am a diplomat and an intelligence officer."

He exaggerated signals—squinting his eyes, rubbing his nose, rolling his eyes—and gave her a wide grin. He held his hand out. She took it with a giggle.

"Pleased to meet you, Herr Gisevius, if that is your real name," she said.

He leaned in again, close to her ear, and whispered, "Don't worry, Brigitte, you won't be a maid for long. I think you'll be good at this." Then he walked past her.

She turned around, but he was lost in the crowd. *What is he talking about? How does he know I'm a maid? How does he know my name?*

She turned to the others who had gathered around. "Who was that?"

"Hans Gisevius," one of the men said, his amiable face lit up with a grin.

"So it's true he's an intelligence officer?"

"And a diplomat. He works with us." He motioned to a man standing next to him—short, graying, dignified, with sharp eyes that never left her face.

She looked from one to the other, searching for flaring nostrils or tightened lips. "Where?"

"Abwehr," the man said. "I'm Hans Oster. This is Admiral Canaris."

She nodded a greeting and went to the bar, a bit awestruck.

That night she had a hard time falling asleep. She retraced the conversation in her mind, wondering about this esoteric circle she had been welcomed into.

Over time, she noticed that the topics became more

focused on specific plans for transforming the political structure, with the conversations becoming more direct.

One evening she sat next to Fabian von Schlabrendorff, who served as adjutant to General Henning von Tresckow. Out of the corner of her eye she saw the general leave his seat to join a few others in the library. Schlabrendorff held her attention, keeping her spellbound with his observations of the three branches of American politics. She kept him equally fascinated with her sharp, perceptive comments.

The exchange continued past dinner and into the drawing room.

"I would rank it the purest form of democracy that exists today," he said, his face bright with fervor. "There are checks and balances to ensure total equality. The judicial branch is no less than the legislative nor the executive. It is a political marvel that their founding fathers engineered such a system."

"And it has been going strong for more than a century and a half," she said. "They must be doing something right to retain a citizen-centric structure for that long."

Schlabrendorff leaned in close to whisper. "We can only hope that Germany will soon return to a similar structure. Imagine it."

She froze. Such remarks were generally *verboten*, at least among the Nazis, and she didn't want to commit herself. Despite the general conviviality of the gatherings, she still wasn't sure whom she could trust, and she couldn't afford to be ostracized again. What was it Dr. Gerhard had called it? *A system that keeps track of wrongs, even perceived wrongs with no basis in truth.*

She was saved from an awkward silence when the library door opened, and the general appeared along with a dozen men. Schlabrendorff was immediately at attention. He bowed, thanked her for a lovely evening, and went to the general's side.

Another time, Dr. Gerhard invited a small group over for aperitifs before an evening at the theater. Brigitte had no plans to attend the show, but she completed her shift as maid, then changed clothes and went into the drawing room for a drink and, she hoped, an inspiring parley.

She picked up a glass of wine and winked at Rolf, the servant holding the tray. He returned a sly grin.

She ambled around the room, nodding and smiling at the guests, then she made her way into the library. Before she knew it, she was engrossed in a lecture that touched on a variety of subjects: religion and patriotism and individual will and cosmic fate and where God could be found among it all. She found herself captivated by the swirl of ideas and ideals.

"We may make our meticulous plans and our carefully constructed campaigns," the speaker said in closing, "but it is almost guaranteed that we will be interrupted by God. In fact, we must be ready to allow ourselves to be so interrupted."

There was a spattering of applause, but Brigitte was too deep in thought to clap. The comment had resonated deeply and brought to mind her nursing career that had been derailed. She had considered it a failure on her part somehow, though she had done nothing wrong. Now she wondered if it was one of "God's interruptions." The thought gave her hope. Her eyes filled with tears, and she swung around to make a dash to the lavatory—and came face to face with Hans Scholl.

"Not everyone is brought to tears by one of Pastor Bonhoeffer's messages," Hans said. "He might be glad to know you were. It shows you were listening."

"I always listen to his messages," she said, wiping her tears. "You look well, Hans."

"So do you." He gave her a quick embrace. "I saw Sophie last week. She misses you."

"And I miss her. Is she starting university yet?"

"Soon, yes." He swung to one side to introduce his friend. "Please meet my friend, Theodore Haerker. He works as a translator in Munich. Haerker, this is Brigitte Bauer."

Brigitte and Haerker shook hands.

"Brigitte is fluent in several languages," Hans said. He winked at Brigitte. "Her bantering with Professor Wichmann was quite the show."

Haerker raised his eyebrows. "You know Professor Wichmann?"

"Not really," she said. "I was friends with his sister, and I studied with her fiancé. I met August only a few times, once at his sister's wedding."

"A few times was all it took," Hans teased. "Sparks were flying between the two of you."

Brigitte blushed. "It was nothing like that."

"I met with him several times to get his opinion on some of my work," said Haerker. "He's quite accomplished in linguistics."

"By now quite accomplished in other things," she said, leading them to a settee. "He joined the SS."

Haerker frowned and shook his head. "I'm sorry to hear that."

Brigitte caught Rolf's attention, and he brought over some drinks. They caught up on what had been happening in their lives.

Brigitte's story was concise: The day after the arrest, she had moved to Berlin and tried to find work, eventually ending up as a maid.

Hans told her about the Gestapo confiscating everything from their house: journals, poems, essays, diaries, song collections—essentially everything that would show them as being members of an illegal organization.

"They still follow us," Hans said. "We're on their lists."

"What lists?"

"Oh, didn't you know? The Gestapo has lists," Haerker said. "The Kreisau Circle. *Die Schwarze Kapelle*—the Black Orchestra." He took a drink. "Even the Schafer Circle."

A chill went down her spine. "This is just a gathering of people. We're not doing anything wr—"

"—It doesn't matter what we're doing," Haerker said. "We're a named list. The Nazis have labeled us. That means they're doing everything they can to find out about us and stop us."

"That's why we came up from Munich," Hans said. "We brought information about what the Gestapo is doing there."

"Is there anything we can do?" Brigitte asked.

"There might be some things we could do," Haerker said.

"I don't want Sophie to do anything dangerous," Hans said. "And whatever I do, she'll end up being involved in it."

Brigitte shrugged. "The written word can be action enough, can't it? Seems a safe way to protest."

~ ~ ~

The day after the gathering, Haerker sent her a note offering her a job doing translations.

"You mentioned the written word being action

enough," he wrote at the bottom. "I like the way you think. Come help us with our action."

She discussed it with Dr. Gerhard. He kissed her forehead.

"I was hoping something good like this would come from your attending our gatherings," he said.

Brigitte continued to attend the Schafer Circle gatherings as often as she could get to Berlin. Sometimes she went with Haerker or Hans, sometimes alone. Though she missed being a nurse, she was reunited with Sophie and Hans, and that made her feel like she was back on track again. *Maybe the past few years were merely a God interruption.*

She knew Pastor Bonhoeffer would understand.

Chapter Fourteen

HEYDRICH SCRUTINIZED AUGUST UP AND DOWN, appraising the new insignia. August endured the inspection with a slight smile, staring straight ahead.

"The new rank looks good on you," Heydrich said.

"Thank you, sir."

"And the reports on your performance have been glowing." He flipped several pages in the folder. "Very effective. And most efficient." He looked up at August and smiled. "I count you one of the best of my staff."

August sat taller and preened a bit. "I hope I can serve in a larger capacity." *Preferably somewhere I can get to the files of where Germans have relocated.*

"In fact, I have something in mind," Heydrich said, pulling a folder to the center of his desk. "Heading up one of our Special Actions groups—"

A quick knock on the door interrupted them. His aide walked in. Heydrich's eyes narrowed at the intrusion.

"We found them," the aide said. "They're at Le Havre."

Heydrich's expression changed. It was good news. "Excellent. Let's get them back."

"We intercepted a coded message," the aide explained. "The British have them at a safe house. They're waiting for a liaison to take them to England."

Heydrich bristled. "We need to get these men back here before they're sent to England."

As he watched the exchange, a flash of inspiration came to August. *If I prove myself invaluable, I'm one step closer to getting information on Helga.* He could feel his heart beat faster.

For a split second, he was afraid it might be a setup to test him, then he quickly dismissed the idea, reasoning that Heydrich could have tested him at any point while he was on assignment. He took a deep breath and seized the moment.

"If I can get there before the liaison, I can pose as him and reroute the men back to Germany," he said.

Heydrich turned back to him and studied him quietly. He saw how calm and composed August was, so sure of himself. He made a decision.

He turned to the aide. "Get Wichmann transport to Le Havre."

The aide nodded and rushed out to carry out the order.

Heydrich turned back to August. "Use force if you have to. Get them to our office in Vichy, then get back here as fast as you can."

August stood and saluted. "I'll see to it at once."

"At which point you will have my gratitude."

Exactly what August wanted to hear.

Chapter Fifteen

THE TRAIN STEAMED ITS WAY FROM MUNICH AND WAS bound for Berlin, the Nazi flags flapping on either side of the engine. The train was only four cars long, but it received priority at all junctions and crossings solely because of its passenger list.

One of the cars, furnished in elaborate decorations—wood, satin, velvet—carried Hitler and two of his most trusted aides: Joseph Goebbels and Alfred Rosenberg.

Goebbels had been with him since the beginning, carving out his mission in the press and in his speeches. Hitler considered his acumen with public relations indispensable.

Rosenberg was another matter. Named head of the Nazi Party in 1923 while Hitler was incarcerated following the Beer Putsch incident, Rosenberg was a staunch member of the party, effective in laying the groundwork for what had become the Third Reich. In fact, Rosenberg was a little too effective for Hitler's comfort, and he kept him on a short leash.

Goebbels and Rosenberg could not have been more different in temperament. The two men stood before Hitler now like attorneys from opposing sides, arguing a case before a district judge.

Goebbels laid out several newspapers on the desk in front of Hitler.

"All of the press in Britain is filled with protests of his arrest," he said with passion. "Damn the clergy! All of them!"

Hitler glanced across the papers. "What is being said? And who is saying it?"

"Bell. Some clergyman from Chichester. He's published several letters about Niemoller's arrest."

"And that he was moved to Dachau," said Rosenberg. "That's the news that tugs at his readers."

Goebbels glowered at Rosenberg in irritation then turned his attention back to Hitler.

"The *point*, Mein Fuhrer, is that Niemoller is damaging to your image," he said. "His execution is the best damage control."

"Nonsense," said Rosenberg. "That would only draw more attention to the case."

Goebbels turned to face Rosenberg. "Perhaps you misunderstand how the public would react. It is, after all, not your area of expertise."

Rosenberg threw a patronizing smile at Goebbels. "Here is what I understand about public relations. Beck's resignation was *bad press*." He emphasized the words with a dark look into Goebbels eyes. "We don't need the situation compounded."

He turned back to Hitler. "People listen to Bell. He's not just a clergyman from Chichester. He's a bishop *and* he's the deacon of Canterbury *and* he's in the House of Lords." Rosenberg finished with a flourish and looked at Goebbels in triumph. He'd done his homework on Bell, something he knew Goebbels had neglected to do.

Hitler looked from one to the other. He turned and looked out the train window, arms behind his back. He turned back to them.

"I agree with Rosenberg."

Goebbels gaped. Rosenberg smiled. "But th-the—" Goebbels stuttered.

"There will be no more discussion," Hitler said. "I have no problem with how Niemoller is treated. But keep him alive."

Hitler dipped his head slightly and stared at Goebbels over the rim of his glasses, waiting for acknowledgment of the command.

"Yes, Mein Fuhrer," Goebbels said quietly. As he turned away, the look he shot Rosenberg was pure venom.

Chapter Sixteen

AUGUST COULDN'T HELP MAKING COMPARISONS. After the arrogant efficiency of Berlin and the fear-laden bravado of Paris, Le Havre was a breath of fresh air.

The air was not only fresh but icy. Situated on an estuary of the river Seine and facing the English Channel, the town withstood a biting cold that blew almost constantly in the weak December sun. August didn't mind. In fact, had he not been on assignment, he might have enjoyed a holiday there.

The name Le Havre literally meant "the harbor" and its history was a valiant tale of a harbor town surviving one calamitous thing after another.

Founded in 1517, a range of mishaps, ranging from plagues to storms to conflicts—both religious wars and battles with the English—had hindered any real progress or development. Undaunted, the town drew strength from centuries of persistence and merely showcased Le Havre's preservation as a picturesque, quasi-medieval town.

August sauntered through the market and focused on faces and voices. The civilian business attire helped him blend in. He hoped it would lead to the men before they were sent into enemy territory. Years ago, he and

Kurt had spent a year at Cambridge. They both loved the country: the old-world elegance, the civilized manners. He smiled at the memory. *Hard to think of them as the enemy.*

He turned his attention to the search. He wanted this assignment to succeed so he could build Heydrich's trust, maybe even his favor. Perhaps Heydrich would be so grateful for the excellent way August handled the assignment that he would allow August to use the means of information Heydrich had at his disposal to find his sister.

He allowed himself a moment to daydream a wildly successful mission and a happy reunion with his family.

Then he steeled himself for the task. Up streets, down alleys, around corners, he sidled up to conversations and listened in, low-key and discreet. He figured the SOE group would want to be as close as possible to an escape route, so he concentrated on the areas close to the actual port.

Later that night, he sat in a quiet bistro on the waterfront. He nursed a drink at a table near the bar, positioned to both stake out the door and overhear customers banter with the bartender. The night wore on.

The next day he strolled through the streets and meandered past cafes. He remained alert and perceptive, attuned to every nuance, his eyes taking in everything. A few stray words caught his ear. English. British accent.

"—like the bloody mess at Dunkirk—"

"—Right. You know what Churchill said about—"

August whipped around and searched frantically. The voices were gone. He eyed the faces, walked briskly among them, and struggled to hear. They were gone. All he could get were snippets of French. *Now what?*

He stopped and looked around at the buildings. A

bank. A coffeehouse. A few nondescript office buildings. Apartments. He zeroed in on the coffeehouse.

He dashed across the street and walked in to find a late afternoon lull. A man and woman at a table on the far wall, a bottle of wine and two glasses in front of them, their heads close together. An ancient resident at the bar looked up at him with weak, watery eyes, then slid his gaze away.

August made his way to a table and ordered a cup of tea. He relaxed into his role. *You're George Middleton. You're from England, expatriated here, and you miss home.*

The afternoon wore on, then the evening. He replaced the cup of tea with a beer and a sandwich. He went back to his hotel.

He came back several days in the afternoon, relaxing at the same table, a cup of tea in front of him. One day, his patience paid off. A man walked in: suit, bowler hat. August sat up.

The man plopped down at a table and caught the eye of a waiter. The waiter ambled over. The man concentrated hard for a moment and enunciated carefully.

"Juh voo-dray une ... oh hell, I just want a bloody cup of tea."

August made his way over to the table. "Allow me." He turned to the waiter. *"Est-ce que je pourrais avoir un thé, s'il vous plaît?"*

The waiter nodded and went to the kitchen.

"Well done you!" the man said. "No telling what I might've ordered."

"My pleasure, Mr. ?"

"Jasper. Ian Jasper. Have a seat."

August sat. *Remember, you're from England, expatriated here.* August held out his hand. "I'm George

Middleton. Pleased to meet a fellow Englishman here on the continent." He spoke with a neutral British accent.

"From hearing you place that order, I'd have taken you for a Frenchman. No offense."

"I've lived here a while. You pick up the language or don't eat."

Ian let out a belly laugh.

Two cups of tea later, they were still talking.

"Let me guess," Ian said. "Your accent has a bit of Home Counties. London?"

"Suffolk originally."

"You don't say? I'm from there."

Damn. What were the odds? August thought fast. "I mean I was born there. Then we moved to Southampton."

"Well, France is all well and good, but better you than me is how I feel about it. I'm only here on business." Ian thought for a minute and revised. "Well, government business. Not the same thing as making money, is it?"

"All doing our bit for king and country, though, right? At least that's the talking point at Whitehall."

Ian lowered his voice to a whisper. "What? Not with MI-6 are you?"

August glanced around, leaned in, and whispered. "Foreign Office just contacted me to get some gents past the Germans. Guess they figured since I know the language and terrain and all. Thing is, I think they gave me the wrong address. They're hid pretty well."

August reached into his jacket for a set of papers. They were forgeries, of course, but he hoped they were close enough to the real thing to get him in the door.

Ian glanced at the papers and jumped up. "You must be the chap we been waiting on. Come with me."

~ ~ ~

August stood near the door of the safe house. In the far corner of the room, two SOE agents grilled Ian, keeping an eye on August. They whispered, but their anger raised the volume and August caught most of the conversation.

"He orders tea for you, and you bring him back here??" the first agent said.

"It's not like that," said Ian. "I found out he's from Suffolk and—"

"So he says. He could be anybody." He turned to the other agent. "Why'd they send us this bloke?"

The second agent shrugged. "They wanted the codes checked out. Who knew we'd get a bungling—"

Ian threw his arms wide. "No, I'm telling you, I know that—"

The second agent leaned in, getting into Ian's face. "What do you know? Hanging out at Bletchley Park, so used to doing nothing but reading code you can't spot the obvious." He waved the documents. "These aren't even our usual papers."

"You know, I noticed that too," August called from across the room. "I asked 'em about it and they said they'd just revised the forms." They turned and stared at August for a moment. He gave them a cheery smile. "You know how it is. Pencil-pushers at Whitehall need something to do."

They eyed him intently, then turned to huddle closer together. They whispered more quietly, reducing to a level August couldn't hear. But he could read their lips.

"Why can't we just send the codes?" the first agent asked. "Because Canaris wants the men sent to England too," the second said.

August perked up at Canaris' name.

"Look, if these papers aren't proof enough, call the Foreign Office and ask for someone else," he said. "All I know is they said time is of the essence with this Canaris business."

The two agents studied August, deliberating. The first agent nodded.

"All right. Since you know the route. Head out after dark." He pointed to Ian. "But he goes with you."

August was irritated at having an extra rider, but he didn't dare protest. He forced a smile at Ian. "Jolly good."

~ ~ ~

Later that night, August pulled up a car to the curb. The first SOE agent looked up and down the street. Coast clear. He brought three men out and put them in the back.

August studied their faces but kept quiet. There'd be time later to let them know he was one of them. Ian handed the men some blankets. He waved his arms in exaggerated fashion and pointed to the blankets.

"You...have...to...hide," he said, slowly, exaggerated. The agent rolled his eyes. "They're German, not deaf!"

Ian looked at August. "You don't speak German by chance?"

"Sorry, old chap. Bratwurst and lager is about all I know."

Ian bellowed out laughter. "Right! Learn the language or don't eat."

August and Ian got in the car. August grinned at the agent. "Cheerio!"

For the first half hour, the miles rolled by quietly.

The three men stayed huddled under the blankets, and not a peep was heard from the back seat. August turned to Ian.

"Did I hear you say you're looking at codes?"

"Yeah. This is what those guys were bringing with them." He pulled a paper out of his pocket. August glanced over and saw symbols, lines, and random letters.

"Looks complicated."

"It is," Ian admitted. He studied the paper. "I should have a go at it."

August turned his attention to the road. Some minutes later, he glanced over and saw Ian's head droop. He lifted it and glanced around in a stupor.

"It's a long drive, old chap," August said. "Don't feel like you have to stay awake to keep me company."

Ian gave a quick smile and sighed in relief. "Thanks."

He leaned against the door. In a few moments he was snoring. August drove on. There were no distractions. He had time to relax and settle back into his own personality.

He turned his thoughts to Helga and the day he took up his commission.

~ ~ ~

He had come into the house in full uniform. Her face turned white. Then she realized it was him. The shock gave way to anger. "What is this?" she demanded.

"How do I look?"

"You look stupid," she spat out.

"Now there's an intelligent response."

"You did it anyway," she said, her tone flat and disbelieving.

He ignored her comment and asked again. "How do I look?"

"I can't believe this." She looked at Kurt for support.

He shrugged. "What do you want me to say? He's made up his mind. He's enlisted."

"Why is this so terrible to you?" August asked. "It's a chance for me to make something of myself, to be someone—"

"You're already someone!" she yelled. "You're my brother. And a professor. Isn't that enough? And the SS?? Good God, you could be killed!"

"Sure. Defending our country," he said. "The most honorable way to die."

He'd said it lightly, expecting her to come back with a witty barb and start a debate.

Instead, her face fell, and she let out a sob. The anger drained out of her, replaced by a flood of tears down her cheeks. He groaned and moved toward her.

"I'm sorry, Helga—"

She ran from the room.

He stared after her, full of remorse. Her passionate anger he could handle; her grief left him helpless. He looked at Kurt.

"I'll talk to her," Kurt said and walked down the hall.

August flopped onto the sofa. After a moment, he bolted upright, mindful not to wrinkle his uniform. He looked around. The insignia on his collar cast a reflection on the walls, like stars twinkling around the room.

~ ~ ~

The road stretched out in front of him. He saw a sign ahead that read *Vichy ... 5 km.*

He looked over at Ian. Still asleep. August saw an

inn ahead and pulled off the road just past it. He spied the code paper lying idle in Ian's hand. He eased it out of Ian's grasp and tucked it into his secret pocket. He got out, went around to Ian's side and pulled out his pistol. He opened the door. Ian almost fell out.

"What's all this--?" Ian looked around, bleary-eyed. He saw the weapon and looked up, his face filled with fear.

August pulled him out of the car. "You stay here. I'm taking them to safety. Back to Germany. It won't be safe for you."

The men in the back looked up. He aimed the pistol at them. "Get down! *Unten!*"

They pulled the blanket over their heads.

"Oh my God, you're a bloody Kraut," Ian whispered.

August ignored him and pulled out a fistful of francs. He handed them to Ian and pointed to the inn. "You can stay there."

Ian threw the money on the ground. "I'm not taking anything from a Kraut!"

"Just take the money. Go to the hotel and call the safe house to pick you up."

"You think I'm stupid?" Ian cried. "Bloody Germans never do anything out of kindness!"

"Ian, I'm trying to help you—"

"—Oh no, I've heard about what you people do. I don't want to end up—"

"—I'm just trying to get these men back to Germany. And that way I can—" He stopped trying to explain, picked up the money, and put it in Ian's hand.

"So, what are you doing this for?" Ian asked. "Trying to curry favor with some higher-up? No German can be trusted, you know. Including you. You're probably going to shoot me in the back as I'm walking away."

"Good luck, Ian." August jumped back in the car and drove on. He looked in the rear-view mirror and saw Ian throw the money down again and point a finger at him.

"I only trusted you because I thought you were an Englishman!"

A few miles later, August eased the car next to the depot and parked. He got out and strode to the platform. An SS guard greeted him.

August pulled out his papers and flashed them at the guard. "Delivering some men as ordered. See that Heydrich is informed."

He handed over the car keys. The guard clicked his heels and held up his hand in the Nazi salute.

August moved onto the train. After a few minutes, the train moved out. August was eager to get back to Berlin and see whether he had curried enough favor with Heydrich to get a search going for his sister.

Chapter Seventeen

LIKE MOST GOVERNMENT BUILDINGS IN BERLIN, the structure was imposing, as it was meant to be. Its thick concrete walls built to withstand the ravages of war that were inevitable, given that they were fighting two fronts with most of the world determined to see their demise. Five stories high, with several stories below ground, the building housed several agency offices, most notably Abwehr headquarters: Canaris' domain.

Inside a small office on the top floor, Dohnanyi and Bonhoeffer huddled together, poring over a stack of files. An agent walked in.

"They're back in Germany," the agent said.

"What??"

"One of Heydrich's men got them. Right under the nose of the SOE." The agent handed him two slips of paper.

Dohnanyi grabbed the papers and darted into Canaris' office, with Bonhoeffer trailing behind him.

Canaris was at his desk, with Oster across from him

"They didn't make it," Dohnanyi said.

"What happened?" Oster asked.

"Intercepted by the SS. Here's the cable that went to Heydrich."

Dohnanyi handed Canaris the decoded message. He read silently and handed it to Oster.

Oster held it up and read aloud. "*Wichmann delivered men to Vichy.*" He looked up. "Who is this Wichmann?"

"Someone very clever, apparently," Dohnanyi said, handing him the second paper. "This went to MI-6."

Oster read aloud. "*Liaison just arrived. We surmise that a bloke posing as one of ours took the men and Jasper. Bloody good ruse. Will await your orders.*" Oster shook his head. "Brazen of him. Devastatingly so."

Canaris looked at Bonhoeffer. "Let your contacts in England know they'll be delayed."

"Right away," he said.

Canaris turned to Dohnanyi. "We need to find out if any of them talked. Any idea whether they're still in Vichy?"

"I'll find out."

Canaris nodded and set the paper aside. He trusted Dohnanyi to carry out the order with precision. He was free to turn his attention elsewhere. He picked up a folder and handed it to Oster.

"Here are plans for the Paris project. Goring and Himmler will be there. Let's try to get both."

Chapter Eighteen

AUGUST WAS BACK IN HEYDRICH'S OFFICE, BUT NOW he was more confident than he'd been at the last visit. Heydrich studied him, a bemused look on his face.

"Do that accent again," Heydrich said.

"I don't know what you mean by accent, old chum. This is just how we Brits talk." The British accent was heavier than what he'd used, but he was performing.

Heydrich laughed. "I thought you'd be going in with force," he said, giving August an admiring look. "But the way you handled it was ingenious. I'll be sure the Fuhrer knows what talent I have on my staff."

"Thank you, sir."

"You deserve a reward for a job well done," he said.

August sat up straight. He had practiced how he should ask for the favor.

Heydrich turned serious. "The last time you were here I mentioned Special Actions. We're improving our methods, and I want you to help with that."

"Yes, sir."

"You'll get to see the next one in person. It's in Poland. At the front. We travel there next week." Heydrich smiled at August. "Consider yourself lucky. Not everyone has such an opportunity."

August left the building deflated and frustrated. He made his way to a beer hall down the street and went in. He scanned the room, spotted someone on the far side, and made his way over to the table.

"What kind of Intelligence officer leaves work early to grab a beer?" August barked out. "Don't you know there's a war on?"

A man looked up at him in alarm, then he saw August laughing and joined him.

"Well, if it isn't August Wichmann. And if my training serves me, I detect that you're not surprised to see me here. Come, join my celebration. I just received orders to Paris."

"So I heard. That's why I'm here." August sat down and motioned for a waiter. He doffed his cap and set it onto the table. He turned to him with a grin. "Barth Klinger never met a beer hall he didn't like."

"Neither did you when we were in basic training," said Barth. "Not to mention those missions we did together. How long has it been anyway?"

"Let's see … the recon in Marseille … three years?"

"Right. What are you doing in Berlin? I thought you were in Paris. I had planned to look you up and have a good time in the City of Lights."

"I was reassigned to Heydrich's team."

"Interesting. Someone with your skills transferred to his team. Wonder why."

August started to answer, but Barth held up a hand. "No, never mind. Tell me nothing, and I'll know nothing at the right time."

They both laughed, then August took a deep breath to quell the tension. He didn't want to sound desperate.

"How about a favor for an old friend? I need to locate someone in France. Confidential, of course."

"Who is it?"

August hesitated. Revealing information could be costly. Could he trust Barth? He took the leap. "My sister and her husband. I lost track of them."

"You're not on the outs with Heydrich, are you?"

"No. In fact ... what do you mean?"

"That's the first question when people are suddenly missing," Barth said. Then he laughed. "In fact, I heard someone say parachuting into London isn't as risky as being related to Heydrich's enemies."

August regarded him for a long moment. "It's nothing like that. I'm on good terms with Heydrich."

"Good. Try to keep it that way." He watched August pull out paper and pen and scribble the names. "I'll have a courier meet you weekly."

August handed over the paper. "It might not take that long."

Chapter Nineteen

THE UNDERCURRENT OF FEAR WAS STILL RIFE in the streets and alleyways of Paris, but pockets of Resistance kept some of the men and women busy with tasks that, they hoped, would return the city to them.

Fritz, a tall lanky Frenchman, was one of them. He walked around an area roped off for an upcoming parade and selected a spot in the empty viewing stands. He held up his hands as if he were holding a rifle and took aim at a spot in the distance. He nodded, satisfied. He made his way back to his apartment.

Once inside the apartment, he locked the door and retrieved the rifle from a closet.

He heard a knock at the door and stashed the weapon away. He opened the door to a cute petite brunette, full of life and energy. Janette. He planted a kiss on each cheek. She slipped into his arms, pressed against him, gave him a long kiss.

"I just checked the area. I can get both Goering and Himmler when they pass the theatre." He looked at her curiously. "I didn't expect you until tomorrow. Aren't you arranging the entourage?"

"No, *mon cher*. That's what I came to tell you. They cancelled the visit."

He shrugged. *Ah well. We'll get them another day. There'll be other chances to wipe the Boche off the face of the earth.* He gave her a sexy grin. "I'm glad you came to tell me in person."

He pulled her inside the apartment and closed the door.

Chapter Twenty

BRIGITTE DASHED OUT OF THE UNIVERSITY AND MADE it to the bus stop just in time. She was running late for her job at Haerker's office. She knew it wouldn't matter if she were late—he knew exactly what was happening in Professor Huber's psychology class—but she wanted to get there in a hurry just the same.

Sophie, with characteristic exuberance, had convinced them to stage a mock protest, hoping to stir up the other students. Brigitte had helped with the planning, and she couldn't wait to show Haerker the designs.

She found a seat on the bus and leaned back, smiling. Things were looking up. She had a good job—granted, translating manuscripts was not the job in nursing she had trained for—but she had reconnected with Hans, Sophie, and Christoph, and through them she joined in activities that gave her an outlet to vent her frustrations against the government.

Things could be worse. In fact, she'd even say she was grateful.

The bus stopped half a block away from Haerker's office, and she was so eager to discuss the protests with him that she ran the distance. She was out of breath when she breezed in the front door.

"Wait until you see what we came up with!"

"Brigitte," Haerker said. His voice held a warning.

She suddenly noticed a man standing to the side, almost behind the door. She saw the Gestapo uniform, and her heart pounded. She was so startled she dropped her bag. The contents spilled out onto the floor.

"My apologies, Fraulein Bauer," he said. "I did not mean to frighten you." He reached down and gathered her things and handed them to her with a smile.

She scanned his face. Where had she seen him?

"Perhaps you don't remember me." His voice was gentle and soft. "I am Agent Koch. We met during an unfortunate encounter at the home of some of your friends."

At Sophie's house when we were arrested. She stared at him, afraid to speak.

"You see, I remember you quite well," he said. "That evening, in the midst of—" He glanced at Haerker. "—the confusion, my hand was injured, and you offered me a bandage. I found the gesture enchanting. And unusual. So unusual that I decided to find out more about this person who took pity on a soldier wounded in the line of duty. As it were."

She stole a glance at Haerker. He was keeping wary eyes on the agent.

"Would you like to know what I discovered?" he asked.

She shrugged her shoulders, not trusting her voice.

He pulled out a notepad, flipped it open, and began reciting. "You were not sixteen years old as you stated that night. You were twenty." He looked up at her. "You are quite young looking. This may be why we were deceived. It's also possible that you were frightened and confused." He waited for her to respond.

"Y-yes."

He looked back at the list. "You are from Frankfurt. An only child. Your father was a clerk in a law office and was killed during the *Sturmabteilung* incident in 1934."

Brigitte looked down at her shoes, not out of fear but to hide her fury. *Incident? The Night of Long Knives an incident? SS bastards. Call it what it was: a bloodbath.*

Koch gazed at her. "I understand your father was simply in the wrong place at the wrong time. A most unfortunate event. The government issued an apology, yes?"

She gave him a cool glance. "Yes." The apology was a half-page letter expressing condolences. *And nothing about him being gunned down in his office with the other clerks because his boss had the same name as another man they were after.*

"This also allowed you to exempt your mandatory National Labor Service project," he said.

"Yes."

He turned his attention back to the notes. "You took care of your mother until her death a year later. After her death you studied to become a nurse." He gave her a warm smile. "A lovely way to honor the memory of your mother."

Haerker came over and put his arm around her. He stared Koch down. "What do you want?"

Koch regarded Haerker for a moment, still wearing a genial expression. "Herr Haerker. I do have a question for you. How is it that you came to hire a nurse to do translations?"

Brigitte started to answer, but Haerker jumped in ahead of her. "She answered my advertisement. She has good skills with languages."

Koch turned to Brigitte. "Most of which you learned while traveling to other countries with your father."

Brigitte nodded. She didn't know what else was in his notepad, but she figured the truth was best at this point.

"What do you want?" Haerker asked again.

Koch kept his eyes and smile focused on Brigitte. "I want to offer an apology. It seems that due to our ... misjudgments ... you were not able to get work as a nurse." He ignored Haerker and stepped closer to Brigitte. "I want to make amends."

He handed her a card. It had his name and title printed on one side and a name and phone number hand-printed on the other.

"Call this man tomorrow," he said. "He will hire you as a nurse. I give you my word."

Brigitte was dumbstruck. She looked at the card, then up at Koch.

"I recognized your talents that day when you offered to help me," he said. "It has been a disgrace that you have been deprived of using those talents for so long."

He bowed to her, continued to ignore Haerker, and left.

She was wary, but she couldn't contain the excitement bubbling up inside her. "What do you think?" she asked Haerker.

"He's Gestapo." He went back to his desk.

"But he sounded sincere about what happened."

He shook his head at her. "You're free to do whatever you want, Brigitte." He turned his attention back to his work. "Just remember he's Gestapo."

Chapter Twenty-One

OSTER WALKED INTO CANARIS' OFFICE AND BROKE the news to him that the Paris project had fallen through.

Canaris looked up sharply. "Why?"

"Someone in the entourage tipped them off. Goering and Himmler cancelled the trip." He eased in, sat down, and took a deep breath before delivering the next news. "They arrested Fritz this morning."

Canaris looked out the window and shook his head. *Another setback.*

"Gather everyone. We need to plan another one as soon as I return." He rose and put on his coat and hat.

Oster thrust his chin toward the coat and hat. "Where to?"

"An invitation to the front. Heydrich's showing off his skills to the General Staff." He rolled his eyes as he said it. "But a chance for us to gather more evidence."

~ ~ ~

Canaris rode in the train car with several generals, including chief of staff Wilhelm Keitel and Heydrich. Canaris took note of the lieutenant seated beside Heydrich.

"A new aide?" Canaris asked Heydrich.

"A new member of my Special Action staff," Heydrich said. "He's here to observe how we do things. Admiral Wilhelm Canaris, meet Obersturmfuhrer August Wichmann."

So this was Wichmann. Canaris held out his hand. "Wichmann."

August took his hand. *So this was Admiral Canaris.* "A pleasure, Admiral. I've heard a lot about you."

"That's not good news to a spy."

Laughter erupted from the generals. August and Canaris measured each other for a long moment. Keitel leaned over toward Canaris.

"So America's in the war, eh, Canaris? It's all part of the Fuhrer's plan."

Canaris frowned at him. "What do you mean?"

"He'll have them where he wants them. On European soil. And he'll crush them," Keitel said. "He outlined it all in a meeting last week."

Canaris stared straight ahead. It was an effort not to roll his eyes at the bizarre logic.

"It's usually prudent not to underestimate an opponent," Canaris said. "Especially before we meet him on the battlefield."

Keitel laughed in his face.

Mid-morning they arrived at the battlegrounds. Signs of war stretched out across the horizon: overturned vehicles, smoke and fire, dead and wounded lying around. The generals whooped it up, giddy at the sight of all their planning manifested before them.

Canaris, no stranger to war, still grimaced at the waste, the needless slaughter. He surveyed the devastation in silence. He cast a quick glance to August and saw stone-face observation. Then he watched as August's jaw tightened and his breath quickened.

Later, they were taken by car to the middle of town. The townspeople stared at them, wild with terror. A truck pulled up and soldiers piled out.

"Watch and learn, Canaris," Keitel called to him. "This is how we make sure not to underestimate an opponent."

The soldiers rounded up the townspeople, about two hundred Jews, and herded them through the town. Among the group were several children.

A little boy toddled by in front of August and dropped his toy. August picked it up and handed it to him. The little boy smiled and flexed his fingers to wave "bye-bye." He rejoined the group.

The soldiers shoved the Jews into the synagogue. They locked the doors and hammered nails into boards across the windows, then they poured gas around the outside of the building.

August looked on in horror, his breath catching in his throat. "What are they doing?" he whispered.

Keitel heard him and laughed. "Sending our opponents up in smoke."

A soldier lit the gas and the building roared into flames. Screams surged out from the building.

August looked around and saw the gleeful faces of the generals. He noticed Heydrich gazing up at the burning building, a wide grin on his face. August inched back and swallowed hard. He turned and saw Canaris studying his reaction with interest. He looked away.

On the train headed back to Berlin, August was seated again with Keitel, Heydrich, and Canaris. Lunch was served, but he refused. He got up and went to the lavatory. He locked the door and stared into the mirror. Haunted eyes looked back at him. He looked away, off into the distance.

He heard the screams. He saw the little boy drop his toy. The little boy turned into his nephew. He saw himself pick up the boy and run.

He blinked, and the vision was gone. His breath was coming fast. His hands were growing numb, and he looked down at them. They were shaking. He deliberately slowed his breathing by taking long, deep breaths. He closed his eyes and saw the little boy again.

A knock on the door brushed away the memory. He opened his eyes, splashed cold water on his face, and hid his face in a towel. He exited back into the train car and bumped into Canaris.

"Pardon."

"Wichmann. You don't look well."

August gave him a wan smile and started to move down the aisle. "I'm fine."

Canaris blocked his way. He took August's arm and led him to a seat away from the others. He spoke in a low voice. "I heard about Le Havre. When you transported some men to Vichy."

"I wasn't aware the Abwehr knew me."

"We make it our business to know a lot of things." They both went silent and studied each other for a moment. Canaris spoke again. "It was daring, what you did. Getting them out of the SOE safe house. Quite a feat."

The color returned to August's face. He smiled. "Thank you."

"You saved the SS a lot of trouble. They'd been after them for weeks. The men kept escaping."

August frowned. "You must be thinking of other men. I was sent to rescue these from British custody. They were—"

"—Heydrich's enemies, on the run," Canaris said. "As soon as you dropped them at Vichy, they were sent to Dachau. I assume you've heard of it."

"The concentration camp?" August's voice was barely audible.

"I heard they're testing Zyklon-B in the gas chamber there. The men you rescued might be among those selected." Canaris stood and looked down at August. "As I said: quite a feat."

The color drained back out of August's face. Canaris turned away. August stood, put his hand on Canaris' shoulder. "Wait!"

Canaris turned around.

"How do you know all this?" August whispered.

"There's not much the spy network wouldn't know."

August took in the comment. "So it would seem." He eyed Canaris, curious. "Suppose I want to verify other information?"

Canaris gave a slight smile. "Feel free to drop by."

Part 3

If you board the wrong train, it is no use running along the corridor in the opposite direction.

~ Dietrich Bonhoeffer

Chapter Twenty-Two

SITUATED ABOUT TWELVE KILOMETERS NORTHWEST of Munich in the state of Bavaria, the town of Dachau rose almost five hundred meters above sea level and was bound on three sides by the river Amper, the Amper glacial valley, and a marshy area called Dachauer Moos. Most would describe it as a charming medieval town.

Not so charming was the concentration camp built near it on the grounds of an old abandoned munitions factory. Opened in 1933 by Himmler, it was the first concentration camp in Germany, and its original purpose was to house political prisoners. It was the model camp and served as the training center for the other SS-staffed camps.

Dachau was later enlarged to include Jews, foreign nationals from countries Germany invaded, ordinary German and Austrian citizens, and just about anyone else who disagreed with the Nazis.

August passed through the gate with the usual double-check of credentials and made his way to the main office. He told them he was there on Heydrich's order to verify that the prisoners had been transferred properly. It was a lie—Heydrich had no idea he was there—but one he felt wouldn't be cross-examined.

Heydrich's orders were rarely questioned, mainly because of what happened to those who questioned them.

His reason for being there was dubious at best, but he had to know whether Canaris was right about the men from Le Havre being sent to Dachau.

It had haunted him for weeks, had haunted his nights—endless nights when he woke in a cold sweat from a dream in which he pulled into the depot at Vichy with corpses that bore his name on their arms.

There was no way he could ask Heydrich about the men. He decided to make a visit to Dachau and see for himself whether the men had been transported there. If nothing else, he hoped the trip would exorcise the nightmares.

August waited an hour while they checked the files for men coming in on that date, but they couldn't locate the men. August had no names for cross-reference, and they did not have photographic files for him to review.

The clerks helping in the search were worried at the report that would go back to Heydrich, but August reassured them that they had been most helpful and he would let Heydrich know.

It was a little white lie ... on top of another white lie ... *When do the stacks of white lies begin to discolor?* he thought as he walked to his car.

"That can't be young August Wichmann."

August started. *Heydrich doesn't know I'm here.* He turned to see a frail old man in prisoner garb smiling at him. As the man walked toward him, August stared, at a loss to place him.

"You don't remember me," the man said as he reached August. "I don't blame you. I'm not easy to recognize in these clothes."

With a flash, August knew him: Pastor Martin Niemoller. It had been years since he'd seen him, long before he went to college, and he was beyond frail now—down to skin and bones—but his smile was still the same: genuine and full of love. August gave a small laugh at the recognition, but he was filled with wonder at Niemoller's attitude. How could he smile at a time and place like this?

"Pastor Niemoller! Of course I remember you," he said. "I'm surprised you remember me. It's been a long time."

"Actually, it wasn't you but your father I saw," he said. "You look just like him."

August's chest swelled with pride, and he gave a broad smile. "Thank you," he said. "That's very kind." He glanced around at the camp, then looked back at Niemoller with embarrassment. "How ... uh ... how are things here for you?"

Niemoller gave a sad smile, with a look in his eyes that August couldn't quite read.

"Not as bad as things are for you," Niemoller said, eying August's uniform.

And then he saw the look in Niemoller's eyes for what it was: pity.

"What do you mean?"

"The things you're having to do," Niemoller explained. "And worse things you've yet to be called on to do..." Niemoller trailed off but he held August's gaze.

"I don't know what you mean," August said with a short nervous laugh. "I'm just—"

"—doing what you're told," Niemoller cut in, "serving your country like a good soldier, protecting the Fatherland. Yes?"

"Something like that," August said.

Niemoller shook his head and grinned. "The young August Wichmann I remember is too smart to fall for that," he said. "What would your father say if he saw you now?"

"I think ... he would be proud to see me in service," August said, but his voice lacked conviction.

"Not in that uniform." And Niemoller's smile had faded away completely. "Look in the mirror and ask yourself why you are wearing it. Then listen for the answer. If, after hearing the answer, you can bear to keep wearing it, then you will know that is the moment you lost your soul. But if you cannot stand to wear it any longer, take it off and bear the consequences."

He started to walk away, then turned back. "I will pray for you, August Wichmann," he said. "Either way you choose, you will need prayer."

August watched him melt into the crowd, then got into the car. Through the windshield he saw the smoke-stacks rising into the air, thick black smoke billowing out the tops.

He stared, riveted, until his mind wandered to the train ride back from the front, when Canaris had looked down at him, his words clear and foreboding: *I heard they're testing Zyklon-B in the gas chamber ... The men you rescued might be among those selected. ... Quite a feat.*

As he drove away, the image from his dreams rose in his consciousness—the lifeless bodies of the men from Le Havre, prostrate in the back of the car, their arms stretched out with August Gunther Wichmann tattooed on their forearms.

His mind raced, searching for a persona that he could hide inside. But none would come.

He looked in the rearview mirror and caught sight

of his visor cap, the new insignia polished and shining. The face stared back with wide eyes, flaring nostrils, mouth agape. No persona. Himself. Alone.

A stab of anguish hit the pit of his stomach. His hands started to shake. He gripped the wheel, then tore one hand loose, grabbed the cap, and flung it across the seat.

Chapter Twenty-Three

THE TOWN SQUARE WAS PACKED FOR THE EVENT, but the crowds were composed and attentive to the speaker. No jostling about, no rabble-rousing, no unforeseen dissent. The armed guards would see to that.

The crowd stared with rapt attention at the speaker: Adolph Hitler, hair falling into his eyes, arms waving wildly. He screamed with enthusiasm. The rise and fall of his cadence seemed to lull the crowd into a feverish trance. They cheered at everything he said, no matter how bizarre the message. He screeched at the microphone, focusing all his will on it.

Across town, inside the Bonhoeffer home, the speech came to them through the wireless. Even through the mechanical box, Hitler's words still blasted through frantic, urgent, and more than a little mad. Bonhoeffer and his father, Karl Bonhoeffer, listened in silence, glancing at each other occasionally.

The doorbell rang, followed by sounds of happy greeting from the foyer. Dohnanyi entered, looked at the wireless, then at them.

"How can you bear to listen to that?"

"I can't," said Bonhoeffer. "Father has a professional curiosity, though."

The voice on the wireless grew louder and more forceful.

"Crazed ramblings of a narcissistic megalomaniac," Karl said.

"Quite fascinating." He listened for a few more moments. "Turn it off. I've heard enough."

Dohnanyi turned it off and joined them. "Enough to make an assessment?"

"Indeed. I've made it." He went to the desk, retrieved some papers, and handed them over.

Dohnanyi glanced through. "Good. Your expertise will help our case."

Bonhoeffer sighed. "A renowned psychiatrist states what we already know: that the man is unbalanced, irresponsible, most definitely insane—"

"—and surrounding himself with other sick men," his father finished up. "A dangerous combination."

Dohnanyi eyed him quietly. *The question was how dangerous and at what cost.*

"Are you afraid of repercussions?" he asked Karl. "It's possible that this assessment could harm your standing at the university."

"It's my professional opinion," he said. "It's the truth. And truth, dear Hans, does not generate fear."

"But lies can generate frenzy," Bonhoeffer said. "You hear the crowds. They worship him." He let out another sigh and shook his head. "While the church remains completely silent. It's baffling."

Dohnanyi gripped Bonhoeffer's shoulder in sympathy. "They'll find their voice soon." He didn't quite believe they would, but he wanted to say something comforting.

"What are the odds of getting Hitler to stand trial?" Karl asked.

"To be honest? Slim," Dohnanyi said. "But we have to try. And we can't arrest him until we've documented enough evidence."

Dohnanyi dropped into a seat and leaned back. That was the dilemma in a nutshell. At the moment it might as well have been shooting the moon.

Chapter Twenty-Four

AUGUST STUDIED HEYDRICH WHILE HE REVIEWED a folder that outlined the Special Action at the front, boasting at the efficiency of the operation. August watched his movements, his expressions, his reactions —and was amazed at how he could have missed the core of evil inside this man.

There was no other way to categorize him: *a man who could laugh as people—young, old, women, children, a little boy carrying a stuffed toy—were shoved into a synagogue and set on fire is a man with a core of evil.*

At the thought of the little boy, a pain shot through his bowels, and he felt a wave of nausea. *Something else. Turn your mind to something else.* He had been so eager to curry favor with this man, and the thought sickened him even more.

What was he doing in this office, listening to this man relish the torture and senseless killing of defenseless people? How did he end up here? His mind raced to connect the dots. He spoke several languages fluently and assumed roles with such ease that he earned trust quickly, and that trust gained information, and those skills had brought him to the attention of this madman, and for a moment he worried that he might throw up on the desk. He almost snickered at the image of Heydrich's desk and uniform covered in his—

"Wichmann?" Heydrich's tone was sharp, irritated. "Are you ill?"

August snapped to attention. "I'm fine."

Heydrich nodded and continued his prattle.

August struggled for a calm, unruffled demeanor. He took quiet deep breaths and focused. *What role am I playing now? SS officer. God help me.*

"We just finished an action in Kiev," Heydrich was saying.

August flashed on an image of Heydrich gazing up at the burning building, a wide grin on his face. "Like the one in Poland?"

"No, more effective than that one," Heydrich said. "Most of this one went well, but we're concerned about containment."

"Containment of what?"

"Our methods are top secret. We don't want any leaks. If we find any, we need to eliminate them. And anyone they know."

August thought back to his conversation with Barth. What had Barth said? *I heard someone say parachuting into London isn't as risky as being related to Heydrich's enemies.* August felt a chill go over him.

"What do you want me to do?"

"Go to Kiev. See if anyone's talking."

Chapter Twenty-Five

AS HE HAD DONE IN LE HAVRE, AUGUST SAUNTERED through the streets in civilian clothes, seeking and listening. He was subtle and inconspicuous, but this time his actions were lackluster, his energy subdued.

He looked down at his clothes, wondering if he was disguised enough. Any clothes besides his uniform would do, he supposed. The thought of his uniform brought back the memory of his meeting with Niemoller, and he could hear the old man questioning his choice to wear it.

If you can bear to keep wearing it, then you will know that is the moment you lost your soul. But if you cannot stand to wear it any longer, take it off and bear the consequences.

He considered the chasm between the two choices, and he began to shake. He stopped in the middle of the sidewalk so suddenly that a woman behind him bumped into him. He apologized and leaned against the building, taking deep breaths to calm down. He scolded himself: *Remember, you're playing a role. You're good at this.*

After a moment he felt able to go on. He pushed Niemoller from his mind and continued the quest.

By the end of the third day, he had a lead. Casual conversations and careful questioning had led him from one person to another, a person here checking on rumors, a person there making a phone call. He made his way to the outskirts of the town, to a small house set back in the woods. August knocked.

A small block at eye level opened for a moment, then closed. The door opened and a woman ushered him in and bolted the door behind him. She led him into the living room and motioned to a chair.

He looked around the room. Safe house. He wasn't sure about safe, but it certainly looked comfortable. It reminded him of his parents' home, the home he had shared with Helga as they were growing up.

Ingrid was muscular and energetic, bustling around the room, drawing curtains tight, keeping up a running chatter the whole time.

"Normally I don't let anyone in, but since Herbert sent you, it's okay. To be honest, Herr ... what's your name again?"

"Lauder. And you are...?"

"Call me Ingrid. Herr Lauder, to be honest, I thought Admiral Canaris was sending someone next week to get Dina's testimony."

At Canaris' name, his heart pounded but he recovered quickly. "Yes. The admiral is always so busy. He must have forgotten to tell me."

"Busy is that man's middle name," she said, fluttering around, breathless. "Well, it was nice of him to wait. When they took the truck driver's testimony, Dina just wasn't ready. They agreed to come back."

"Right, right. The truck driver." He snapped his fingers, pretending to recall the name. "What was his name again?"

"Hofer."

"That's right. Hofer."

A knock pulled their attention to the door. Ingrid went over and looked through a peep hole, then opened to a woman holding a medical bag.

"Thank you so much for coming again," she gushed, ushering the woman in. "I'll get her. Come on in and have a seat."

The woman entered the room, spotted August—and stopped.

It was Brigitte, her hair an ash blonde pulled up into a bun, but the eyes were the same, and August recognized her at once.

He found his voice. "Hello, Brigitte."

She turned away, her face flushed. She looked at the door, the window, the hallway. Any exit would do.

Ingrid leaned over and patted August on the arm. "No, this is Traute, a nurse who helps us out sometimes."

"Traute," August said. "My pardon. You look like someone I used to know."

Ingrid turned to Brigitte. "Admiral Canaris sent Herr Lauder here to interview Dina."

Brigitte held out her hand and locked eyes with August. "Herr ... Lauder?"

It was August's turn to do an awkward glance around for the exit.

They heard a noise down the hall, and Ingrid dashed away.

Brigitte and August locked eyes again.

"So. Traute the nurse," August said.

"And Herr Lauder the ... Abwehr agent?"

"I ... not exactly. I'm here for Intelligence."

She studied his face, searching for truth. "Are you in the military? Or did you decide not to go in? I saw the Gestapo arrest you in Paris."

"That was—a"

"—Let me guess. A ruse? A deception?"

"A strategic maneuver."

She rolled her eyes and looked down at his clothes. "Please. Spare me the propaganda. At least you rid yourself of that disgusting uniform."

He studied her face, searching for truth. "Why are you in disguise? A nurse has nothing to hide."

"It's a long story."

"I'd like to hear it."

She turned away and paced around the room. "What do you hear from Helga?"

After a moment of silence, she turned back and saw the fear in his eyes. She dropped her guard and took a step toward him.

Just then, Ingrid returned with Dina, a small, frail woman in her early twenties. She was bundled in a thick robe, her left wrist in a cast. She crept into the room and curled into a ball on the sofa, hugging her knees.

Brigitte brought her bag over and gave Dina a brief check. She nodded to Ingrid, then moved to a chair across the room, ready to observe.

Ingrid placed a blanket beside her and whispered into Dina's ear, then nodded to August.

Dina avoided his eyes. Her voice was weak, halting, almost monotone. She started without preamble.

"I was in the fifth group," she said. Her voice was so quiet he had to lean toward her slightly to hear. "I knew what to expect. I knew bullets would rip into me and I would die. But I got to the edge, and I looked down. Bodies were stacking up. I saw it was not far to fall."

She started to shiver, but she kept talking. "I heard the guns, and I threw myself in. I fell on top of the bodies." Her voice rose as the memory resurfaced, a metallic tenor on the edge of panic. "When the soldiers came into the ravine, I closed my eyes. I pretended to be dead so they wouldn't shoot me."

The shivers grew more violent, and her teeth chattered. "One of the soldiers stepped on my wrist and broke it. But I didn't cry out. It was agony. But I didn't cry out. I stayed silent. I didn't want to die."

The shivers wracked her body. August rushed to her and lifted the blanket to wrap it around her. She screamed and pushed him away. He dropped the blanket. She shook her head back and forth, screaming and screaming.

Brigitte jumped up, put her arms around Dina, and pulled her into the other room. After a few moments, the screaming stopped.

August turned to Ingrid, his eyes wide. "What just happened?"

Ingrid motioned for him to sit back down. She took a deep breath and spoke quietly.

"After her group was shot, they used machines to push dirt on top of the bodies. She had to dig her way out." She gave him a helpless look. "She feels suffocated when things are put on top of her."

"Oh my God."

Ingrid brushed away the incident. "Don't worry, you didn't know."

The problem was that August did know. He had listened to the stories in town. He knew there was some truth to them. And he had deliberately sought out this place on Heydrich's orders—to find out who was talking. He looked down at the floor.

"You didn't know," she repeated. "No one would have guessed what she endured at the hands of the SS."

He looked up at her. *At the hands of the SS.* The words slammed into him.

"I'm sorry," he whispered.

It wasn't just empathy for her suffering; it was an apology. He didn't commit the horrors that she'd experienced, but he belonged to the group that either committed them or made them possible.

I'm sorry. Did the apology assuage the guilt? Would it restore Dina's life? Would it make her feel safe again?

"I'm sorry," he said again.

And this time he was apologizing to his sister as well. Helga had known the truth long ago. So had Brigitte. She had told him that day at his house that the SS killed her father. How had she endured his company?

Ingrid led him to the door. "Thank you for letting her speak. She believes she's alive because she was silent. Now she has to learn not to be silent. We all do."

August looked behind her, toward the hall. Brigitte was not there. He waited a moment, hoping she would come out. She didn't. He couldn't stall any longer. He nodded to Ingrid and left.

~ ~ ~

On the train headed back to Berlin, August sat in a dimly lit compartment alone. He let the darkness and the silence wash over him, grateful for the respite from human contact. *I let Dina speak. But how many others are staying silent?*

The landscape rolled by: trees, mountains, streams, but he barely noticed. He had much to think about.

He had been given a command to find witnesses and bring their names back to Heydrich. What would happen to those witnesses?

August had an inkling. A series of images flashed through his mind:

No one would have guessed what she endured at the hands of the SS.

The little boy dropped his toy. August handed it to him. The little boy waved "bye-bye."

In front of the synagogue, Heydrich gazed up at the burning building, a wide grin on his face.

On the train with the generals, Canaris had led him away from the others to talk to him.

Canaris. Ingrid said something about Canaris sending someone next week to get Dina's testimony. *Canaris knew about this?* What was it he said on the train? *There isn't much the spy network wouldn't know.*

He reached into his secret pocket and pulled out the code page he'd taken from Ian. He studied it, wondering what Canaris' people would do when they met with Dina—arrest her or rescue her?

He looked out the window, wondering how long before he was back in Berlin. He had things to do.

Chapter Twenty-Six

IN THE SPACIOUS STUDY OF GENERAL BECK'S HOME, Gehre sat across from Beck and marveled at the transformation. Where Beck had been worried and tense at the meeting at Canaris' house, he was once again the strong, firm, capable commander he had been during his glory days.

The transformation was due solely to his resignation from the Army—which, despite Canaris' pleading, he had done within a year—and only one incident had marred his departure from the military: the other generals had refused to resign *en masse* with him. He shrugged it off and left anyway.

His days now were spent planning a post-war and post-Hitler Germany and had become the Resistance's most ardent supporter. Gehre had come by to deliver secret documents, taking a circuitous route to avoid being seen by the Gestapo.

"The problem is that we need more people to join with us, more willing to take a stand," Gehre said. "They should want to join us. What we're doing is right. I can't understand why we can't generate more support."

"Full picture, Gehre," Beck said. "It's risky for a lot of people.

It's not yet time for them to take a stand."

Full picture was Beck's key phrase. The man had a perfect grasp of the entire operation, yet he could see down to minute details—even Gehre's tendency toward rash action.

"But isn't that rather a sign of cowardice?" Gehre asked. "To be overly concerned about risk?"

Beck took his time answering. Gehre was impatient to get to the promised land of a Germany without Hitler and his henchmen. Beck knew that and considered it admirable. But he also knew it was likely to get Gehre arrested—and then he'd be no good in the effort.

"Think of it this way," he said. "At this point all action is voluntary—and must be so for some time before we can take the reins. It's a vast endeavor. And no room for error."

Beck raised his eyebrows at Gehre, checking to see whether he understood and agreed.

Gehre nodded. He understood perfectly well, but he didn't agree. But he was careful not to voice his disagreement with the man who would be the next leader of Germany. Not at this point.

"I understand sir," Gehre said.

Beck nodded, satisfied. "Good. Let's get some coffee, shall we?"

Chapter Twenty-Seven

WHEN AUGUST ASKED TO SPEAK TO ADMIRAL CANARIS, the receptionist went pale. Instead of picking up her phone, she dashed into the inner offices. After a few moments she returned with Oster.

"This is the admiral's deputy," she said.

August took in the civilian clothes, easy grin, piercing gaze. He held out his hand. "August Wichmann."

A glint of recognition shone in Oster's eyes, a hint of a raised eyebrow. He took August's hand.

"Hans Oster. I'll let the admiral know you're here. Please wait."

August looked around the room, noticing everything—the layout, the doors, the position of the windows. His being there was a ruse, but it was also a reconnaissance mission for him. *Get in the role: officer in the German military, the son of a Naval enlisted man, and you and Canaris both witnessed the horror at the front; he told you to feel free to drop by.*

Oster returned and led him back into Canaris' office. On the way in August studied the door lock. Oster retreated, closing the door.

"Have a seat," Canaris said.

August sat and looked around, taking in the details.

A portrait of Generalisimo Franco hung on the wall. *Franco? Are Canaris and Franco that close?*

He kept a straight face and studied the file cabinet across the room. He noticed the lock at the top.

He looked back at Canaris. He knew he was in front of an expert interrogator. Could he play his role long enough to get information out of him? It would have been so much simpler if he could ask direct questions of Canaris, but could he trust him?

August realized Canaris probably had the same reservations about him.

"Everyone here seems so hard at work," he smiled. "They looked up when I came in. I hope my visit isn't disturbing them."

Canaris nodded to August's uniform. "They probably think you're here to investigate them. Our departments don't always see eye to eye."

August realized that's what had alarmed the receptionist. "Do you have many agents?"

"Worldwide, thousands. Here in headquarters, a few hundred."

"This is quite a busy place. Do they all work round the clock?"

Canaris narrowed his eyes, and August realized too late that he must have sounded like a reporter investigating a news story or a prosecutor gathering evidence.

"What can I do for you?" Canaris asked, his tone sharp.

August dropped the forced geniality. "I'm curious. The agents in Le Havre working with SOE—are any of them ours?"

"Why do you ask?"

August pulled out the code paper and handed it to him.

"This was on one of the men. I wondered if it came from your agency."

Canaris looked at the paper for long moment. When he looked up there was no expression at all.

"I'll pass it along to our code department," he said.

August leveled his gaze on Canaris. "Of course, if those were your codes, I'm guessing they would be secret."

"We are the Abwehr," Canaris said with a half-smile. "We do keep secrets."

"And you keep secret the fact that you're keeping secrets." August's tone was bantering.

Canaris couldn't help smiling. "Excellent point, Wichmann."

"Call me August."

"August. You may call me Admiral. I worked hard for the title."

August laughed. "Admiral. I'm a fan of the Navy. My father served on a U-boat in the Great War."

"So did I. It's possible we knew each other."

"Probably not. He was only a seaman."

"I was a captain. And I know that those 'only' positions are what keep you afloat. Where is he now?"

"He died at sea. My mother died soon after. Of a broken heart, they say."

"Hearts do that. Are you married?"

"No. The military keeps me busy."

"And relationships are harder when one is a professional liar."

August was taken aback. He didn't see that one coming. "I ... suppose that's true."

Canaris grinned at his reaction. "It goes with the job. At least you have no one to accidentally tell. It can be a powerful temptation."

"How do you handle the temptation?"

"Why do you assume I'm tempted?"

"It goes with the job. So you said."

Canaris smiled. It wasn't often he came across someone bold enough to banter with him. "My wife has learned not to ask. And if I feel the need to talk, I have my dogs. They've yet to betray me."

Canaris stood. Meeting over.

August was disappointed. He realized that he liked the admiral's company and would have enjoyed talking to him a bit longer.

He decided to play one more card. He remained in his seat and looked up at Canaris.

"I went to Dachau to locate the men from Le Havre," he said. "They weren't there."

Canaris shrugged. "That's no surprise."

"However, I did see Martin Niemoller," August said. "You knew him, didn't you?"

"Yes." Canaris' face held no expression. "How do you know him?"

"Father served under him."

Canaris took in the detail. "How was he?"

"Emaciated," August said. "As one would expect a political prisoner to be."

He stood and looked Canaris in the eye, searching for grief, wariness, confusion, *anything* that would give him a clue how to break through, at least enough to find a common ground for trust. With a shock, he realized that the old man's face was a mirror to his ponderings. Canaris' eyes were roaming over his face, searching for evidence of truth.

It was a stand-off. August might have been a pro, but Canaris was a master. Without breaking eye contact, Canaris extended his hand. August took it.

"Thank you for letting me drop by, Admiral."

Canaris watched him walk out, then looked down at the code page.

Chapter Twenty-Eight

IT TOOK AUGUST A WEEK OF SURVEILLANCE TO FIND the patterns of entry and exit and the routines of the guards in the Abwehr building.

He picked a night and returned to the building. He waited in the shadows across the street in civilian clothes and a fedora, carrying a folder. He scanned the area and waited. He saw a movement to the right. Two men, heading into the building. He dashed over and followed them, blending in. They glanced back at him and nodded. The fedora and folder kept his face in shadow. They all went inside the building.

The two men went to the elevator. August walked on, located the stairwell, went in, and jogged to the top floor.

He was in the outer offices. He looked around, saw people concentrating on work. Noses to the grindstone. No one looked up at him.

He moved quickly to Canaris' office and glanced left and right. No one around. He pulled a lock-pick out of his pocket. A few moves and he opened the door, slipped in, and closed it slowly behind him.

He pulled out a tiny flashlight, made his way over to the file cabinet, picked the lock, opened, and flipped through some files. Not there. He opened the next drawer, flipped through. There were many files, but not the one he was looking for. He went through the entire cabinet. Nothing.

He moved to the desk and picked open the drawers. No files were inside.

He looked around. His eyes landed on Franco's portrait on the wall. He pulled one side of it. It was on a hinge. He moved the portrait away from the wall. Behind it was a safe. He looked at his watch.

"Damn. No time."

He started to move the portrait back, but he noticed how thick it was. He moved his hand across the back and looked up.

He spotted the lock at the top. He grabbed a chair and stood on it to reach the lock. He picked it and slid a panel. Several folders tumbled out. He spread them on the floor, opened each one, glanced at the contents, and set each aside.

He opened one with a cover sheet that read:

Statement of Truck Driver Hofer about the Massacre at Babi Yar Copies to go to Vatican and Allied liaisons via MI-6 courier.

He flipped a page and scanned down it. His eyes landed on a few words: *...made aware of his situation by the Leipzig Strasse butcher, who has successfully located many individuals for us...*

August stopped and looked at the words again: *...the Leipzig Strasse butcher, who has successfully located...*

August's heart started to beat wildly. *Could the butcher find Helga?*

He heard a noise outside the office, looked up, and

waited, holding his breath. Nothing. After a moment, he looked down at the page again and decided to stay on task and get the hell out of there.

He flipped the page. The testimony started.

> *I was on the road near the ravine. I had a delivery in Kiev that day.*

As he read Hofer's words, the images came alive for him.

~ ~ ~

Hofer, a big and burly man with hands that were calloused from hard work and tough times, maneuvered his truck down a road near the forest. He passed a crowd of people miles long being herded by soldiers with machine guns.

> *I was driving past and seen people going to the ravine. Thousands of 'em. Little kids too. Guns at their backs. Pushing 'em along.*

He pulled into the woods, parked, and eased out of the truck, closing the door quietly. He snuck along the edge of the woods.

> *I parked in the woods and ran back. I stayed in the woods so they wouldn't see me. And I saw what they was doing.*

The people stopped at stations along the way and handed over their belongings: suitcases here, coats there, shoes next, and at last, clothes.

The soldiers stripped 'em, one piece at a time.
Even underpants.

The women huddled together at the ravine. Some clutched children to their bare bodies. The men tried to shield the women.

By the time they got to the ravine they was
naked. Some protested. But them that did was
beat up.

They lined the edge of the ravine, naked, shivering. Their lips moved in silent prayer. Suddenly shots filled the night air.

They shot 'em! Just lined 'em up and shot 'em
again and again.

The bullets tore into the people, sending them tumbling, arms outstretched and flailing, into the ravine.

The people ... the way their bodies jumped ...
it looked like they was dancing on the edge of
the ravine. And then ... the men went into the
ravine, shooting the bodies. Just making sure
they was dead. Walking on the naked people.
On top of 'em!

~ ~ ~

August gaped at the words on the page.

You could hear their ribs break under their
boots.

He stared off into the distance. His hands shook. The paper rattled. The noise jarred him.

He looked at his watch. It was getting late. He put the papers back in the envelope, returned the envelopes to the hiding place, and replaced the portrait.

He left the way he came in—stealthy, anonymous, spectral. He raced to his apartment, putting as much distance as he could between himself and the building that held the document and its vile contents.

~ ~ ~

Later, he sat on the sofa in his apartment in his underwear and t-shirt, his eyes red and raw. He stared straight ahead at nothing, drained, depleted.

He glanced down and noticed a stack of unopened mail. He flipped through and came to a thick envelope, official government stamps on the corner. He opened. A medal fell out: gleaming, gold, shiny. In the shape of a star. And a note:

> *For outstanding service at Le Havre. The work of a rising star in the Third Reich.*
> *~ Obergruppenfuhrer Heydrich*

For a moment he was at a complete loss over what to do with it. He wanted to throw it, to send it back to Heydrich, to burn it. In the end, he just dropped it on the coffee table and headed to the bedroom.

Chapter Twenty-Nine

DOHNANYI, OSTER, AND BONHOEFFER GATHERED in Canaris' office with the door closed.

"He just stopped in for a talk?" Dohnanyi asked.

"He gave me the codes," Canaris said. "But he was here for something else. I don't know what yet."

"What was your impression of him?" Oster asked.

Canaris thought hard for a moment. "Actually, I liked him very much. He's personable. Intelligent. Very smooth."

"And that bothers you," Dohnanyi said.

It wasn't a question. Canaris smiled.

Bonhoeffer looked from one to the other. "Is it possible that he's simply a likable person?"

"In this business? No," Dohnanyi said.

Canaris thought about his meeting with August and the overwhelming urge he had to let down his guard and have a normal discussion, a one-on-one with him, to share views and opinions.

He couldn't point to a logical reason to trust August or to want to work with him. It was something in his gut, an intangible, that made him want to take August into his confidence and find out what he thought of the rash of atrocities that were occurring across Europe.

As usual, he kept such thoughts to himself. He merely looked up at the others and gave a nod.

"I agree," Canaris said. "There's something more going on." He looked at Oster. "Put a tail on him."

Chapter Thirty

THE COFFEEHAUS WAS BUSIER THAN BRIGITTE thought it would be. When Sophie called, Brigitte had suggested the place because of its casual, quiet ambiance. But when she arrived, she was stunned to find it brimming with customers. She scanned the tables looking for the bright smile and pixy haircut she remembered. She made her way to the back, turned around, and inched along, scrutinizing each face as she returned to the front.

"Brigitte! Here!"

She turned to the voice. At first she didn't recognize the drawn and listless face. She sat down and eyed her friend.

"I'm glad you called," Brigitte said. "I've been wanting to talk to you."

"I have news too. My—" The waiter approached, and Sophie looked up with a shadow of a smile. "Two coffees."

When the waiter left, she leaned across the table. "My father was arrested," she whispered.

Brigitte gasped. "Oh my God. Why? When?"

"A month ago. For anti-Hitler remarks."

"Who reported it?"

Sophie shrugged. "It doesn't matter. There's no doubt he said it.

"How long will—"

"Four months," Sophie said, tears rolling down her face. "They sentenced him to four months."

"Where is Hans?"

"The Russian front. Alex and Willi too. They needed medics." She gave a short bitter laugh. "He finally gets to do what he wanted. Thanks to the war."

"War always generates a need for medics," Brigitte said.

Sophie blew her nose. "I got a job in a munitions factory. My stint in the National Labor Service. So I could—"

She stopped when the waiter approached with the coffee. She waited for him to leave before she continued.

"I thought it would be a way to support Hans, but it felt so ... " She groped for the right words. "The hypocrisy was too much. So I staged a slowdown strike and they fired me." She heaved a sigh. "Here I am."

Brigitte reached across the table and squeezed Sophie's hand. "I'm so sorry."

Sophie forced an air of vague enthusiasm. "How are things at the hospital?"

Brigitte hesitated. She had seen and heard troubling things at the hospital, but now she wavered on how much to say.

Located on the outskirts of Munich, the six-story building surrounded by a ten-foot-high stone wall was more fortress than infirmary. At the back of the building, a ramp led down into a basement warehouse, and a brick pathway led to the far side of the property, where a towering brick furnace had been newly constructed.

Brigitte was assigned to process new patients and

assess the severity of their injuries. It was a fairly rote task, but she was willing to overlook any moments of monotony. In truth, she was thrilled just to be in the nursing field, eager to take on any role.

She shared her enthusiasm with Erika, a recent graduate of the nursing school who had started work the same day. They soon became fast friends.

When Erika invited Brigitte to stay at her apartment a few blocks away, she was glad to lessen her commute. They worked the same shift, and every day after work, they walked together to the apartment, comparing notes on the work, the staff, and the patients.

It was Erika who first pointed out some of the discrepancies: that many of the people who came in were not sick at all, that most of them were admitted and were sent to the sixth floor, that the sixth floor housed the mysterious T-4 project, that the ill who were released were not sent to other facilities but had simply disappeared.

Brigitte kept all these things to herself. She had planned to share her concerns with Sophie, but seeing her friend so distraught, she decided to spare her. Sophie's troubles seemed so much larger than the incidents that were disquieting her.

She gave a dismissive shrug. "I'm still getting used to it all. But it's fine."

Sophie gave a slight nod and looked off into the distance with damp, downcast eyes.

Brigitte sipped the coffee and studied Sophie covertly over the rim of the cup, her heart filled with unease.

Chapter Thirty-One

THE NEXT FEW WEEKS WERE BUSY ONES FOR BRIGITTE, with a sudden surge of patients coming into the hospital. But she thought of Sophie often and found herself fretting over the events that had transformed a bright, spirited young girl into the despondent figure she saw in the coffeehaus. She felt an urgent need to check on Sophie and make sure she was okay. She decided to pay a visit on her next day off.

As it turned out, Sophie called first. Erika took the call while Brigitte was at the market on her way home from work.

Erika met her at the door and took the bags from her. "Your friend Sophie called. Three times. She insists you come right away."

A tremor of anxiety seized Brigitte. "How did she sound?"

Erika frowned, not understanding. "Impatient for you to get there. As I said, three calls."

"I mean ... did she sound ... desperate?"

Erika busied herself unpacking the grocery bags. "Desperate? No. More like impatient." She looked up from the bags. "Go on. I'll take care of this."

When she arrived, she saw that Erika was right: Sophie was excited. Hans had returned from the front, and Sophie had arranged a party to celebrate.

When Brigitte arrived, Sophie gave her a tight hug. "Oh, Brigitte, I'm so glad you're here! So very glad!" she sang out. "I have so much to tell you. We've started back up. Getting the protests going. And there are some people I want you to meet. Wait until you see what we've been doing."

It was the old Sophie—the upbeat, passionate girl Brigitte knew. Sophie's entire demeanor had improved, as if her brother's return had rehabilitated her. Brigitte was relieved.

But then she discovered there were other reasons for Sophie's exhilaration. Sophie led her into a back room. A sheet was draped over a bulky form in the corner. Sophie yanked the sheet away to reveal a mimeograph machine.

"A friend gave me the money," she said.

Brigitte stared in awe. "This is amazing."

Sophie got a pamphlet from the table and handed it to Brigitte. "We're starting the protests."

Hans steered two men into the room to see the machine and the pamphlets. Brigitte tucked the pamphlet into her bag and greeted him.

"Welcome home," she said, kissing him on the cheek.

"I heard they allowed you to practice nursing," he said.

She smiled. Now wasn't the time to bring up her concerns about the hospital.

He introduced her to the men: Falk and Arvid Harnack, two brothers whom he had met during his tour of duty in Russia.

Haerker wandered into the room and greeted Brigitte with a warm hug. He nodded to Arvid.

"I see you've met one of the leaders in *Die Rote Kapelle*." Brigitte studied the man. *Die Rote Kapelle*. The Red Orchestra. She remembered Haerker mentioning *Die Schwarze Kapelle*, the Black Orchestra, at one of Dr. Gerhard's gatherings. She assumed they were similar groups. What was it he had said? *We're a named list. The Nazis have labeled us. That means they're doing everything they can to find out about us and stop us.*

Haerker introduced her to Arvid. "I met Brigitte at one of the Schafer Circle meetings."

Arvid gave a slight bow. "Dr. Gerhard was a great man," he said.

"Yes, he—" she stopped, her voice suddenly hoarse. "Was?"

Harker regarded her with sad eyes. "Arrested last month. He and his wife."

"Where are they now?"

"A concentration camp. Most likely."

Brigitte looked down, blinking rapidly to forestall the tears.

Sophie grabbed her hand and nodded toward the pamphlets. "All the more reason why we have to continue our protests. We have to defeat them."

Brigitte sighed. "Yes. Of course." The news about the Gerhards had doused her mood. She thought of the kindly old doctor and his sweet wife being dragged away to a concentration camp, and doubt gripped her heart. What benefit would a few words on paper be now? How could that help defeat the Nazis? The mimeograph machine in the corner, the gallons of ink, the stacks of paper—what good would a mock protest do?

She stayed only a few minutes more, then begged off with the excuse that she had to work the next morning.

She caught a bus back to the apartment. As the bus took off, she leaned back in the seat and pulled out the pamphlet. On the cover was a drawing of a white rose under a headline:

The Manifesto of the Students of Munich.
We will not be silenced!

As she read the text, she was suddenly energized. This was no mock protest. They were deadly serious.

Chapter Thirty-Two

THE AIDE USHERED AUGUST INTO HEYDRICH'S OFFICE.

"The Obergruppenfuhrer is in a meeting upstairs," he said. "He asked me to get you seated. Can I get you anything?"

"I'm fine."

The aide nodded. "He won't be much longer." He closed the door.

August cracked his knuckles and tapped his leg. He noticed the tense movements, stopped, and took a breath.

It wasn't nerves as much as bottled-up rage at Heydrich. He was taut, like a rubber band, ready to snap.

He took a deep breath and focused. *Remember, you're an SS officer. You're on the rise. Heydrich trusts you.*

He looked across the room. Heydrich's file cabinet was slightly open.

August turned back to the door, looked at the file cabinet again. He got up and moved over to it.

He pulled open the drawer. He looked at the door, looked back at the folders.

He flipped through them, pulled out a few, opened them, scanned the contents, and replaced them.

Three floors up, Heydrich walked out of a meeting and headed to the elevator.

~ ~ ~

August flipped through more folders. He stopped at one and opened it. Photos. The faces of the three men at Le Havre. A red stamp on the photos: *Eliminated*.

~ ~ ~

In the elevator, Heydrich looked at his watch, then looked at the descending numbers.

~ ~ ~

August replaced the folder. He flipped through a few more. He read through name after name. He stopped at one and opened: A photo of Helga, Kurt, and Gunther.

August froze.

A noise outside the door startled him. He dropped the folder.

Papers went everywhere.

~ ~ ~

In the outer office, the aide stopped Heydrich and showed him a paper.

~ ~ ~

August looked at the door. He gathered the papers, frantic.

He looked at the door.

He shoved the papers back in the folder and stashed the folder back in the file cabinet.

He looked at the door.

He eased the file cabinet drawer shut.

Heydrich swept in.

August stood, his back to the file cabinet, admiring a painting on the opposite wall.

"Ah. One of Cezanne's finest," Heydrich boasted. "I had it brought here from Paris."

"Magnificent."

August went back to the chair and sat down opposite Heydrich.

"What did you find in Kiev?"

August stared at him for a long moment. *What did you think I'd find, you bastard? Wreckage and ruin, lives shattered or ended because of you.* His natural instinct to take action rose up. He wanted to leap across the desk and punch Heydrich in the face. The only thing that stopped him was the folder he'd found of his family. *Parachuting into London isn't as risky as being related to Heydrich's enemies.* He swallowed the desire for action and kept his face calm and impassive.

"No one is talking. The operation apparently was very effective." He might not be able to take action, but he wouldn't hand Dina over.

"Excellent." And with one word, Heydrich dismissed an entire town and its people. "I'm going to set up a series of meetings to go over our procedures. I'll have my aide inform you when they'll take place. I want you there too."

SS officer on the rise. "Very well."

August saluted and walked out, hating the man he worked for and loathing the man he was forced to be.

Chapter Thirty-Three

AFTER THEY HAD BEEN THERE ONLY A FEW WEEKS, both Brigitte and Erika were promoted to the prestigious T-4 project on the sixth floor. They learned that the work had increased so much that they were recruiting for more nurses to work in the program.

First they had to go to the administrator's office to fill out paperwork for their transfer. The clerk assigned to help them was Herr von Trent, a short balding man with horn-rimmed glasses, a thick mustache, and bushy eyebrows. Brigitte had seen him a few times around the hospital, always silent and observing. She found him intimidating.

He kept an eye on them as they filled out the paperwork. Erika tried to make small talk, but he just stared at her, and she went quiet.

When they got to the sixth floor, they were assigned to release the patients. Brigitte assumed she would be preparing paperwork to send the patients home.

She soon discovered that the hospital had its own vocabulary, much like the political and military language that called pogroms "special treatments" and executions "special actions." She had learned of such euphemisms at Dr. Gerhard's salons and in her work with Haerker and long ago when she was arrested with the Scholls.

She never thought she'd encounter such blatant deceits in the medical field, yet here she was, along with Erika, receiving orders to strap down patients and inject them with needles that had been filled with a serum she was afraid to identify.

The head nurse gave the orders in a bored, mundane tone. "After their release, you must count out five minutes, then check for a pulse. If you detect one, administer another dose and repeat the procedure. When there is no pulse for five full minutes, declare time of death."

Brigitte and Erika looked at each other in horror.

"I won't do it!" Erika said.

"It's an order," the head nurse said. "You cannot refuse."

Erika pointed to the bed. "This is murder! I can refuse to do that!"

A doctor swept in. "Is there a problem?"

The head nurse jutted her chin toward Erika. "She disobeyed a direct order."

The doctor made an efficient half-turn to face Erika. "If you're a professional, you will do as you're told."

"I can't do this!" Tears were streaming down Erika's face. "This is wrong. How can this be happening? Doesn't anyone know about what's going on here?"

The doctor gave a curt nod, strode to the door, and called for guards. Within moments they were in the room. The doctor pointed to Erika. "Please escort this young lady out."

The guards clicked their heels, grabbed Erika's arm, and led her out. Brigitte was shaking as she watched her friend leave.

"She can leave by the back gate," the doctor called

out after them.

He swiveled to Brigitte and peered at her, his jaw clenched firm. "Can you take orders?"

She nodded, too nervous to answer.

"Good. You will have to make up for the time we just wasted." He stomped out the door.

The head nurse nodded to the bed. "Strap her."

Brigitte stepped over. An elderly woman lay there, tossing her head back and forth. Drool was running down her cheek and neck. Brigitte took the straps from the table—and at that moment, she heard three sharp cracks in rapid succession. It jolted her. She looked around.

"What was that?"

"It was nothing," the head nurse snapped. "Continue your work!"

But she couldn't help thinking about it. *What was that sound? Was it a gun? What else makes a noise like that?* She chased the thoughts around in her head as she strapped in the woman. An assistant handed her the needle. She looked up at the head nurse, who gave a sharp nod. She pressed the needle against the woman's skin. Her hand was trembling so hard she kept missing the vein. At last she got it in and pressed the plunger until the serum was all gone.

It took only a few minutes to work. When the woman breathed her last, Brigitte started to tear up.

"You'll need more fortitude than that to work in the nursing field," the head nurse barked.

Brigitte blinked back her tears and stood there stoic, watching the clock on the wall, counting out five minutes. She checked the woman's pulse. Nothing.

"Time of death eight-fourteen," she murmured.

The head nurse led her to the next bed where a young

girl lay. Brigitte guessed she was about twelve, with long blonde hair and bright blue eyes—a lovely, cheerful child who happened to have misshapen, short stumps instead of arms, with small hands where her elbows should have been. She flashed a brilliant smile at Brigitte.

"Good morning," the young girl said.

"G-good m-morni—" Brigitte stammered.

"Don't talk to them," the head nurse interrupted. "They aren't the same as us. They're not really human."

It was obvious the girl understood. Her beautiful face formed a confused frown. Brigitte felt sick.

The head nurse handed over the straps. Brigitte adjusted them for the girl's size, positioning herself so the head nurse couldn't see her face. She gave the girl a warm, encouraging smile. When she administered the dose, she placed her hand on the girl's stump, pretending that she was configuring the needle placement, but she was actually moving her hand in place so the girl could grip her finger—which she did and held on to it while the serum took effect.

Brigitte watched the clock for five minutes, checked for a pulse, and declared time of death.

Then she excused herself, went to the lavatory, locked herself in the stall, and cried—a gut-wrenching, silent flood of grief. *I can't do this. This is wrong. Erika knew. She was right. I can't stay here.* And then she remembered the gunshots she heard earlier. *Were those gunshots? It couldn't have been. They wouldn't do that. Would they? I have to leave.*

She splashed water on her face, dried her eyes, and went out to the corridor. Guards were positioned beside the elevator and the stairwell door. She turned and went back to the ward.

By lunch time they had "released" fourteen patients,

and any time she showed any emotion, she was scolded. She went with the other nurses to the cafeteria, but she had no appetite. All she could think of was getting out of there.

After lunch she was sent to the first floor to the supply room to get more serum. A guard escorted her. The door was locked, and she jiggled the handle in exasperation. She knew she was in for another reprimand for not anticipating that the door was locked. She turned on her heel and bumped into Herr von Trent.

"I need to get more serum," she said in a shaky voice.

He eyed her over the rim of his glasses. "Where is the requisition form?"

She sighed. Another mistake. Without a word, she started for the elevator.

"Wait!" he called. "I'll get the form later."

He opened the door, then waited while she got several bottles of the serum. On her way out, she flashed a warm smile of gratitude.

He glanced from her to the guard, his eyes cold and gray behind the horn-rimmed glasses and bushy eyebrows. She shook her head and went to the elevator. *How can everyone here be so cruel?*

Somehow she made it through the rest of the day. In all, she had helped "release" twenty-seven patients. When her shift was up, she rushed downstairs and found the closest exit. It led to the back entrance.

As she plodded her way across the grounds to the sidewalk, she saw a patch of blood-soaked grass. Her mind raced back to the three gunshots. *Erika?* She realized with a shock that her friend had probably been killed that morning. This was probably her blood. She fell to the ground and threw up.

As she steadied herself, she caught a glimpse in one

of the windows: horn-rimmed glasses, bushy eyebrows.

Her eyes widened in terror. *They'll think I'm pro-testing like Erika did.* She ran away.

Herr von Trent eyed her all the way down the street.

Brigitte went back to the apartment. Erika wasn't there, confirming her worst fears. She couldn't stay there. She couldn't go back to the hospital. She thought for a moment. There was one place that might be safe. She packed a bag and dashed out the door.

Chapter Thirty-Four

AUGUST HAD NO TROUBLE SPOTTING THE COURIER. The man was a half block ahead, bobbing his head and whistling a tune, clutching the envelope that, August hoped, carried news of his sister from Barth's sources. August rolled his eyes. The courier was only slightly less conspicuous than the bright yellow stars on dark coat sleeves that used to be found around the city.

As he made his way to the courier, August looked back and saw a man turn abruptly to look in a window. The man's face looked familiar. Where had he seen him? And then he recalled several other incidents when he would turn and see a man suddenly interested in something else—a window display or a car horn or a dog on the sidewalk.

August frowned. An agent, obviously. But whose? And why? If it was one of Heydrich's men, he had to keep him away from the courier.

He glanced around. A coffeehaus was a few doors down. He dashed in and scanned the room. A group of teenage boys were at a table. August walked over and motioned to one of them.

"See that man out there?" he asked, pointing outside. "Would you go tell him the meeting's in here?"

"Why should I?" the boy said with a swagger that drew a few snickers from his friends.

August wanted to grab him by the collar and explain exactly why it was in his best interest to assist an SS officer when requested to do so. But he resisted the temptation. *No. I may have to stay in the role for now, but I will not become one of them.* Instead, he dug into his pocket, pulled out a few Reichmarks, and handed them over.

It was reason enough. The boy smiled and sashayed out the door.

August moved to the window, looked down the street, and saw the agent trying to look discreet on his stakeout. *The courier should take lessons.* August turned back to the pantomimed conversation between the boy and the courier and watched the courier trudge into the coffeehaus. He handed August an envelope.

"There you are!" the courier said.

"We were being followed, you idiot," August said. "This is confidential. Remember?"

"What? Where?"

August ignored him and opened the envelope. A handwritten note:

> *Sorry we're having trouble locating her.*
> *Should we continue? ~ Barth*

August shoved the paper in his pocket. Barth's sources weren't doing the job. He'd have to find another way to locate her. But first things first. He stepped out into the street and headed away from the agent, walking in and out of shadows and between buildings.

The agent's eyes darted around, searching for him. Suddenly August appeared next to him and slammed him up against a building.

"Who are you with?"

"I don't know what you mean," the agent said. "I'm just on my way home."

August saw the man's eyes go to the insignia on his uniform. "Yes, you know who I work for," he said. "Now tell me who sent you."

No answer. August pressed harder.

The agent winced in pain. "Abwehr."

August's eyes widened in surprise. *Canaris?* A wave of disappointment swept over August. *Canaris and I had a rapport. Didn't we? Was I wrong about that?* He released the agent and gave him a hard look.

"Tell the admiral to stop sending snoops. If he wants to know something, he can drop by."

August released the agent and walked away.

Chapter Thirty-Five

CANARIS AMBLED DOWN THE STREET, A MAN WITH no purpose or path, a man with a lot of time on his hands and nowhere to be. At least it seemed that way.

Those who knew Canaris knew that he was never without purpose or a path toward an achievement.

Those who knew him well would realize he had already detected the man following him and that he had discovered the man's identity.

Those who were on intimate terms with Canaris knew he was a spymaster and that he was damn good at it.

He meandered into a men's clothing store. He nodded to the proprietor, went through the store and out the back door. He paced half a block and entered the back door of a house to find Dohnanyi sitting at a table with Karl Sack sipping coffee.

For years Sack had practiced law in his hometown of Hesse. In 1934 he joined the newly established Reich Military Court and rose to a prominent position, where he was able to provide assistance with legal matters for those in the Resistance circles.

In his capacity as jurist, Sack had to walk a fine line, but he was often able to score a win for the Resistance through sheer enforcement of law. He was so effective that no one yet suspected he was secretly working with the Resistance and that he wanted Hitler dead. In fact, Hitler had recently named him Judge Advocate General of the Army. Sack and Canaris met often to share secret plans. He was one of the few that Canaris trusted without question.

Canaris closed the door and joined them. A woman appeared from the other room with another cup of coffee, then disappeared. "Karl and I worked out some of the details while we waited,"

Dohnanyi said. "We think we'll have a solid case to depose Hitler within months."

"Good," Canaris said.

"What took you so long?" Sack asked. "You're never late."

"I was followed." He gave a slight grin. "By August Wichmann."

"You're joking!" Dohnanyi said.

"Who is he?" Sack asked.

"SS. Working with Heydrich," Canaris shrugged. "I use the word 'working' lightly. I think there's more to him than SS dogma."

"Why was he following you? Do you think Heydrich put him up to it?"

"I doubt he would resort to putting a tail on me."

"I don't know. Heydrich has his moments of paranoia."

"True. But he wouldn't use someone I've met."

"Whatever the case, we need to stop Wichmann," said Dohnanyi. "Sooner or later he could stumble on something that will ruin us."

"Is he that good?" Sack asked.

"He followed me today," Canaris admitted. "And I

barely spotted him."

"If he's that good, why not try to turn him?" Sack reasoned. "Get him working with the Resistance."

Sack, knowing Canaris as well as he did, had hit the nail on the head. Canaris wished it were as simple as offering the man a job.

"I'm not sure we have time to sift his loyalties." Canaris drained his cup. "Speaking of time, I have a full day. As you two have already worked out the details, I'll get back to the office."

He nodded to them, went out, and retraced his steps to the clothing store. The manager was waiting for him. He handed Canaris a bag as he went by.

Canaris nodded his thanks and kept moving.

Chapter Thirty-Six

THE BUTCHER SHOP WAS EMPTY. AUGUST WALKED IN and went straight to the counter.

"I understand you can find people."

The butcher looked at his uniform. "I cut up meat. That's what I do."

August let out an exasperated sigh. What he wouldn't give for just one moment of basic trust, one human being to another.

"Ignore the uniform. I'm here on personal business." He handed the butcher a note. "This is my sister, her husband, and their son. And that's their last known address. I'd like your help."

The butcher didn't glance at the note. "Sorry, I cut meat for a living."

"This conversation goes no further. What do you need to trust me?"

"Where did you get my name?"

"On an official document."

"I need a name."

August groaned. *The man needed a name. Fine.* "You located the truck driver Hofer."

The butcher looked down at the note. He took his time reading it. "I'll be in touch."

Back at his apartment, August trudged up the stairs. He pulled Barth's note from his pocket and read it as he made his way up the steps. A shuffle of boots. A shadow. He stopped and looked up. A figure barred his way. August recognized him as one of Heydrich's aides.

"Are you Wichmann?"

August's heart hammered in his chest. He couldn't find his voice. He nodded.

"Come with me," the agent said.

The aide led him to a car. August climbed into the back. He tried to bolster himself, but it didn't work. His heart was still drumming wildly. Had Heydrich learned about his visit to Dina? Had the agent reported the incident to Canaris? Was he being arrested? He leaned forward.

"Where are we going?" he asked. The aide looked at him in the rearview mirror then looked straight ahead.

August sat back and glanced around at the scenery, wary and alert. They passed a church. August saw a bride and her father out front. He remembered a day like that.

~ ~ ~

August waited in the narthex with Helga, a vision in white lace and satin. On the other side of Helga, Brigitte stood as maid of honor. She leaned back and made a face at August's uniform.

"I can't believe you wore that," she said.

He returned her look with mock injury. "Madam, I stand here as an example of the clothes making the man," he said. "A model of success and heroism."

"Heroism? In the SS??"

August dropped the charade. "Those stories are exaggerated."

"No they're not," Helga chimed in.

An attendant peered through the door and motioned for them. August looked at both girls and placed his hand on his heart.

"Can we call a truce?" he pleaded. "Just for today?"

Helga and Brigitte looked at each other and shrugged.

"Very well," said Helga.

"For today," said Brigitte.

He kissed them both on the cheek and held out his arm for his sister. Brigitte entered the church ahead of them.

~ ~ ~

She had protested his uniform, the symbol of the SS. She had told him stories of the SS, and he dismissed them all as wild exaggerations, because he thought there was no way anyone could commit such atrocities in this day and age. He had believed that Helga made it all sound worse just to annoy him. If he found her again, he would let her say "I told you so" for a week.

Not if ... when, he corrected himself. *When I find her*.

The car pulled into an immense courtyard and eased around to the entrance. August stared wide-eyed at the Reich Chancellery, a former palace and now Hitler's state offices. A footman opened the door and August climbed the stairs.

Heydrich was waiting at the top. August braced himself.

"Special occasion, Wichmann," Heydrich said with a grin. "We're dining with Hitler tonight."

Chapter Thirty-Seven

BONHOEFFER AND DOHNANYI STOOD OUTSIDE THE church and watched Canaris dodge traffic. Churchgoers moved past them into the sanctuary. Canaris hurried over, the exertion transforming his breath into a steam engine in the cold night air.

"Trust you to pick a venue like this, Dietrich," Canaris said.

"A Vespers service is tonight," Bonhoeffer said. "And it's safe. I doubt any Gestapo or SS men will be here."

Canaris looked at Dohnanyi. "I take it the Americans are inside."

"With some MI-6 agents," Dohnanyi said. "They've come a long way to meet you."

"Let's join them."

They trekked up the stairs and into the narthex. They waited for a moment between groups gathering for the service, then Canaris and Dohnanyi slipped through a door to the right into a supply room. Bonhoeffer stayed in the narthex, on lookout.

Four men were waiting. Canaris studied them.

"Admiral Canaris, Rand and Geldon you know from MI-6. This is Bill Haynes and Jim Stafford from the OSS," Dohnanyi said. "Gentlemen: Admiral Canaris."

Canaris nodded. The men nodded.

"Roosevelt sends his regards," Haynes said. "Along with a message that must be delivered in person."

Canaris nodded.

Haynes took a deep breath. "He says he recognizes your efforts toward a peaceful resolution to hostilities and that he will gladly receive any information you deem valuable that can aid and assist the complete downfall and elimination of the current regie of Germany along with its current leadership."

Canaris studied him for a moment. "Is that everything?"

Hayes shook his head. "The president also said I should make it clear that all communication should be in verbal form, no documentation kept, and that this meeting never happened."

"I understand," Canaris said, turning to Dohnanyi. "We have several things to share now."

"I'll take care of it, Admiral," Dohnanyi said.

Canaris looked at the men. "We have safe houses and a special route you can use to return home."

He moved to the door and turned back. "Glad to have you on board."

He went out into the narthex.

Bonhoeffer was still waiting. He pointed to the sanctuary. "Care to join me?"

Canaris smiled. Contact with the Allies had put him in a good mood. *The Munich project is soon. It might not hurt to get divine guidance.* "Why not?"

~ ~ ~

The event in the Reich Chancellery was a small gathering. Hitler sat at one end of a large table in the vast dining room. To his right was Heinrich Himmler and Josef Goebbels; to his left, Heydrich and August.

It may have been supper, but it was hardly appetizing. They ate only when Hitler ate, which never happened when he was talking. The food grew cold. Fortunately, the wine stewards at either side of the table kept the glasses filled.

Heydrich had called it a special occasion, but August would label it interminable vexation. They were forced to watch while Hitler held court, his logic thin and fragmented, his proclamations confusing and contradictory. Worse was watching the other men smile and nod assent throughout the discourse.

"'A date that lives in infamy!'" Hitler said. "Roosevelt is a braggart and a fool!"

"Very true, Mein Fuhrer," Goebbels said. "He has nothing but words to fight with. It's a foreign war to them. There will be no public support."

August studied Goebbels' face, brows drawn down with confusion. Hitler noticed and pointed to August.

"You disagree?"

All eyes turned to August. Heydrich spoke up quickly. "Wichmann is here to observe."

August had recognized within minutes of their arrival that he was there to showcase Heydrich's department. It made August feel like a show dog, and he resented it. Throughout the evening, he had pushed away the resentment and listened to the conversation. But as the evening wore on, he fought the urge to look at his watch and calculate the minutes until he was released. Now, with Heydrich's vague dismissal, his resentment flared up again. He didn't like anyone speaking for him, especially Heydrich.

"But didn't you introduce him as a bright young

member of your staff?" Goebbels chided. "How bright is he? Let's find out." He turned to August. "Wichmann, your thoughts."

August looked around. Goebbels smirked. Himmler's face was cold and impassive. Heydrich downed half a glass of wine. Hitler leaned back, glassy-eyed. August took a deep breath.

"American might have been complacent so far," he started, "but they'll change their minds."

"Are you a mind-reader as well?" Goebbels challenged.

"No, but in my studies—"

"Yes, that's right," Goebbels said. "You were a college professor, teaching languages."

"Not only languages," August said. "Cultures too. And yes, I do feel that I understand the American mind-set."

"Perhaps you can tutor Goebbels," Himmler smirked.

Himmler and Heydrich laughed. Goebbels leaned across the table.

"I repeat: There will be no support. This is a foreign war to America. And if I know anything, it's that they grew weary of fighting other men's battles twenty years ago."

"But it's not foreign when you're attacked," August reasoned. "They will mobilize. And we have to be prepared—"

Suddenly Hitler laughed and slapped the table.

"Yes, yes!" he said to Goebbels, getting right in his face. "I never said they would not respond, only that his boasting was foolish. Preparation is our only course of action. We have to arm even more."

Hitler drained his glass. A waiter rushed to refill it,

diluting with water and adding a spoonful of sugar to the red wine.

August watched the crystals swirl around in the glass. He kept his face impassive.

Goebbels glared at August.

~ ~ ~

Inside the church, the organ rang out the last few notes of the final hymn. The congregation filed out. Canaris and Bonhoeffer stayed seated. Neither spoke, even after all were gone. The silence was comforting.

"Do you feel closer to God at a time like this, Dietrich?" His voice was barely above a whisper. It seemed fitting to be humble in the sanctuary, even if only in tone and volume.

"Inside a church, do you mean?"

"I mean when blatant evil rises up. How does one fight it?"

Bonhoeffer glanced at Canaris and saw the confusion in his eyes, the anguish. He knew the questions were rhetorical, but he looked at the cross anyway, searching for answers.

"Faith leads me to God," he said, simply. "And to truth."

"Faith. I always thought it the last bastion for those unable to act."

"I've always considered faith the strongest action one can take."

Canaris thought about that for a moment. "I can't recall the last definitive action I took that made me proud," he said. "Our work is fraught with deception. Around every corner, another ruse."

"But look what we're up against." Bonhoeffer looked

at Canaris. "At least we're not guilty of evil."

"But is that enough?"

Bonhoeffer had no answer. He turned back to face the cross.

~ ~ ~

Outside the Reich Chancellery, August descended the long stairs with Heydrich. When they reached the bottom, Heydrich turned to August and grinned.

"He's pleased with you. Very good. I called you a rising star, didn't I?" He slapped August on the back. "As a reward, I am sending you to Paris to take a look at the Special Action files from that office. That will prepare you for the next steps. Wait for a package from my aide. It has to go with someone I can trust."

~ ~ ~

Bonhoeffer pulled some papers from his coat and handed them to Canaris.

"This is something I'm planning to send to our fellow conspirators," he said. "Something to remind us of how far we've come. And what's at stake."

Canaris read silently at first, then aloud. "We have been silent witnesses of evil deeds ... learnt the arts of equivocation and pretenses ... experiences have made us suspicious of others ..." He stopped and looked at Bonhoeffer. "Do you really feel this way?"

"Yes."

"Good. Those are the perfect qualifications for the job."

Bonhoeffer smiled.

Canaris read a few more lines silently, then aloud.

"Will our inward power of resistance be strong enough, and our honesty with ourselves remorseless enough, for us to find our way back?" He folded the paper and looked up at the cross. "Remorseless honesty with ourselves. Where do we find someone like that?"

"I don't know. But when we do, I will be his friend." Bonhoeffer turned to Canaris. "Admiral, please know that I pray for you constantly."

They sat a moment in silence. Then Canaris stood.

He looked down at Bonhoeffer with a weary smile. "I wouldn't think to ask for prayer. But I'm grateful to have it."

Chapter Thirty-Eight

BRIGITTE FOUND SANCTUARY IN SOPHIE'S APARTMENT. She made herself useful by doing the grocery shopping, cooking, and cleaning. At first she didn't dare venture out, but after a while she grew restless and had to leave. She was afraid of being tracked down, so she couldn't look for work, but she was able to resume her translation work with Haerker.

Her life had settled into a comfortable routine. She went to Haerker's office on Mondays to pick up manuscripts and brought the completed translations back on Fridays. Afterward she went to the market on the way home. Before long she began to hope that the people at the hospital had forgotten about her.

One Friday as she was heading to the market, she noticed someone walking alongside, keeping pace with her. She looked over and saw horn-rimmed glasses, thick mustache, bushy eyebrows. Herr von Trent.

With a cry, she darted the other way, but he grabbed her arm and steered her into a waiting car. The car sped away. A dark glass separated the front and back seats, and she couldn't see the driver. Her breath was coming fast, and she thought she might faint.

Herr von Trent put his arm on hers. "You must trust

me." He removed the horn-rimmed glasses and pulled at his bushy mustache and eyebrows, removing them inch by inch until his face was transformed into a round, clean-shaven, pink moon. His eyes were still bright and intense, but without the dark foreboding glasses, they weren't at all mysterious and dark. In fact, he looked like he could be someone's jovial uncle.

He looked at her and smiled. "And you must call me Bogart, dear girl." His voice had transformed into a distinct British accent.

"B-b-bogart? Like the American actor?"

"Precisely."

"Why must I trust you?"

"I understand your reluctance, especially after what you were asked to do at the hospital."

"Am I under arrest?"

"No, no, my dear. I'm here to offer you a job."

"I will not go back there!"

"That's not what I mean."

He asked her a series of questions: *Did she want to make a difference? Did she want to end the suffering she saw in the country? Did she want to get rid of the corruption she saw?*

She said yes to each question.

"I thought so." Then he explained that he had been following her for several weeks and had discovered her patterns. "That's not good, by the way. Having patterns. You must do better. And I'm sure you will."

He told her what he knew about her: where she was staying, who she was staying with, what they were doing.

"The White Rose group has a lot of energy, a lot of magnificent ideas. Their pamphlets and their planned protests are quite worthy." He took her hand and squeezed it. "But you, my dear, are destined for more serious work. Things more worthy of your skills."

She looked out the window as the town of Munich rolled by. "What kind of work?"

"You'll find out soon enough. But first I want to introduce you to some colleagues."

She turned back to him. "Colleagues from where?"

It was his turn to stare out at the scenery. He seemed to be holding an inner debate. He turned back. "You must understand that everything you are to learn—and you will never know everything, only what you need to know in case you're ever caught—you must always keep secret. Agreed?"

"Yes."

"We're a section of the Special Operations Executive. SOE. Based in England." He told her about the variety of missions and the various groups they worked with, both internal and external, from time to time. She found herself warming to him. Believing him. And believing in his mission.

"What do you want me to do?"

"Several things," he said. "First, we often have need of a medic. We can't just pop into the local hospital, now can we? Your skills would come in handy."

"I can do that."

"Good. That's where we'll start. First things first. I'll need to show you where to find the safe house, but there's a particular route you have to follow to get to it."

He saw her frown and leaned in toward her. "I cannot stress enough how critical it is to follow the exact route I give you so you won't be followed."

She nodded. "Understood."

He looked her up and down, then asked, "How good are you at role-playing?"

Out of the blue, August Wichmann came to mind.

She thought about the afternoon at his house in Munich, when he showed them archery and she teased him with the accents she could do. She looked over at Bogart, batted her eyelashes, and pushed her lips up into a flirty pout. *"Moi? C'est bonne."*

Bogart laughed. "You'll do, my dear. Oh, yes, you will most certainly do."

Chapter Thirty-Nine

AUGUST STROLLED DOWN THE CHAMPS-ELYSEES, dressed in civilian clothes with a cravat around his collar, his hair parted on the side and combed back. He carried a briefcase.

He turned onto the Place de la Concorde and glanced around furtively. He had to avoid running into people he'd known before. Like the group he'd been meeting with when the Gestapo "captured" him years ago. A group of Jews seeking ways to hide their heritage so they wouldn't be targeted by the Nazis. He had called the meeting to discuss methods for getting around wearing the yellow Juden star.

At least that's what he told them in his French Jew Jean Louis Mardot persona. The reality is that he was uncovering their ways and their means of disobedience.

His reasoning had been simple—the law required them to wear it; those who didn't were disobeying—and in retrospect, his reasoning was incredibly naïve. He assumed the Jews who disobeyed were deported. He didn't know the star marked all of them for transport to concentration camps.

At least he hadn't known at the time. *How could I have not known? Why didn't I see what was happen-*

ing? It occurred to him that the people in the café's cellar that day—those twenty people who trusted him—were probably imprisoned or dead. His shoulders slumped.

All the buildings in the Place de la Concorde were flying swastika banners. He made his way to one in particular and dashed up the stairs. Inside, a few people glanced at him with curiosity. He ignored them and moved with purpose down the hall and into an office.

Behind the desk, Barth looked up when he entered and laughed. "You look like a damn Frenchman," Barth said.

"Good," August returned the bantering tone. "Because I'm in France." He held out the briefcase. "Confidential from Heydrich."

"You got my note about your sister?"

"Yes. I have another source looking. You can stop the search."

"As you wish," Barth shrugged, opening the briefcase.

August studied Barth's face as he pawed through the contents of the briefcase. He had known Barth for years, and they shared many interests. He ached to have someone to have a serious conversation with, to unload his fears and the desperation that crept into his soul. *But can I really trust him?* He took a deep breath and took the plunge to find out.

"Barth, how much do you know about what really goes on?"

"About what really goes on where?" Barth said, distracted by some documents. "It's a big war we've got going on here."

"Well ... about the Jews, for instance."

Barth's head shot up and he narrows his eyes at August. "Don't tell me you've become a Jew sympathizer.

Not you!"

"No, no, I was just—"

"Because I can tell you now, my friend, Jew sympathizers don't last long in this organization."

"No, I was just—"

"Wait!" Barth laughed. "It isn't some girl you're crazy about, is it?"

"Never mind, Barth. It's nothing."

Barth looked at him for a long moment, a speculative look in his eyes. "Okay, fine. It's nothing," he said. "Want to have supper tonight?"

"I'm busy."

"I know that tone. What's her name? Please tell me it's not a young French-Jewish princess who's captured your heart."

August laughed merrily, reminding himself that Barth knew him as a loyal SS agent.

"Don't be absurd!" He rolled his eyes at Barth and headed for the door. "See you tomorrow."

~ ~ ~

August paused before knocking on the door. *What if she didn't live there anymore? What if she wasn't alone? Would she remember me?* He took a deep breath and knocked. His pulse quickened as he waited. The door opened, and Janette stood there. Her eyes grew wide, and she threw herself into his arms. He breathed a prayer of thanks. At last, someone he could share with.

She drew him in and closed the door.

~ ~ ~

Later that night, they lounged in front of the fire.

A bottle of wine sat on the table, half empty. Janette was curled in his arms. August leaned over, kissed her hair, and downed his glass of wine. He leaned up to pour more.

"What did they do to you?" Janette asked.

"Hmm? Oh, when they arrested me?" He hurried to brush away the deception, trying to maintain a sense of trust between them. "Just a lot of questions. They had nothing, so I was let go."

"Do they know where you are now?"

He realized she was worried about his safety. He smiled. "Don't worry. They won't find me."

She sat up, looked into his eyes, and laughed softly. "Always so sure of yourself. The resolute Jean Louis Mardot."

"Actually, I'm—" He stopped. Could he trust her? He still wasn't sure. He wanted to tell her the truth, but how would she feel at being deceived all this time? He caressed her cheek. "I'm glad to see you again."

"I missed you, Jean," she said. "I've been so lonely. No one to talk to. No one to trust. You don't know how hard that is."

Oh, but he did. He pulled her close.

"How have things been for you?" he asked.

She pushed away and refilled her glass. She took a drink and shrugged. "Terrible. The *boche* have taken over all of Paris. They delight in destruction. They take things that are beautiful and tear them down."

"I know," he whispered.

"And what they do to people is worse. Even if you escape death or torture, they can break you."

August gazed at the fire. *Yes, I've met someone they almost broke. Dina.* He could still see her curled up on the sofa, telling her story, her arm in a cast because a soldier stepped on it and broke it. But they didn't break her spirit. What was it Ingrid had said? *She's alive because she stayed silent. Now she has to learn how not to be silent.*

August shook his head, brushing away the memory. He looked at Janette. *I can't be silent either.*

"I want to tell you something," he said.

She moved into his embrace again and kissed him. "Tell me everything, my love."

"Not long ago, I found out—"

The phone rang. Janette went to answer it, mumbled a few words, and hung up. She turned to August.

"A friend needs my help." She held up her hands in a helpless gesture. "I must go."

He kissed her. "Hurry back."

Chapter Forty

ERIK MEISNER WAS AN EXCEPTIONALLY DRIVEN MAN, a zealous anti-Nazi with no moral dilemmas about taking a man's life for a cause. Just the man for the job.

He walked into the beer hall in Heidelberg carrying a package under his arm. His eyes darted around the room while he made his way to a column beside the podium. Making sure he wasn't noticed, he crouched behind the column and opened the package. Inside was a bomb, the detonator set to 9:15. He moved a small piece of wood in the column, put the bomb inside, and replaced the piece of wood.

He ambled outside, crossed the street, and blended into the shadows to wait.

At 8:45 Heydrich and Himmler arrived. Hitler's car pulled up behind it with several guards. They all entered.

Across the street, Meisner stared at the building.

At 9:10, Hitler exited, followed by Heydrich, Himmler, and several others.

Meisner lurched toward the building, stopped, looked at his watch, then looked around wildly. The entourage sped past him.

The bomb exploded. Windows shattered. Pieces of debris flew out in all directions.

Chapter Forty-One

DOHNANYI AND BONHOEFFER WERE IN CANARIS' office when Oster swept in with the news.

"They were called away to a meeting," he said. "The bomb missed them by a few minutes."

"Where's Meisner?" Bonhoeffer asked.

"In Gestapo custody," said Oster. "They picked him up at the Swiss border."

Canaris looked up at the ceiling, pensive. "Maybe we should recruit Wichmann."

"Can we trust him?" Dohnanyi asked.

"He handed over the codes," Canaris said. "He caught the tail we put on him. He broke in here and looked at some of our files." He brought his eyes down from the ceiling and leveled his gaze on Dohnanyi. "And he's revealed none of it."

Dohnanyi glanced at the portrait of Franco. "How do you know he broke in?"

"He gave the butcher Hofer's name."

"Which no one knows about," Dohnanyi said.

Canaris nodded. "He has enough on us to cause problems. Recruiting him would be prudent."

"We're already tailing him," Dohnanyi said. "We could see what the Gestapo has on him."

Canaris thought through the potential risks and repercussions.

He nodded. "Do it."

Chapter Forty-Two

WAITING FOR JANETTE TO RETURN, AUGUST POURED another glass of wine and paced the room. He saw a paper on the floor by the desk, picked it up, and opened the drawer to replace it.

Inside the drawer, he saw a book, paper, and pen. The paper had symbols, lines, and random bits of letters on it. Where had he seen something like that before?

All at once he knew. *On the way to Vichy.* Ian's papers. He picked up the book and opened it. A code book. *Was Janette a spy? Or a double?* He sat, grabbed another paper, and decoded the message.

After a few minutes, he looked at the decoded message:

> *He's back. Might have information. I'll try to keep him here a few days. What do you want me to do?*

He looked around the room, his breath coming fast and anxious. *I trusted her. How could I have trusted her? Who can I trust?* He leaned over, head in hands. *I almost told her about Dina. Oh my God. I almost told her.*

He looked back at the paper, weighing options until he narrowed to one: *I want to kill her.*

A dead chill came over him. He eased up from the chair and slipped on his coat, his mind gripped with careful deliberation.

He took the code book and papers and flung them into the fire, then bolted out the door.

The streets were filled with people bustling around, getting on with their lives despite the occupation.

August made his way toward the Place de la Concorde, a hollow dread growing in him.

Chapter Forty-Three

CANARIS HAD KEPT A FROZEN SMILE ON HIS FACE FOR hours. It was the only way to get through an evening with Heydrich.

They had been neighbors for years. Besides the morning horse rides, the Canaris and Heydrich families visited each other's homes, usually on holidays and other special occasions. For Canaris it was a means of gathering information, although the more he learned about Heydrich's activities the harder it became to keep up a pretense of hospitality and warmth.

The Heydrichs had invited Canaris and his wife over to their house. Canaris' wife had made such a fuss over the specifics that Canaris knew something was up. He figured it was a surprise for his birthday, which was a week ago and which he thought he'd passed without pomp and ceremony.

After dinner, as their wives puttered around removing dishes, Heydrich turned the conversation to politics.

"I supposed you've heard the news about the Navy," Heydrich said.

Canaris had heard the news—that Hitler had announced that he would operate as head of the Navy and would operate from Berlin. But Heydrich was trying to get a rise out of him, so he feigned ignorance.

"What news is this?" he said. "I've been away."

"Your staff doesn't keep you apprised?" Heydrich needled.

Canaris gave a slight smile and said nothing. Heydrich gave up on the badgering.

"The Fuhrer has taken personal control of the Navy," he said, watching for Canaris' reaction.

Before Canaris could react, the women brought in a cake with a great deal of fanfare.

"Happy birthday, Willi!" his wife said.

"We should say *belated* happy birthday," said Lena Heydrich.

"You were away on your birthday," his wife said, "so we planned a surprise for tonight."

"They didn't believe me when I said how hard it was to get you here," Heydrich smirked. "I had to bait you with news of my latest campaign."

Canaris smiled. "Nonsense. I wouldn't miss your wife's cooking." And he turned his attention to the cake.

~ ~ ~

After cake and coffee, the men rose and went into the living room. Heydrich resumed the conversation.

"What do you think about Hitler commanding the Navy?"

Canaris shrugged. "It doesn't affect my department."

Heydrich persisted. "How would you feel about it if you were still at sea?"

Canaris took a while to answer. He didn't want to debate the issue, but he also didn't want to kowtow to Heydrich's game.

"Generally speaking, it's better to have a seasoned commander at the helm. Someone who's fought in sea battles."

"Ah, but you can't fault the man's insight, though," Heydrich said. "Or his cunning and drive."

"Such as it is."

"And he values loyalty. I expect to be rewarded handsomely for the objective we're launching soon."

"Which objective?"

"Tackling the Jew problem."

Before Canaris could ask what he meant, the women joined them and Heydrich dropped the topic. He poured four glasses of brandy.

Canaris sat down and wished the evening were over. He tried to catch his wife's eye and signal to her that he was ready to go home.

But then Heydrich brought out two violins, and Canaris knew it wouldn't be an early evening.

His wife's eyes lit up as she took one of the violins. She and Heydrich both were accomplished violinists, and Heydrich's wife was a pianist, so the evenings usually ended with a flourish of classical music.

As they played, Canaris studied Heydrich and marveled at how a person could bring forth such exquisite music and yet be responsible for the brutal acts he had committed. It baffled him.

Twenty minutes later, they finished and Canaris applauded. They smiled at him, then were lost in their own conversation about the pieces they'd played.

Canaris took the opportunity to excuse himself. He went down the hall toward the bathroom. He waited, walked back toward the living room, listened, then dashed into the study.

He opened drawers and rifled through the files. His

movements were swift and silent. He opened a drawer and found a paper. At the top:

Agenda ... Location: Wannsee

He saw a numbered list of items to discuss and a roster of attendees. He glanced down the list, taking it in as fast as he could. One phrase caught his attention:

Final Solution

He heard footsteps and put the paper back, easing the drawer shut.

"What are you doing?" Heydrich's voice was strained.

Canaris turned around slowly and smiled. "Looking for the good scotch."

Heydrich gave him a long look and pointed to the other corner. "The bar's over there."

Canaris went over and mixed two drinks. For a few moments, the tinkling of ice cubes was the only sound in the room. He handed a glass to Heydrich and held up his in toast.

"Zum Wohl."

Heydrich didn't return the toast. He drank, staring over the edge of the glass. "What were you looking for?"

Canaris took a long drink. "The good scotch." He swirled the ice. "And I found it."

He moved to the door. Heydrich grabbed his arm, edging and breathing hard, his eyes wide.

"Looking for secret documents, weren't you?" he asked. "Building a case. Gathering evidence for—"

Canaris took some satisfaction in the look of fear on Heydrich's face. After all the terror the man had caused others, Canaris thought Heydrich deserved this moment of discomfort.

"On you?" Canaris asked. "Why would I ever do that?"

Canaris walked away.

Heydrich stared after him, his face taut with fear.

Chapter Forty-Four

HEYDRICH STOOD IN FRONT OF HIMMLER'S DESK AND watched him align items on his desk from one side to the other and back again. Himmler's eyes were icy, his lips thin and hard. One silent glance from Himmler had been known to make grown men soil themselves. Heydrich could never withstand a face-to-face meeting with Himmler without frequently looking away.

"We'll be at Wannsee. All confirmed," Heydrich said, looking out the window.

"Good."

Heydrich turned to face him. "We should consider a preemptive movement against the Abwehr."

Himmler's hands stopped. It was like a shout. "I thought you two were close."

"We're neighbors," Heydrich assured him, looking down at his shoes, avoiding Himmler's curious look. "Nothing more."

Heydrich and Himmler didn't always find common ground on everything, but one thing they shared was a hatred of Canaris. Himmler's cold eyes bore into him.

"The Abwehr will be under your command soon anyway."

"Yes, but I want to send one of my men to look into

what they're doing now."

"Be sure it's someone you can trust," Himmler warned.

Heydrich could feel Himmler's eyes on him, but he avoided the icy stare.

"Wichmann hasn't failed me yet," Heydrich said.

"Very well." Himmler considered the problem solved. His hands resumed their silent ballet, moving things around his desk in a continuous motion.

Heydrich nodded, keeping his eyes on Himmler's desk.

Chapter Forty-Five

AUGUST WALKED INTO THE BUTCHER SHOP AND WENT straight to the counter.

"Nothing yet," the butcher said. "I'll send word when I hear something."

August nodded and looked down. *They didn't fall off the planet. They're somewhere. Patience.* He took a deep breath, mustered his strength, and looked up.

"I'll be away a few days," August said. "I'll stop in when I return."

"Back to Paris?"

August shook his head. "A conference in Wannsee."

~ ~ ~

August and Heydrich sat in the back of the car, a glass between them and the driver. Heydrich had insisted on August attending this meeting, which he had said would revolutionize the Special Action methods. August kept his face impassive.

"This meeting will be confidential," Heydrich said.

"Yes, sir."

"I know I can trust you, Wichmann. That's why I invited you."

August gave a short nod. It was taking all his energy to play the role of a dedicated SS officer.

"Not everyone can be trusted," Heydrich said. "Not everyone is loyal to the Third Reich. There are threats everywhere. We have to eliminate them."

"Threats everywhere? What do you mean?"

"The Abwehr, for instance. They keep files on everyone." He leaned over to August. "Did you know only a few of their agents are Nazi party members?"

"Is that so?" August had no idea why that mattered.

"They cannot be trusted. Especially Canaris. I know. I've lived next to him for years," Heydrich said, his eyes narrowed in disgust. "He's such a small man. You met him. Did you notice how small he is? He's not Aryan, that's obvious."

August turned to him, frowning. *A small man? Not Aryan? What the hell is he talking about?*

"We're here," Heydrich announced.

The car pulled into the Am Grossen Villa at Wannsee. August looked out the window at the spacious grounds and the mansion in the middle. A layer of snow covered the grounds, giving it a storybook ambiance.

August looked back at Heydrich, wondering what his obsession with Canaris was about.

Chapter Forty-Six

CHRISTOPH AND HANS WERE TINKERING WITH THE mimeograph machine, up to their elbows in blue ink, when Sophie came in and tossed a half ream of paper on the table.

Christoph glanced at the paper. "We'll need more."

"They wouldn't let me have more." She slumped into the chair. "Wonder if there's any in Ulm."

Hans looked at Sophie. "Can you make a trip home tomorrow?"

She nodded.

"Be sure to take an empty suitcase to bring the paper back in," Christoph said.

"I know that!" she said, folding her arms across her chest. Christoph raised his eyebrows at Hans, then turned to Sophie.

"I'm sorry. I know you know what you're doing."

Brigitte came out of the bedroom and looked around at them. "What's going on?"

Sophie slapped her hand on top of the half ream. "They're rationing paper now. Can you believe that? I couldn't get more than this. They're afraid we'll do something like—"

"Like exactly what we're doing," Hans said. "Waking

people up to what's going on right under their noses."

Sophie noticed Brigitte was in her nurse's uniform. "You're going back?" she asked, her voice shrill. "After what they made you do?"

"It's not what you think," Brigitte said. "And the less you know about what I'm doing the better."

They regarded her with sober, serious faces, but no one asked any more questions. She tossed them a quick smile and picked up her satchel bag.

~ ~ ~

She made her way to the SOE safe house the way Bogart had taught her: a series of turns down alternating streets, a backtrack to a certain corner, through a store into the alley behind it, into a house and up the staircase to a secret passage leading to a room in the safe house next door. What would have been a fifteen-minute walk took more than an hour, but Bogart insisted she take that route to avoid being followed.

She closed the door to the secret passage—a full length painting of an aristocrat from days gone by—and walked into a library. She went across the room to another door and gave the prescribed code: knock-knock-pause-knock-knock-pause-knock. She sat down to wait.

Bogart came in with another man. Brigitte first noticed the man's hawk nose and beady eyes, then she saw the SS uniform. She jumped up and ran back to the painting.

"Wait! Don't be afraid!" Bogart dashed over, caught her hand, and brought her back to the man. "This is Otto. He's one of us."

Otto shook her hand. "I apologize for frightening you. Bogart deserves the credit for my disguise."

"Why don't you introduce yourself?" Bogart said to her.

She realized he was testing her to see if she remembered which name to use for which identity. *Traute is the nurse, Karin is the socialite, Petra is the school teacher.*

"Hello, I'm Traute," she said.

Bogart beamed at her.

"That's a marvelous disguise," Otto said. "It fits you well."

"That's—" she started to say "that's because it's my actual nursing uniform," but she noticed Bogart studying her and remembered his instructions. *Never give more information than you need to, even to friends. One day they may be tortured and tell all.* She looked back at Otto. "That's very kind of you." Bogart gave her a quick wink.

He sat her down and went over the plan. They would wait until midnight, after the night shift went on duty. Otto would walk her to the side of the building.

She frowned. "I know where it is. I used to work there."

"He has to be there," Bogart said, "in the unlikely event you're caught."

She felt a quiver of discomfort. *The other day it was a foolproof plan. Now it's an unlikely event I'll be caught. We'd better hurry before it becomes a suicide mission.*

"If anything happens," Bogart continued, "Otto will be waiting outside and will assume custody of you, then he'll bring you back to the car."

"I understand," she said.

He resumed the details of the plan. She would use Bogart's key to get in. She would go to the supply room and fill her satchel bag with the list of supplies he had given her. She would exit as quietly as possible and lock the door behind her.

She nodded.

Bogart studied her face. "You understand why I need you to do this, don't you?"

She shrugged. "I assume it's because you can't get supplies out during the day. They do searches when you leave. Every bag, as I recall."

"And every pocket," he said. "And they would question my being there after hours."

"Okay," she said.

"And they wouldn't question a nurse being in the supply room."

"Okay," she said again, wishing they would leave. She looked around the room. It was getting dark, but they still had hours before they left.

Bogart pointed to a chaise in the corner. "Get some sleep. I'll come get you when it's time." He and Otto left.

She was too nervous to sleep. She paced the room for a while, going over the scenario, trying to remember exactly where the supply room was, whether she had to pass a nurse's station on the way to it, what she would say if she ran into anyone.

She sat on the chaise and forced herself to think rationally. She knew where the supply room was. It was on the ground floor, and there was no nurse's station nearby.

She tried to calm herself down. It was impossible to sleep, but she would see how long she could sit still.

~ ~ ~

She was walking in a park with August Wichmann, telling him about the plan and how afraid she was. He stopped and put a hand on her shoulder.

"You can do this, Traute."

"Why are you calling me that? You know my name is Brigitte."

He just smiled and shook her shoulder. "Traute."

She woke with a start. Otto was shaking her shoulder. "Traute. It's time to go."

It was after midnight when they got to the hospital. Bogart parked a block away, and Otto walked Brigitte to the entrance.

"I'll be here," he said, then disappeared into the shadows.

At the door, her hands were shaking hard, making the keys jingle as she fumbled with the lock. *Oh God, please don't let anyone hear*.

Once inside, she hurried down the corridor to the second hallway on the left, then to the third door on the right. She flipped to another key on the ring, opened the door, and slipped into the room. She leaned back against the door and stuffed the keys into her pocket. She was in.

She raced around the room grabbing items and stashing them into her satchel bag: gauze, antiseptic, merthiolate, spirits of ammonia, aspirin, penicillin, chloroform, terpin hydrate, arsenic, opium, quinine, petrolatum, milk of magnesia, mercury.

Brigitte heard a key in the door. She ran to the closet at the far corner of the room, pulled back the curtain, and squeezed herself into the bottom of it. She heard the door open, then footsteps walking around the room. The footsteps got closer. She looked around for something to cover her. There was nothing but shelves with bottles and jars.

She could feel her hands getting numb. She looked down at them and saw they were shaking. Her chest hurt. *I'm having a heart attack. I'm going to die in here.* She felt faint. *No, I'm just hyperventilating.* She forced herself to take deep, slow breaths.

The footsteps receded. She continued her slow deep breathing, looking around at the shelves. Her eye caught the name on one of the bottles: Aktion T-4. It held the serum used to euthanize the patients. She took two bottles and stashed them into her bag.

After a few minutes she heard the key turn in the lock and the footsteps move down the hall. She moved the curtain and left her hiding place. She dashed around the room collecting the other items on the list. She found a box of needles and grabbed a handful.

She opened the door, looked up and down the hall, eased out, and locked. She took a deep breath and moved toward the exit. *I did it. I can't believe I did it. Bogart will be—*

She heard footsteps behind her. She stole a glance back. A nurse was carrying a stack of folders, flipping through and reading the labels. She hadn't spotted Brigitte yet.

There was no way to get back to the storage room—it was locked now anyway—and Brigitte couldn't make it down the hall and to the outside door without running. She tried to speed up her walk, but the satchel bag was heavy and bumped against her leg. A door was coming up on her right. She tried the knob, and it opened. She darted in.

It was nothing but a landing and stairs. She inched her way down two flights to the basement. It was a massive warehouse with bare concrete walls, dimly lit and cold. Canvas-covered crates filled the room. On the back wall was an office, the open door spilling out harsh bright light into a rectangle on the gray slab floor. Beside the office were two elevators and a door.

She calibrated her bearings and figured the door would lead to the back of the building. She thought it might be safer than going back upstairs. She prayed it was unlocked.

She crept toward the door between rows of crates. A rat scuttled across her path. She jumped and fell back against one of the crates. She spun around and saw a word stenciled on the side of the canvas:

Verbrennungsanlage. Incinerator.

She pulled back the corner of the canvas.

At first she thought they were dolls. Naked bodies stacked chest-high in the crate, tiny cherub faces with eyes closed, swaths of hair in a variety of colors, arms and legs tangled together.

And in one swift, mind-numbing instant she realized they weren't dolls. These were children. *Had been* children. *Oh, dear God. Holy God in Heaven. WHY???* Her mind screamed out, begging for reasons.

And then she leaned in and scanned the faces. Cleft palates. Deformed eyes and noses. Facial characteristics of mongoloid condition. A few with stumps instead of hands. Some with enlarged heads. She remembered the twenty-seven people she had helped "release." They all had had some imperfection. A voice echoed in her mind, the head nurse describing those who received the T-4 treatment: *"They aren't the same as us. They're not really human."* She backed up and bumped into another crate with the same stencil on the canvas. Under that canvas were more young bodies, but these looked to be pre-teen.

She could feel a scream rising in her throat, and she struggled to hold it in. She turned toward the door and caught sight of the full extent of that den of cold, raw evil: row after row of canvas-covered crates. She had known that they were killing people they considered undesirable, but now seeing the full scope and magnitude of what they were doing in front of her gutted her.

"Aaaaaaahhhhh!" A long wailing sob of grief escaped her.

The sound brought a hulking figure out of the office. "What are you doing down here?" the man yelled.

She bolted for the door. *Please, God, let it be open.*

"Hey, you! Get back here!" the man called out, lumbering after her. "Hey!"

The satchel bag was heavy, hampering her speed. She reached the door and threw her weight against it.

It opened. *Thank God!* She was outside. She jogged up several stairs to ground level.

"Otto!" she screamed, her chest heaving. "Otto! Back here!" She sprinted to the street, the bag bumping hard against her leg.

The man's voice was getting closer. "Get back here, you bitch!"

Brigitte didn't stop. She rushed past a tall figure and realized it was Otto. She slowed down, but he yelled, "Go! Go! Get to the car!"

As she shot away, she heard a series of muffled blows and a loud crackling noise, like someone stepping on a bundle of dried twigs.

She was all the way to the car before she realized it was the sound of bones being shattered. She leaned against the car door, shaking and sobbing.

~ ~ ~

Back at the safe house, she unloaded the items onto a table, but she kept the needles and serum in her bag.

"Come," Bogart said, leading her to another part of the house. She expected a reprimand. She hadn't been able to follow the plan, she was almost caught, and there was an injured, possibly dead, staff member that Bogart would have to deal with tomorrow.

She had apologized over and over in the car, but he waved his hand at her, refusing the apology.

"Bring some antiseptic and bandages," he called over his shoulder.

She grabbed the items and followed him into a room where two girls were lying on cots, conscious but wincing in pain. They had bruises and lacerations on their faces and hands. One had a bullet lodged in her leg.

"I need you to work on them," Bogart said.

The girls were young, about sixteen or seventeen. She closed her eyes and saw the bodies in the crates. She started to cry.

Bogart pulled her into the hallway. "Are you able to do this?"

"The crates in the basement," she sobbed. "The T-4 program. So many—"

"—Yes, I know."

"How can ... how ... how could you..."

"I have no part in what they're doing. I'm merely there to document proof of what they're doing."

"But how can you go into that building every day?"

He grabbed her shoulders. "Listen to me. I am in place there to observe and document. I don't like what I see and hear, but I have to be there to report on it."

"I won't go back. Ever."

He nodded his head. "Very well. I will not force you to go back." He pointed to the room with the young girls. "Can you tend to them?"

She got to work cleaning, bandaging, stitching. She

commandeered Otto as her assistant, ordering him to fetch various tools and medicines from the other room.

After she pulled the bullet out of the girl's leg, she treated Otto's hand. It was scraped and bloody, and she knew that whatever body part he hit was in worse shape. It sickened her to think about it.

When she finished, she stumbled back to the library and fell onto the chaise fully clothed.

She slept for most of the day. When she woke, Bogart was standing over her in his administrator disguise, with bushy eyebrows and mustache and horn-rimmed glasses. The transformation unnerved her, and she sat up.

"I'm sorry about last night. I didn't—"

"—No more apologies," he said. "You did well with the girls."

That put an end to it. She nodded.

He pulled a chair up. "Why did you retrieve two bottles of serum and some needles?"

"I—uh—" she started. "I thought about ... I thought there might be ..."

He folded his arms, waiting. She took a deep breath.

"I thought I might have to defend myself at some point," she said.

"I see." He nodded. "I can obtain a gun for you."

"No," she said. "If I have to carry around a weapon, this would be best. And it's—" She stopped.

"What is it?"

"It's ..." she marshalled her thoughts. "Well, it's just that if I ever have to kill someone, I wouldn't want it to hurt. If I inject this, the person dies peacefully."

He stared at her so long she grew uncomfortable, almost wishing he would go ahead and laugh or scoff and get it over with. He nodded.

"You are a good medic," he said, then got up and left.

She checked on the girls, then found Otto and checked his hand. Her tasks done, she headed back to Sophie's apartment.

On the way she passed a stationery store. On a whim she went in and told the man she had been sent by the hospital to buy paper.

He regarded her uniform. "How much do you need?" "Four reams," she said.

He went into the back room, brought back the reams, and put them on the counter.

"Can you send the bill to the hospital?" she asked.

"Of course."

She brought the paper to Sophie's house and put it on the table next to the half ream.

Chapter Forty-Seven

THE WHITE ROSE PAMPHLETS WERE DISTRIBUTED TO the citizens of Munich. Some had never heard of the atrocities and were surprised at what was written. Others were afraid to have it in their possession and got rid of the paper. A few tracked down the White Rose members and asked to join.

Inside the pamphlet, Hans and Christoph had written a stirring portrayal of the crimes that were being committed by the government:

Since the conquest of Poland three hundred thousand Jews have been murdered in this country in the most bestial way...

In the Jewish ghettos, German officials rounded up the Jewish people at gunpoint and herded them onto trucks bound for concentration camps, many of them to face death. The few brave enough to protest were shot on the spot.

The German people slumber on in their dull, stupid sleep and encourage these fascist criminals...

At Auschwitz, the red brick chimneys rose high above the facilities. Smoke billowed out of the incinerators nonstop.

Each man wants to be exonerated of a guilt of this kind ... But he cannot be exonerated; he is guilty, guilty, guilty!

At the hospital, another shipment of T-4 serum was delivered, along with another bus full of people who had been deemed undesirable by the regime. They were destined for "release" within days.

Chapter Forty-Eight

OSTER STUCK HIS HEAD INTO CANARIS' OFFICE AND waved a paper. "Weather report just in. Stormy."

Canaris looked up. "The butcher has something." Oster nodded. They left together.

~ ~ ~

When Canaris and Oster entered, the butcher came from behind the counter to greet them. He handed them a note.

"This is who he was seeing in Paris. And here's her address." Canaris nodded at him in thanks and turned to leave.

"He's headed to Wannsee," the butcher said.

Canaris turned back to him and narrowed his eyes. "Did you say Wannsee?"

"Isn't that what was on the document at Heydrich's house?" Oster asked.

"Yes." Canaris handed Oster the note. "Have her picked up."

It wouldn't hurt to have leverage when he and August crossed paths again.

Chapter Forty-Nine

THE CAR DROPPED AUGUST OFF, AND HE LUMBERED up the steps. His shoulders sagged. Every breath, every movement was an effort. He felt stunned beyond coherent thought. The conference had done that to him. He wasn't sure how he'd be able to exorcise it from his thoughts.

He went inside and locked the door. *First things first. A drink.*

He stopped, looked around, listened. He wasn't alone. He pulled out his weapon and stalked his way into the living room.

Canaris was sitting on the sofa, a glass in his hand. A folder sat on the sofa beside him. A bottle of scotch was on the coffee table with an empty glass beside it.

"We have some things to discuss, so I dropped by. How was Wannsee?"

"The butcher told you? Damn it!"

"Of course he told me. He's my asset."

August eyed Canaris, leaning back on the sofa, a glass of scotch in his hand. There was no threat. August put away his weapon, took off his coat, and sat across from Canaris. His movements were slow and thoughtful. By the time he sat, he was focused, calm, and collected.

"So you know I went to Wannsee," he said. "What else do you know? Or want to know?"

"What else do I know? Let's see..." Canaris took a drink and looked up. "I know your apartment isn't bugged. We swept it this morning. So we're free to talk." He looked back at August. "I know you're intelligent. And capable. We could use that."

"We? You mean the Abwehr?"

"I mean the Resistance. A group of us who are committed to restoring honor to Germany." He studied August. "You've already encountered it."

August leaned forward and studied him. "The men at the SOE house. And the testimony from Dina and Hofer."

"Yes."

"This is a lot to reveal. How do you know you can trust me?"

"I don't know that I can yet. I'm gambling on your sense of moral outrage at what you've discovered." Canaris took another drink before continuing. "And I'm paying you the compliment of not trying to deceive you."

"How do I know I can trust you?"

"Because you have no choice."

"Sure I do. I could tell Heydrich about this conversation."

"But you won't," Canaris said. "You want to be part of this. You want to see Germany restored."

"You seem very sure of yourself."

Canaris gave a slight grin. "Actually, you're already working with us."

"What do you mean?"

"You've kept it all secret."

"Including that I have a secret."

"Exactly."

August got up and paced around the room. He shook his head.

"I'm not buying this," he said. "The head of the Abwehr comes to me personally—pardon, breaks into my place —"

"—Like you did at my office."

August stopped and lowered his head, acknowledging the offense.

"There were things I needed to know. To ... to verify. I know I probably—"

"—Apology accepted," Canaris broke in. "That's not why I'm here. Sit down. There's more."

August sat. Canaris poured scotch into the empty glass and held it out to him.

"No thank you."

Canaris shrugged and put the glass in front of him anyway.

"We pulled the Gestapo's files on you," he said. "It has information on your family."

August tensed up. "Wh-where are they? Are—are they—"

"Your sister and nephew were sent to a labor camp. Theresienstadt."

August took in the information with a frown. "And Kurt?"

Canaris looked down. "Killed. By Heydrich's men."

August started to shake, his breath quickening. Canaris reached over and put the drink in his hand. August took a gulp and put it down.

"Are you sure? How did you find out? Maybe it was someone else. Maybe—"

"It's confirmed." Canaris handed him the folder.

August opened it and flipped through the pages of official documents. After a few moments, he closed the file and cowered back in the chair, covering his eyes.

"I tried to avoid this," he said in a small voice. "Doing everything I could to stay in his favor so I could find my sister. My God, I feel sick just saying that."

He sat up and looked away, trying to hide his wet tears. Canaris noticed anyway.

"I'm sorry, August."

August tossed the folder over to Canaris. He downed the rest of the scotch, slammed the glass down, and glared at him.

"And you had to deliver the news yourself. Come to gloat? Are we even now for the office break-in?"

Canaris looked at him for a moment, then gathered the two glasses and took them into the kitchen. August heard running water, tinkling of glasses, cabinet doors shutting. Canaris came back, stood over August, and pointed to the kitchen.

"Never reveal you've had a guest that the Gestapo would find interesting."

August glanced toward the kitchen. "I see."

Canaris sat on the couch and leaned forward. "I want to recruit you. I came because the request comes with devastating news. I'm paying you the compliment of not trying to deceive you."

August took a deep breath and nodded. "I take back what I said. It was ... just ... a shock."

"I know."

August gave a weak smile. "Yes. You're the Abwehr. What is there that you don't know?"

"What was discussed at Wannsee."

August looked away. "You don't want to know."

"Where can I get the documents?"

"Eichmann has the only copy."

"We'll have the butcher get a copy."

August started to tell him that it would be impossible to get a copy. But then he realized there wasn't much that was impossible to this man.

Canaris stood. "Come. We have work to do."

They walked to a car parked down the road. Oster was waiting behind the wheel. August and Canaris got in the back.

August turned to Canaris. Time to set terms.

"Admiral, if I'm going to do this, I want to be sure we can trust each other," August said.

"I value what you can do, August. But trust costs more."

"You value what I can do?" August gave a short laugh. "Says one professional liar to another."

Canaris looked out the window to hide his smile. How many were bold enough to counter his statements? It was refreshing. Yes, he liked this August Wichmann very much. He hid his smile and turned back to look August in the eye.

"I will never deceive you. You have my word," he said, his voice quiet and firm. "I expect the same courtesy from you."

"Then there's something else you should know," he said. "Heydrich is placing me inside the Abwehr to spy on you."

Canaris smiled. "Yes, I know."

Chapter Fifty

AT ABWEHR HEADQUARTERS, AUGUST SAT IN A ROOM with Dohnanyi and Bonhoeffer. Several dossiers were open in front of them, and more folders were stacked on the corner of the table. The table was crowded with empty plates and glasses, and ashtrays overflowed with cigarette butts. It had been a long day.

Dohnanyi stood and put on his jacket. "We'll continue tomorrow. Good to have you on board, August."

August watched him leave, then turned to Bonhoeffer. "The admiral mentioned the two of you are related."

"Yes. He and my sister are married."

"He also said you were a clergyman."

"Let me introduce myself properly," Bonhoeffer said. "I'm 'Dietrich' to family and friends. 'Pastor' to my former seminary students. 'That Damn Clergyman' to Himmler and Heydrich."

"Not popular with the Third Reich, I take it."

"Heydrich sent his thugs to shut down Finkenwalde Seminary," Bonhoeffer said. "All my students were conscripted. I complained and they forbid me from preaching."

"Does your work with the Abwehr conflict with your faith?"

"I'm an ordained pastor working with our country's spy network in a secret group planning to overthrow it, all to drive away evil. I could argue this is precisely my faith in action."

"Does it bother you, planning a coup?"

Bonhoeffer laughed. "My father is a psychiatrist. He would be very impressed with you."

Then Bonhoeffer grew serious. "Does it bother me? Certainly. But God's calling is irrevocable. And it's mutually agreed: God calls me to action; therefore I must battle evil. That's my confession. What's yours?"

August thought for a moment. "I think I'm more at ease planning assassinations than I should be."

"Welcome to the Resistance."

Chapter Fifty-One

CANARIS AND SACK MET WITH GEHRE AT THE SAME house behind the clothing store. With both the Gestapo and the SS tightening operations against the Abwehr—the three agencies had always been at odds but not until recently had two ganged up against one—Canaris felt that the clandestine arrangement was necessary.

"Let me get this straight," Gehre said. "You want me to help generate some legal issues that will warrant Heydrich's full attention?"

"Exactly," said Canaris.

"And I'll see to it that the courts will have more than enough problems for him to deal with," said Sack.

Gehre looked from one to the other. "All this just to keep him from finding out that one of his officers is working with us?"

"It's not just one of his officers," Canaris said. "One of his favorites."

"I see." He pondered the matter. "You consider this man that valuable?"

Although Gehre had directed the question to Sack, Sack turned to Canaris and waited for his answer.

Canaris didn't answer right away. He took time to get the proper tone in his voice, not wanting to give away just how valuable August was. He gave a slight nod.

"He has the potential to be one of our best," Canaris said.

Gehre shrugged. "I'll do what I can to keep Heydrich in legal trouble."

Chapter Fifty-Two

CANARIS ENTERED THE SHOP, CAUGHT THE BUTCHER'S eye, and nodded. The butcher was helping a customer, but when he saw Canaris, he immediately went into the back and returned with a thick packet.

Canaris held out his hand, but the butcher clutched the packet to his chest. He grabbed Canaris' shoulder, pulled him over to a corner, and leaned in, his voice low and urgent.

"I slaughter things for a living. I cut into flesh. I drain blood from carcasses. I do it every day, and never once has it bothered me."

He thrust the packet into Canaris' hands. His face was twisted into a grimace.

"This made me sick."

~ ~ ~

Canaris rushed back to his office and called in Dohnanyi, Bonhoeffer, Oster, and August.

Canaris, Dohnanyi, and Bonhoeffer sat as they read the report; Oster paced. August looked out the window. He had no desire to look at the record of the meeting he had attended.

The others read silently, their faces becoming more repulsed as they made their way through it.

Oster gasped. "What kind of mind would think of—"

"They actually held a meeting about how to execute masses of people in the most efficient way possible," Bonhoeffer said, wonder and disbelief in his voice. "I cannot fathom this."

"Did no one at this meeting object??" Oster asked.

"This will be added to the case against them," Dohnanyi said in his usual practical manner. "When we finally get them to trial."

Oster continued to pace, engrossed in the details. "I can't believe this. Heydrich says they need to get people into the chambers naked to avoid waste."

August was there. He remembered.

~ ~ ~

It was a large dining room with an oversized table. A dozen men in uniform from various military branches were seated.

A secretary sat at a nearby desk. Heydrich sat in the center, in charge, commanding attention. August sat against the wall, observing quietly.

"We have to get their clothes off first!" he stressed. "Easier to retrieve their valuables that way. Imagine the senseless waste of jewels and money going into the crematorium."

August looked around the room. They were all nodding in agreement. No one expressed indignation or shock.

August took a deep breath and reminded himself that he was just role-playing. It took a long time to focus.

~ ~ ~

Bonhoeffer looked at August. "It must have been hard to hear this."

August gave him a sad smile.

Bonhoeffer turned to Canaris. "Can we get August transferred to the Abwehr?"

"No. We need him to be eyes and ears on Heydrich." Canaris looked at August. "It's not a pleasant role, but it's one we need you to play. For now."

August heaved a sigh and nodded.

Canaris turned to Bonhoeffer. "Get a copy of this to the Vatican."

Meeting over. They filed out. Canaris watched August leave, his brow furrowed in concern.

Bonhoeffer caught up with August at the door. "You look like you could use a reprieve. Come for supper tonight."

Chapter Fifty-Three

WHEN THE DOOR OPENED, AUGUST WAS SURPRISED to see Bonhoeffer's broad smile. There was no trace of the revulsion and horror that had shadowed his face a few days earlier as they read through the Wannsee document. August had been able to think of little else since, and he marveled at Bonhoeffer's fortitude.

But then he stepped into the Bonhoeffer home and began to understand the transformation. From the moment August entered, it was as if a soothing balm was washing over him. From the foyer he could feel waves of delight and glee reaching out to engulf him: happy chatter among the clink of dishes being set, a roar of laughter from another room, children giggling. He thought of Helga and Kurt and baby Gunther and how lucky he was that he once had enjoyed such moments of pure delight. He tried to remember the last time he laughed. The realization made him want to weep.

The giggles grew louder, and suddenly three small children appeared in the foyer and dashed past them.

Bonhoeffer smiled. "I would tell them to mind their manners around a guest, but how can one admonish children happy at play?"

The children dashed through the foyer again at full

voice. One of them noticed the uniform and came to a halt mid-giggle when he spotted the skull insignia on August's cap, the mark of the SS. The other two children ran back and stood in front of August. He threw Bonhoeffer an embarrassed glance and removed his cap, covering the insignia. But the children still stared, wide-eyed and silent.

The sudden silence brought the adults from the other rooms. With a glance Karl Bonhoeffer sized up the situation and held out his hand.

"Ah! You must be Dietrich's friend. Welcome to our home." The greeting worked like magic on the children. They ran off, giggling and playing again.

"Allow me to introduce everyone," Bonhoeffer said. "August, this is my father and mother, Karl and Paula Bonhoeffer." He motioned to the others. "My brother-in-law Hans you already know. His wife, Christine. The children running through here belong to them. Although, we're not sure, some of them may be from the neighborhood. It gets hard to keep track sometimes."

They all laughed. As the laughter died, an uneasy pause grew with furtive looks at the uniform. August mustered up an apologetic grin.

"Forgive me for having to wear this," August said. "Heydrich's men follow me everywhere."

"Not to worry," Bonhoeffer said. "Here, at least you have no need to wear a mask. Welcome!"

It was one of the most pleasant evenings August could remember in a long while. It was a warm, joyful time—a lot of laughter, jokes going back and forth. He relaxed and joined in the fun. He shared stories of his days as a professor and had them roaring over his imitation of an Englishman, an Italian, and a Frenchman bidding on a painting at an auction.

After dinner, the men moved into the living room. Karl poured brandy for them.

"Herr Wichmann—" Karl began.

"Please. Call me August."

"August, then." Karl handed him the drink. "Do you still maintain any relationships from the university?"

August shook his head. "It's been several years." He glanced down at his uniform and took a sip of the brandy. "They probably wouldn't recognize me."

Karl eyed him with keen interest. "I find your teaching methods quite interesting. Not merely introducing languages but also adopting cultures and philosophies."

"Yes. I found that it helps to embrace the language if one embraces a particular culture's view of the world." August took another sip of the brandy. Over the rim of the glass he could see the others studying him, sifting every word. "Why did you ask about the university?"

Dohnanyi, Bonhoeffer, and Karl Bonhoeffer looked at one another, gauging the trust level. They each gave a faint nod and turned back to August.

"We've heard rumors about student activities in Munich," Dohnanyi said. "We think they're being watched. We want to get word to them to be careful."

"What activities?" August asked.

"Printing pamphlets that criticize the Nazis," Dohnanyi said.

"And distributing them around Munich," Bonhoeffer added.

August stared at them. "That's it?"

Bonhoeffer forced a sad smile. "Times have changed. What once was mundane could now be a capital offense."

August nodded. He well he knew that fact.

"Perhaps you could bring word," Dohnanyi said. "On the pretext of visiting old colleagues."

"Who would I be looking for?" August asked.

Dohnanyi shrugged. "We don't have names, but they call themselves the White Rose Movement."

"Very well." August drained his glass.

"Tell me, August," Karl said, refilling the glass, "when you embrace a particular culture's view of the world, I assume it is a temporary embrace."

"Of course," August gave a short laugh.

Karl rejoined with a short laugh. "For instance, one does not become French permanently by embracing the French culture. I bring this up out of curiosity for your methods. In my line of work, I've found that some people find it difficult to release a viewpoint once embraced in such a holistic manner."

August thought of his Jean Louis Mardot persona. He had them convinced. But that didn't make him French. In fact, he had remained very much a German. He thought of the names he had given to his superiors, and a pain shot through his stomach. He put the glass down.

"I must be getting home," he said. "Dr. Bonhoeffer, thank you for a pleasant evening, one of the nicest I've had in a long time. Dietrich. Hans."

He bowed to them. Karl held his eyes on the double-bolt insignia on August's lapel.

August noticed. He measured his words, then spoke with deliberation. "I find it no trouble at all to let go of another view, especially if it's counter to my own."

"Quite admirable." Karl said. "You will forgive my inquiries. As a psychologist I tend to bring my work everywhere I go. But I am also interested in your views."

"Of course," August said.

"I have enjoyed meeting you, August. You are welcome in our home any time."

As soon as August left, Dohnanyi turned to Karl. "What do you think?"

"The man is wrapped in secrets," he said. "Keeping a secret is one thing; wearing it all day is another. What do I think? I think it will make or break him."

Chapter Fifty-Four

BACK IN HIS APARTMENT, AUGUST REMOVED HIS uniform and hung it up. He slumped on the sofa, retrieved the photos from the secret pocket, and stared at them. The discussion with Karl Bonhoeffer about different points of view reminded August of the day Helga and Kurt had left Germany. It had been a sharp difference of viewpoint.

~ ~ ~

Helga and Kurt gathered up items and stuffed them in the suitcases. They walked around August, who stood in the middle of the room. He pleaded with them quietly.

"You can stop treating them," August said to Kurt. "You have other patients."

"I took an oath," Kurt said. "And it says nothing about race or religious beliefs."

"The Nazis have already started harassing him," Helga said. "Did you know that?"

The baby cried from another room. Kurt went in to get him. August turned to Helga.

"Where are you running away to?"

"Away from here." She busied herself with packing.

"Where??" he pressed.

She took a long time to answer. "Paris."

Kurt carried his son in. August took the boy and cradled him. "I'll try to get assigned to Paris."

"That would be wonderful," Kurt said. "Oradour-sur-Glane is only a few hours away."

August turned to his sister. She avoided his look. He handed the baby to Kurt, then moved over to Helga. He took her by the shoulders and searched her face.

"Why did you lie to me?"

She shrugged and tried to turn away, still avoiding his gaze.

But he held her in place. "Look at me, Helga." His voice was a whisper, hoarse with checked emotion.

She looked at him, her eyes flooded, lip quivering. One glance at the worry etched on his face and the tears spilled down her cheeks.

"Please don't make this more difficult," she sniffed through her tears. "And please don't tell anyone. I don't want them to know where we're going."

He dropped his hands to his side, stunned. "Who do you think I'm going to tell?"

Released, she turned away. Out from under his gaze, she mustered her resolve.

"You know we have to leave," she said.

"I know you have reasons you want to leave," he said. "I don't agree with them. But that doesn't mean I would—"

"I have no idea what you might do," she said, her voice breaking.

"How can you say that? I'm your brother!" He slapped his hand flat on his heart.

Helga watched his hand press into his chest, and even though she knew it was an unconscious gesture, it flashed into her mind that her moving away was breaking his heart. She burst into tears. "But you're an SS officer," she sobbed. "I know what kind of loyalties they demand. How can I trust you?"

~ ~ ~

He gazed at the photos, and the self-recriminations rushed at him before he could stop them. *I could have helped them. Why didn't I? Why did I have to press the issue again? I knew it would end up in an argument.*

He stowed the photos away and leaned back on the sofa. It occurred to him that his sister would still think of him as the quintessential SS officer. He squeezed his eyes shut.

Chapter Fifty-Five

SEVERAL HIGH-LEVEL MILITARY OFFICERS SAT AROUND
the table, among them Canaris, Himmler, Goebbels, and
others. Hitler stood, paced, ranted, and screamed.

"These generals in the field!" Hitler yelled. "What
do they know? Naysayers, all of them! We are going to
open another front to crush America! Smash them to
bits! There is no place for second guessing in the Third
Reich!"

It was interminable. No one interrupted. No one
said a word or moved.

Canaris locked eyes with a general across the table.
The general raised his eyebrows slightly. Canaris gave
a slight nod. They both looked around, assessing reactions, gauging which others were as fed up as they were.
They needed to recruit more. Another attempt was imminent.

Chapter Fifty-Six

IN A HOTEL IN SWEDEN, AUGUST AND BONHOEFFER watched the growing horror on Bishop Bell's face as he flipped through the Wannsee document. August could tell which parts Bell was reading by the shades of green in his complexion.

Bell finished and put the document down with shaking hands. "We're hoping this will be enough to gain support," Bonhoeffer said. "I've brought two copies. One must go to the Vatican. We need military support, of course, but we're also hoping for worldwide church support."

"Yes, yes," Bell said, his brow drawn down. His distraction and reluctance were obvious, but neither August nor Bonhoeffer were sure exactly why.

"Or we can get it to the Vatican by other means," said Bonhoeffer.

Bell took a deep breath and looked at them.

"I'll be honest, Dietrich. I'm not sure this will be enough," he said. "It's difficult to convince the military that there are Germans who can be trusted."

"Are we talking trust again?" August burst out. "We're giving you proof of these atrocities and you say it's not enough?"

"It's more complicated than that."

"Of course it is!" August said. He stalked to the window and looked out. "I'm just frustrated."

"Aren't we all, though?" Bell said with a trace of wry humor. "It's a frustrating war."

There was silence for a few minutes, the weight of the world on their shoulders, the plight of millions of God's people burdening their thoughts.

August turned around. "If we were to ... to work to ..." he groped for the right words. "... to somehow eliminate a common enemy ... would that be proof enough?"

Bell stared at him wide-eyed. He was worried that he'd disgusted Bell with his hints. Clergy are not supposed to be involved in assassination plots. But he realized that the look on Bell's face was not shock but intrigue.

"Can you share details?" Bell asked.

"Not at this time."

Disappointed, Bell flipped open the folder again. "Eliminating evil is a noble endeavor," he said, looking up. "I think it would help."

"It's already in the works," August said.

~ ~ ~

After Bishop Bell left, August and Bonhoeffer stood side by side at the window and gazed down at the street below.

"All I can think of is how to get rid of Heydrich," August said, "and I know how horrible that must sound to you. I just want to take action."

Bonhoeffer grinned at him. "Do you think I'm shocked?"

"Well, I'm no saint, that's for sure."

Bonhoeffer pondered for a moment. "Let me tell you a story. Years ago, I had a wonderful discussion with a young French pastor about what he wanted to do with his life. He said he wanted to become a saint." He looked at August. "If he was in France when it was occupied, he is likely among the saints now."

August thought back to the days when he had gathered information from the Jews in the basement of the French café. *Gathered information? Call it what it was: betrayal.* He lowered his head in shame.

"It was an intriguing view, but I disagreed," Bonhoeffer continued. "I believe it's a better use of time to learn to have faith."

August looked up, confused. "What do you mean? Aren't you already a man of faith?"

"One does not acquire faith through ordination nor through living a holy life."

"Then ... how?"

"By living completely in this world," Bonhoeffer said. "That is the only way to learn faith."

August found himself engaged and energized. He had participated in this kind of debate in his days as a professor at the university. He realized now how much he missed it.

"At what point is the lesson complete?"

"At the point of death, I believe," Bonhoeffer said.

"I don't understand," August said. "You are completely in this world until your death anyway. Right?"

"What I mean is that it's important to stop trying make something of yourself." Bonhoeffer turned and paced around the room, chasing his thoughts. "Stop trying to be a saint like the Frenchman wanted to be. Stop working so hard to be a righteous man. Or a converted sinner, which is worse." He stopped pacing and turned to look August in the eye. "We all must live without reservation or hesitation. We must live with complete abandon in our experiences, all our successes, all our failures."

"Be men of action, you mean," August said.

Bonhoeffer flashed a broad smile at him.

"Yes." He gazed at August for a moment, studying him intently. "You're right, you know."

"About?"

"About the desperate need to take action," Bonhoeffer said, his eyes shining. "When we do, we throw ourselves into the arms of God. And then we are not our own anymore. At that point, we must take seriously that our sufferings are nothing compared to the sufferings of God in the world."

Bonhoeffer went back to the window and looked out. But August left the window and sat in a chair, his breath caught in his chest, stunned into silence.

"When ... uh, when do we head back..." August stammered, his voice rich with emotion.

"Our transport will be ready tomorrow," Bonhoeffer said. "We'll stay here tonight."

Bonhoeffer smiled into the growing darkness outside. He had heard the gravity in August's voice. It was an answer to his prayers, an affirmation that August's heart was in the right place. He was glad that their return to Berlin was delayed. There would be time to talk and to listen. They were on holy ground. Nothing was more important at this time.

Chapter Fifty-Seven

THE RECEPTION DISPLAYED ALL THE GAUDINESS AND glitz due a key member of the regime. Nazi officials strode around the room, their starched crisp uniforms and flashes of medals glittering across their chests.

In a small circle on the far side of the room, Heydrich held court. He had risen higher in Hitler's favor and had been appointed Deputy Reich Protector of Bohemia and Moravia, where he had set up the Jewish "model" ghetto at Theresienstadt. The party was a celebration of Himmler's inspection of the facility, which he called the most efficient in the Reich.

From across the room, August curled his lip in disgust. His sister and nephew had been sent to that same labor camp, and the last place he wanted to be was celebrating how well it was run. But the admiral had asked him to attend this party to gather intel. He adjusted his expression and made his way to the guest of honor.

Heydrich leaned over and threw his arm around August.

"Ah, my rising star, August Wichmann! So you've come to celebrate my achievements?"

August held up his glass. "Congratulations, sir."

They all drank. Heydrich turned to the others.

"I hand-picked Wichmann here to head up our Special Actions division. A busy group. Bigger and better things are coming soon."

A few murmurs of praise and congratulations. Heydrich turned to August.

"But I might have a better task for him. Something more in line with his incredible abilities." Heydrich raised his glass to August. "Perhaps head of the Abwehr."

The group turned to August. At first he couldn't speak. "I b-beg your pardon?" he asked.

"I told the Fuhrer we needed new blood in the Abwehr. He agreed. I'll need someone I can trust to run it."

"What about Admiral Canaris?"

Heydrich threw his head back and laughed. "I'm sure he'll be too busy with other things soon. Get ready, Wichmann, we have much work to do. More special actions. More crematoriums to build." He drained his glass and drifted off to another group.

August was stunned. *Why did he just say that in public? What is he up to?*

He circumnavigated the room with deliberate purpose, inching his way back to Heydrich's circle so he could overhear without being noticed. His eye roamed the room at large, noticing who was where and talking to whom. The admiral would expect a full report.

His eye caught a familiar face and stopped. He appraised the shimmering dress, upswept hair, formal gloves, sparkling earrings. He had never seen her in formal wear like this, and her hair was a lighter shade than he remembered, but there was no mistaking the sapphire eyes. There was no doubt it was Brigitte.

She caught his gaze and strolled over, flashing a bright smile. "Are congratulations in order for you too,

Herr Rising Star?"

She stretched out her arms toward him. He took hold of her hands, massaging her fingers through the silky gloves. No ring. He gave a broad smile. For a moment Heydrich and his treachery toward the Abwehr was forgotten.

"Brigitte Bauer. This is ... I'm so ... It's good to see you." He was unsettled. And the fact that she could unsettle him was unsettling. He found the thought amusing.

He noticed that she was glancing around the room as if uneasy. *Did I unsettle her too?* But something told him it was more than that. He laughed to regain his bearings. "I never thought I'd see you at an event like this."

It was a slight barb—and intentional. He wanted to draw her out and find out why she was here. The last time he saw her, she had been fierce and unwavering and completely anti-Nazi. He wondered if her beliefs had changed. The thought doused his spirits.

She ignored the barb and instead flashed another bright smile. "How are Helga and Kurt?" she asked. "I lost track of them. Did they move away from Munich?"

Again he was caught off guard and fought to keep his face impassive. But when he heard their names, his face transformed into a mingle of shock and grief. It was a struggle to keep eye contact. He drummed up every ounce of training he could muster. *Play the role.*

But it didn't work. He dropped her hands and looked away. "Yes, they did. And they had a baby a few years ago. Gunther. My middle name. And his grandpapa's too. Father would be impressed, such a brilliant little—" *Am I babbling?* He stopped, plastered on a smile, and gave a nod to her dress. "And how are you? Quite a festive outfit. Nothing like the nurse's uniform I thought you'd be in by now."

She swept her hand around at the room. "The occasion calls for some formality."

"Of course," he said. *But why? Why are you here?* He was desperate to know what she was doing at this farce of a celebration. What had changed in her life to make her want to be here?

"I heard Kurt ran into trouble with—" she scanned the room "—the authorities."

He hesitated. He wasn't sure how traumatic the news about Kurt might be for her. And he could barely bring himself to talk about it. He thought of a way to skirt the truth.

"Helga and the baby are at a facility," he said, hoping to leave it at that. No one knew that he was aware that they were in Theresienstadt.

"Which facility?" Her face was white and strained. He decided not to tell her. He gave a brief shrug.

But she pressed him. "Was the baby ... normal?"

"Normal?" He was baffled at the question. "What do you—"

"Karin Werner! *Liebling!*"

One of Heydrich's assistants came up to Brigitte, took her by the shoulders, and kissed her on each cheek. Then he looked her up and down. "You are a vision, as always. You become more glamorous each time I see you. Where is your husband? I am most anxious to speak with Herr Werner."

Brigitte's cheeks flushed. *I have to get away before August kills my cover.* "He couldn't make it, but he sent a message for you." She flashed a bright smile to August. "If you will excuse us."

She slipped her hand through the assistant's arm and led him to a corner of the room. She positioned herself so she could keep an eye on August. He was frowning at her. She hurried to conduct business.

From across the room, he watched her pull a note card out of her purse and hand it to the man. In return, he handed her a note, and she stashed it in her purse. Some more conversation, and the assistant went on his way. August was well acquainted with the man and the heinous acts he had committed. *What was she doing with him?* A frisson of unease came over him.

August strode over and leaned in slightly to whisper, "Outside. Left. One block."

He watched her take a circuitous route out of the room. He meandered in another direction, easing his way to the exit.

Outside, he turned left and paced his way to the end of the street, glancing around as his recon training kicked in. Brigitte was waiting. He scanned the surroundings. They were alone.

He faced her. "So."

She paced back and forth, her head down.

"The facts as I see them. Just to clear up the confusion." He raised his eyebrows at her. "You changed your name—first *and* last, apparently. You're no longer a nurse. You attend parties with high-ranking Nazi officials. How much is correct so far?"

She opened her mouth but paused, still debating with herself how much to reveal.

"Oh yes, and you obviously overcame your loathing of the uniform," he spat out.

"You're angry—"

"I'm not angry, I'm completely mystified." He frowned. "I thought that you—when did you get married?"

"August, I'm—"

"And why did you want to know if Gunther is normal? What kind of question is that?"

Tears started in her eyes. She blinked them back. "A lot has happened to me in the past few years."

"A lot has happened to all of us."

She smirked at his uniform. "You look the same."

"I'm not what you think."

"Maybe I'm not either." They measured each other.

"Who are you working for?" he asked.

"I can't tell you anything."

"You can trust me."

"I just heard you being praised by Heydrich. Rising higher in the ranks." She flung her arm in the vague direction of the ballroom. "Apparently you're one of his favorites."

"It's not what you think."

"What do you mean it's not what I think? Look who you're working with. How can I trust you?"

Helga had said almost the same thing when she and Kurt were leaving for France. *But you're an SS officer. I know what kind of loyalties they demand. How can I trust you?*

Grief over his sister delivered a gut punch. The need to gain Brigitte's trust overwhelmed him. He dealt with distrust in his work all the time, but he didn't think he could bear it from her.

"Talk to me. Please." His voice was soft, tinged with despair.

She looked up at him, her eyes soft. "I *want* to."

He searched her face. If he confided in her, would she open up to him? He searched his mind for anything he could tell her that wouldn't compromise someone else. How much easier it would be if she would just believe him. What would it take?

In a moment of desperation, he seized her shoulders, intending to deliver an impassioned plea, but before he could stop himself, he pulled her into an embrace and his lips found hers and he felt her arms slip around his neck and he wanted nothing more than to hold her and protect her.

He broke the embrace suddenly and turned her face up so he could look into her eyes. She was as strong and fierce as he remembered. He knew she didn't need his protection. Fine. He would just hold her. *Is she working with the Reich? Dear God, I pray she isn't. If she is, I'll do everything in my power to turn her. Or die trying.*

He was out of breath, and his heart was pounding. He noticed she was breathing as hard as he was. He steeled himself to calm down. He had to look away to do it.

"They sent Helga to Theresienstadt. Gunther too."

"What about Kurt?"

He shook his head. He couldn't say the words, that his best friend was dead. Instead he tossed his head back toward the building. "I'm not eager to rise in the ranks with the man who did that to my family."

Her eyes flashed understanding. She nodded.

"I heard he was going to—" A car pulled up across the street. The driver glanced around, saw Brigitte, nodded. She nodded back. "I have to go."

"Wait! How can I reach you?" he asked.

"I can give you a number." She dug into her purse for paper and pen. "Don't use my name. Ask for Karin. And if it's urgent, ask for Petra. Leave a number and I'll call you back."

She was talking fast, almost babbling. August kept his attention on the car. The driver had a beak nose and beady eyes. He wondered who he was. He was going to ask, but then something clattered on the sidewalk. He bent down to pick it up while she wrote the number.

It was a needle, filled with fluid.

She reached for it. "That's mine."

"What is it?" he asked.

"It's ... something I carry for protection," she said, holding out her hand.

"Protection from what?"

"Can I have it back?"

"Tell me what it is."

The car door opened. They both turned and saw the man get out.

Brigitte looked back at August. "It's T-4 serum."

"T-4? From the euthanasia program?" He had learned about it at Wannsee meeting, more than he ever wanted to know.

"Oh, you're familiar. Yes. Now please give it back."

"Absolutely not," he said. "Do you know what would happen if they found it?"

"I don't care," she said. "If I have to use it, it means I would have rid the world of a great evil. Sometimes it takes a great risk to accomplish a greater good."

August stared at her for a moment, completely at a loss for how to respond. He put the needle in his coat pocket.

She stretched out her hand. "Please give it back."

"You could be arrested just for having this on you," he said. "I don't want anything to happen to you."

The man started across the road. Brigitte handed August the phone number.

"I have to go," she said.

"Wait, one question."

She looked back.

"Are you married?" he asked.

"No," she said and dashed over to the car.

August watched them drive off, a smile spreading across his face.

~ ~ ~

Otto looked over at Brigitte as he drove away. "Who was that?"

She shook her head. "Someone I knew a long time ago."

"Is he a threat?"

"No."

He relaxed. "Did you get the intel?"

She opened her purse and found the note the man had given her in the ballroom. "Yes."

He nodded and turned his attention to the road.

Brigitte looked out the window. A flood of emotions swirled around her. Grief over Kurt. Concern for Helga and her baby. She touched her fingers to her lips. *August. What is he doing? Is he working with the Resistance? I need to see him again.* She looked at Otto.

"Where are we taking the intel?"

"Abwehr."

Chapter Fifty-Eight

CANARIS OPENED THE DOOR TO AUGUST. HE HELD UP a finger: *Wait*. He grabbed two leashes and whistled. Two dogs ran up. He hooked the leashes and led them outside to where August waited.

He pointed to the dogs. "Don't worry. They can keep secrets."

August didn't laugh. Canaris looked sidelong at him. "How was the party?"

"He's celebrating his new post," August said. "Which will give him control of the Abwehr. And he's planning more mass executions. More crematoriums."

Canaris digested the news with a nod. "Good information."

"He's also planning to implicate you in something. I don't know what. Something to put you in prison."

Canaris concentrated hard. "Then we need to implicate him first with—"

"We need to stop thinking we'll remove him through legal action. That could take years. Think how much damage he can do before then."

"Don't get me wrong, August. I'm not opposed to a kill. But it would have to be planned and executed well."

"I can do it, Admiral!"

"No. We need you for other things."

August gritted his teeth. They walked in silence for a while.

A figure appeared in front of them, out of nowhere. Shimmering dress, upswept hair, sparkling earrings.

August was thrown off balance. "Wh-what are—? How did you get here?"

She ignored August and kept her eyes on Canaris. "Bogart sends his regards," she said.

Canaris nodded toward August. "It's okay. He's one of mine." He turned to August. "Brigitte is with the SOE."

August and Brigitte eyed one another with deep interest. August raised his eyebrows and grinned. Brigitte flashed him a bright smile.

Canaris looked at one then the other. "Though it seems you might already be acquainted."

"We knew each other a long time ago," August said.

Brigitte handed Canaris the note the man gave her at the party. He opened and read the contents. While she waited, she leaned down to the dogs.

"Kaspar! Sabine! What good puppies you are," she cooed.

August was stunned. *He knows her real name, and she knows his dogs. How well does she know the admiral?* He felt more off balance.

"Who is the SS officer you're with?" he asked.

Brigitte looked up at him in surprise. "What?"

August nodded in the direction of where Otto was hiding behind a wall. "He was the driver. Correct?"

Brigitte was flustered, but she recovered quickly. "Yes. Otto. He's ... he accompanied me here." *The less said the better.*

Canaris finished reading the note and pocketed it. Brigitte stood up and pointed to the dogs. "I see you brought your top secret-keepers to the meeting. What secrets were you discussing?"

Canaris smiled at the dogs, then grew serious. "August told me some of Heydrich's plans. This intel has more details." He patted the pocket that held the note.

"I think we should deal with him now. And for good," said August. "I offered to do it."

Canaris shook his head.

"The admiral thinks we need to come up with a more advanced plan," said August.

"I agree," said Brigitte. "And I think I can help." They looked at her with interest.

"I know two men who can do it," she said. "They're in England with the SOE. We can have them in Prague in a few weeks."

Canaris took a moment to deliberate. "Get me their dossiers."

She nodded, stooped to pet the dogs, then walked toward where Otto was waiting. August gave Canaris a quick glance, then followed her.

Halfway down the block, he caught up with her. "Brigitte, wait," he said.

She turned. He pulled something out of his pocket and held out his closed fist. She thought he was returning her needle, but when she held out her hand, he placed a necklace in it.

"This was Helga's. I want you to have it."

Brigitte looked at the pendant. A miniature hand mirror on a silver chain.

"I remember this. Helga told me when she was a little girl, you gave her this to remind her of how beautiful she was." She looked up at him. "Thank you."

"It was the only thing I found when I went to look for them after they disappeared," he said.

She gave him a sad smile.

He touched her cheek softly. "You look beautiful tonight."

"Thank you, August," she whispered.

He gazed at her for a long moment. "I'm glad I found you again."

"You didn't. I found you."

He grinned. "Even better."

He watched her walk away, then turned to find Canaris a few feet away, staring at him.

"Apparently an introduction was not necessary," Canaris said. "You know each other?"

"She was Helga's best friend. And she was in medical school with Kurt. I haven't seen her in years."

"You weren't aware of her work with the Resistance?"

"Not until now. And I'm guessing there's still a lot I don't know. Like who Bogart and Otto are."

Canaris pulled the leashes, leading the dogs back home. He took a moment to answer August. "Bogart runs the division she works with. Otto is her handler. She doesn't need one, but Bogart insisted."

"Interesting," August said. "All it took was a few minutes with her for you to agree to a plan about Heydrich."

"You sound jealous."

"No. I'm intrigued. I've been saying the same thing for months and you killed the idea every time. And now—"

Canaris stopped and looked August in the eye.

"I don't know the history between you two, but this much I know: She's endured more than most men on the front. And she's transformed that experience into something of value for the Resistance. I trust her judgment, and I would trust her with my life. Understand?"

August stepped back, awed by Canaris' sudden vigor.

"Yes."

"She—by herself—has eliminated quite a few of our enemies. The ones who are dangerous, the ones who are difficult to get to."

"By 'eliminated' ... do you mean—"

"—I don't have time to brief you. Get to know her again. If she trusts you, she'll tell you herself."

Chapter Fifty-Nine

At half-past midnight at an airfield in England, an RAF pilot stood beside the plane with an MI-6 agent. A car dropped off two men. They nodded to the pilot and climbed on the plane.

"Your passengers," the MI agent said. "Off to do some dirty work in Prague."

"So they're really giving us clearance to get these guys in?" the pilot asked.

"Got word from Canaris himself. Don't you know? They want to be rid of the bugger as much as we do."

"Sure. And my mum's the Crown Princess. Nobody should ever trust a Kraut, especially the spymaster of the bleedin' Third Reich?"

"Right. That's enough. Leave the politics to us. Just do your job and drop 'em at the coordinates."

~ ~ ~

Prague was a picture of perfection in springtime. The combination of light breeze and bright sun of early June made the city especially appealing.

A balance of progress and preservation had helped the capital of Czechoslovakia to maintain its old-world charm through ages of capture and settlement, while her fortunes waxed and waned through her thousand-year history. Prague was an important trading site for all of Europe and was known for several important moments in history: It was the seat of two Holy Roman Emperors, and for a while it was the capital of the Holy Roman Empire, playing major roles in the Protestant Reformation and the 30 Years War.

After today, the city would be known for an entirely different reason.

Two men waiting in the shadows didn't even notice the ambiance. They were on a mission. One held a gun, the other a hand grenade. A car rounded the corner. Its driver looked around, alert. The top was down. Heydrich sat in the back, his arm across the top of the seat. He leaned back, relaxed and carefree.

Out of the shadows, one of the men jumped in front of the car and held up his weapon. The driver stopped, pulled a gun from the seat beside him, and aimed it at the man.

The other man came from the side and threw the hand grenade into the car. The hand grenade exploded. The two men ran away.

~ ~ ~

August and Bonhoeffer sat in August's living room trying to relax, two mugs of beer on the coffee table. They both kept glancing at the clock on the wall.

"Did they give a time?" Bonhoeffer asked.

August jumped up and paced around. "No. Just that they'd send word."

Bonhoeffer nodded. "Relax, August. Enjoy your beer."

August gave a short laugh. "Confession time again. I feel guilty for not feeling guilty about this."

Bonhoeffer raised his beer in salute. "Congratulations. You still have a conscience."

"But it's not guilt. I'm worried that the plan will fail."

"Ah. But your concerns are for a greater good. That's still—"

The phone rang. August answered, listened, and hung up. He closed his eyes and leaned against the wall.

"Let's get to Prague."

Chapter Sixty

IT WAS LIKE ANY OTHER HOSPITAL IN ANY OTHER CITY: clean, efficient, dedicated to health and healing. The only difference were the Gestapo agents standing guard and the edginess of the staff—all due to the special patient in room 302.

Canaris and Himmler stood at the foot of Heydrich's bed. Heydrich was unconscious. The doctor checked his vital signs and turned to the two men.

"We've done everything we can for him, but his wounds are very serious."

"You will restore him to health," Himmler said quietly. It wasn't a question, and Himmler didn't look for confirmation. "Or we will find another doctor."

The tone of Himmler's voice caused the doctor's eyes to grow wide. He twisted the stethoscope in shaking hands. "W-w-we're doing e-everything to ensure that he s-survives."

Himmler gave a slow solemn Nazi salute over Heydrich, then left the room. Canaris nodded to the doctor, then walked out after him. As they left the building, Himmler turned to Canaris.

"We need tighter security. We'll discuss it on the way back."

"No, I'm late for a meeting in Munich," Canaris said. "I called for my car. We can discuss back in Berlin."

Himmler nodded and left. Canaris walked down the street and slipped into the back seat. Oster, August, and Bonhoeffer were waiting.

"Serious injuries. I doubt he'll survive."

"We need to finish this," August said.

"This problem will finish itself. We don't need to do anything. Besides, he's heavily guarded."

"I can get past them. I'll go in—"

"We've done all we can do."

"I need to finish this!"

"And I need you to stay alive!"

August opened the car door and gave a quick grin. "That's the plan."

August sprinted to the hospital. Canaris shook his head. "Pray, Dietrich."

~ ~ ~

August emerged from a room with his hair slicked back, wearing a pair of thick glasses, white coat, and stethoscope.

He reached into his pocket and touched the needle he had gotten from Brigitte.

He made his way to Heydrich's room. The guards scrutinized him. He ignored them and went in. He stood beside the bed and looked down at Heydrich. This was the man who had sent his sister and nephew to unknown horrors, who had his best friend killed in cold blood.

He thought back to when he got the news, the day he saw the full weight of Janette's betrayal. He remembered the pain in Canaris' eyes when he told August the truth about them. *Sent to a labor camp in Theresien-*

stadt. And Kurt? Killed. It had hurt Canaris as much as it hurt him. And the monster lying in this bed was responsible.

He wished there were something terrifying he could do to Heydrich. He wasn't sure what. He just knew that he wanted this bastard to suffer cruelly. The viciousness of his thoughts shocked him, but he didn't reprimand himself. The man lying in this bed had led him to such thoughts. All the more reason to rid the earth of him.

He pulled the needle out of his pocket and jabbed it into an arm vein. Heydrich's eyes fluttered open. August leaned down.

"This is for Kurt," he whispered. Heydrich frowned, not understanding.

"And for Dietrich. For what you did to his friends at Finkenwalde," August said.

August leaned closer. "Canaris is a bigger man than you. Bigger than you ever could be." August leaned over ever farther, getting into Heydrich's face. "I want that to be the last thing you hear in this life."

Heydrich's eyes widened in terror. There. That was the look August was after. He was vindicated. The scales were in balance. He pushed in the syringe delivering T-4 into Heydrich's vein. He watched for a moment, savoring the end of the person the Resistance had dubbed the Butcher of Prague.

Outside the room, the guards glanced at him as he left. They turned their attention to a nurse going in. August meandered down the hall. The nurse ran out.

"Help!" she yelled. "He's not breathing! Get the doctor! Hurry!"

The guards raced into the room. August took off the glasses, coat, and stethoscope and tossed them into a room as he passed. He strode down the hall.

He was out the door and into a different persona before the guards raced out looking for the doctor who'd been in Heydrich's room.

August made his way to the car, jumped in and slammed the door. "It's done," he said, his breath fast and hard. "Thank God."

Canaris and Bonhoeffer both stared at him speechless. Canaris gripped August's shoulder.

"Okay," Canaris murmured.

He looked at both of them and frowned. "Okay? That's all you can say? We've rid the world of a great evil! It's marvelous!"

Oster smiled. "Well done, August."

August returned an unsure smile. Oster started the car and drove away. August turned back to Bonhoeffer and Canaris.

"Do you think it's callous to rejoice over his death?" He eyed both of them. "Because if you do, I'll remind you of what he's done."

Bonhoeffer stared out the window for a moment, pondering. "I do have pangs of conscience when I think of what we're doing."

"We need more than pangs of conscience," August said, his brow drawn down. "You can't simply wait for the devastation and busy yourself with burying the dead and comforting the wounded."

Bonhoeffer started to argue his point, then closed his mouth, pondering the truth of August's words.

"What would you have me do?" he asked, his voice quiet and solemn.

"If you see a crazy man driving a car, what would you do?" August asked.

The answer came at once. "Wrestle the wheel from his hands," Bonhoeffer said.

"Exactly," August said. "And I don't know if that would be enough."

"Enough for what?" Canaris asked.

"It doesn't seem enough to be guiltless of the atrocities." He turned to Canaris, his eyes filled with grief. "How does one atone for believing the lies? For not seeing truth sooner?"

August turned to look back out the window.

Canaris kept his gaze on August, his eyes now filled with the same grief. How well he understood August's pain. He knew what it was to want to do something and have to hold back, to be helpless in the role you were required to play. Canaris put his hand on August's shoulder again.

"Make yourself inconspicuous for a while. We don't want you to be identified."

August nodded, keeping his eyes on the passing landscape.

Part 4

I only did my duty to my country when I tried to oppose the criminal folly of Hitler.

~ Admiral Wilhelm Canaris

Chapter Sixty-One

AUGUST SLIPPED INTO THE THEATER AND GLANCED around in the dark. Images flashed on the screen and lively music played from the speakers. For a moment he felt a crazy impulse to snap his fingers and move to the beat. He was in a good mood. After months of feeling the weight of the mask he was forced to wear working for Heydrich, the lightened mood was a panacea. He reveled in it.

He spotted Dohnanyi, made his way to the aisle, and slid into the seat next to him. Dohnanyi leaned over to whisper.

"Any word on Heydrich's replacement?"

"Not yet."

Dohnanyi handed him a packet. "Some Jews need immediate transport to Switzerland. These are the forged papers and money."

"I'll take care of it." August was glad to have a project.

"We need to get them past the guards. Canaris wants you to help them pass for Abwehr agents."

The theatre erupted in laughter. It punctuated Canaris' demands perfectly. They both glanced at the screen. The comedian on screen did a jig. August smiled into the darkness, feeling precisely the same way.

Dohnanyi reached into his coat pocket for another paper and handed it to August. "We intercepted this from one of Himmler's men."

It was a memo detailing the White Rose activities at the University of Munich, along with a list of names of people they were investigating as dissidents. August was dismayed to see a few names he recognized: Hans Scholl, Sophie Scholl, Christoph Probst. And further down the list: Karin Werner. He thought about Heydrich's party, when an aide had called Brigitte by that name. He folded the note and slipped it into his coat. He had to go to Munich to find out if she was safe.

~ ~ ~

August stood before the seven—five men, two women—in a face-off, with them studying him as intently as he was studying them. He knew from their dossiers that they were former neighbors of Canaris. They knew nothing about him except that Canaris had sent him to help them escape.

August could see the trust in their eyes. They eyed him eagerly, hanging on every word and gesture. He was their lifeline. They reminded him of the men and women in the basement of the café in Paris. He saw the same trust in their eyes. Regret washed over him, and he vowed to atone for those actions. His earlier mistakes had been made through ignorance, but he would make sure these seven people got to safety.

"A quick lesson in how to be Abwehr agents." He walked over to one of them and ripped the yellow star from his sleeve. "You won't need these anymore."

A moment of shock, then it gave way to smiles and

snickers and giggles and a round of belly-laughs. A simple act of ripping a patch was hardly a comedy, but the reaction was infectious. August joined in the boisterous activities and before long the merriment caused his sides to ache and tears to run down his face.

Eventually the glee ran its course and their laughter slowed to heavy breaths behind wide grins. The moment of silliness had broken his shackles. For the first time in years he felt carefree.

Chapter Sixty-Two

IN THE PRIVATE OFFICE OF THE CHIEF SURGEON AT THE hospital in Prague, the atmosphere was anything but joyful.

They were gathered in a tight circle: the doctor, two nurses and the guards who had been on duty the day Heydrich died. All of them wore frantic looks. One of the nurses chewed at her fingernails.

"We have to be together in this," the doctor said and eyed each of them. "If Himmler even suspected that—"

He didn't have to finish. The guards nodded in unison. The nurses nodded. The nail-biter stopped chewing long enough to pose a question.

"What do we say happened?"

The doctor thought for a moment. "Infection. From his injuries."

They all considered, looked around at each other, and nodded.

There was no question of anyone leaking the news. They all knew what Himmler was capable of.

Chapter Sixty-Three

AUGUST STRODE ACROSS THE COURTYARD TOWARD the main building of the University. Here were the same buildings, the same walkways, the same statues. He took a deep breath, savoring the surroundings. He was home.

The campus hadn't changed much in the six years since he taught there. It was mid-February, and a layer of snow covered the grounds while the sun beat down on his face with a hint of the coming spring. He felt the urge to stand immobile, close his eyes, and let the warm memories resurface.

And then he remembered the memo in his pocket, and his tenure as Professor of Linguistics, Faculty of Languages and Literatures, seemed like just another role he'd played.

As he hurried toward the main building, he saw that the courtyard was littered with papers. He picked one up and recognized it as one of the White Rose pamphlets.

He heard a commotion in the colonnade. The janitor was trying to wrench away a briefcase from a woman. In the struggle, the briefcase popped open, and more pamphlets spilled out onto the ground.

With a jolt, August recognized the woman's face. *Brigitte*. He headed toward them.

Just as he reached the colonnade, he heard a squeal of tires, car doors, boots. He hid behind a column and peered around at the car. Gestapo insignia.

His heart raced, spurring him into action. He dashed over, grabbed Brigitte's arm, and gave the janitor a brief glance.

"This is the woman I'm looking for," he said.

"She's one of them," the janitor said. "I saw her. She was—"

"Yes, and she's in my custody now," August said. He gave Brigitte a significant look. "Come along, miss."

He led her into a back corridor that circumvented the campus.

"I have to find Sophie," she said.

"No. We have to go," he said.

She pulled back. "The Gestapo is here. I have to—"

"—Yes, they're here to arrest all of you. I have to get you away from here."

"But Sophie and Hans are in there. And Christoph. We can't just leave—"

"—Listen to me, Brigitte!" He turned her to face him. "They are going to be arrested. We can't prevent it. We can't help them now. If you go back in there, you'll be arrested too. And then you won't be able to do anything for them." He let the words sink in before he continued. "Let's get back to Berlin. I'll do what I can to get them released."

Her shoulders relaxed. She nodded and followed him to the car.

~ ~ ~

It was a long ride back to Berlin, and Brigitte slept most of the way. They passed through three checkpoints, but each time August accounted for his passenger by saying his girlfriend had had too much to drink. The guards, regarding his uniform, laughed it off and let him through.

Back in his apartment, August was exhausted, but Brigitte was wide awake and keyed up. He opened a few beers and drew her into the living room.

The conversation was tentative at first. "How well do you know the admiral?"

"Who?"

"Canaris."

"Oh." She thought for a moment. "I met him years ago at a Resistance gathering. When I started working with the SOE, I met him several times. Delivered documents to him. Most of what I do is transport documents."

He nodded and took a drink of beer.

She looked at him. "Why do you ask?"

"Oh, nothing. It's just that you seemed to know each other well that night. Remember? After the party? When you followed me to his house?"

"I didn't follow you," she laughed. "I was delivering intel."

"You mean you weren't pursuing me? Now I have to give up that daydream."

"You can pretend I was," she said.

"That's what we do. Pretend."

She sighed. "Yes it is."

"What was in the note you gave him? Or can you tell me?"

"It was intel. Can we leave it at that? I'd rather talk about something more interesting tonight."

They sat in silence for a few minutes. He took another drink. "You heard that Heydrich's dead?" he asked.

"Yes. I'm glad."

"I did it."

She turned to him, eyes wide. "What do you mean? He died of infection."

"No, I went to the hospital and finished him," he said.

"How?"

"I dressed up as a doctor—"

"—White coat and stethoscope, right?"

"Of course."

"I bet you looked very medicinal."

He laughed. Then he took another drink. "I got into his room. And then I injected him with your needle."

She took a long look at him, then touched her beer bottle to his. "Well done."

He grinned. "Couldn't have done it without you."

She laughed and took a drink.

He opened more beer, and they spent the rest of the evening swapping stories of their missions. They started out laughing and grew more serious. She told him about the horrors of the hospital. He told her about the burning of the synagogue in Poland.

For a while they were silent, holding hands. After a while exhaustion took hold and they ended up reclining on either end of the sofa.

When August awoke the next morning, she was gone. He found a note on the kitchen table.

I have to check on my friends.

He crumpled the paper and headed to the Abwehr building. His first order of business was to try to get the Scholls released.

Chapter Sixty-Four

THE GESTAPO TOOK SOPHIE, HANS, AND CHRISTOPH into custody and charged them with treason. By the time Brigitte returned to Munich, the trial had begun.

The presiding judge was Roland Freisler, chief justice of the People's Court of the Greater German Reich. He had been hand-selected and sent from Berlin.

Robert and Magdalene Scholl tried to get into the courtroom to see their children, but they were forbidden.

"But I'm the mother of two of the accused," Magdalene begged the guard.

The guard sneered at her. "I wouldn't brag about that. You should have brought them up better."

Robert forced his way into the courtroom, yelling that he was there to defend his children. The guards seized him and dragged him toward the door.

"One day there will be another kind of justice," he cried out as he was pulled from the room. "One day they will go down in history!"

The guards allowed Brigitte into the courtroom. At first she offered to stay with Robert and Magdalene, but they told her to go in.

"You can be our witness," Robert said.

The trial lasted only a few hours. The Gestapo had found additional boxes of the pamphlets in their rooms, and none of the accused denied the charges.

However, there was no mercy from the judge. Freisler was the grand inquisitor, and he alternated between questioning their motives and mocking them for their actions.

At one point, he yelled out, "I call down eternal damnation on the heads of the three irredeemable heretics standing before me." Brigitte looked around the courtroom. No one seemed as appalled witnessing the spectacle as she was.

When it was Sophie's turn to give testimony, she gave a quiet, simple statement. "Somebody had to start. What we wrote and said is also believed by many others. They just don't dare to express themselves as we did."

Freisler's face went red. "You impudent little girl! You're just—"

"—You know the war is lost. Why don't you have the courage to face it?"

Brigitte was proud of her friend for being so bold, but she was also terrified of what she imagined would be the consequences for such boldness.

She didn't have long to muse over outcomes. The repercussions were immediate. Sophie's words were the last straw for Freisler. He pronounced judgment: guilty of treason.

Their sentence was execution, to be carried out immediately.

~ ~ ~

The three were escorted to Stadelheim Prison. Hans and Sophie were given one last visit with their parents.

Afterward, through a flood of tears, Magdalene told Brigitte about the visit. Brigitte gripped the woman's hand, trying to give her strength.

"I won't see her again," she cried. "She'll never come through the door again."

Magdalene was grieved about Christoph as well. "No one visited him. His wife is still in the hospital. She just had their third baby. How awful that no one came to see him. I tried to see him, but they wouldn't let me."

She told Brigitte about the execution, details she had learned from a guard.

"They sent them to the guillotine one by one," she said. "Sophie was first. The guard said she faced death without flinching."

Brigitte held on to her, and the two of them cried.

Magdalene pulled back and took a deep breath. "The guard had to whisper to me what Hans said just before he died." Fresh tears ran down her face.

"What did he say?" Brigitte asked.

"Long live freedom," Magdalene said. And a shadow of a proud smile lit up her face.

~ ~ ~

Brigitte reeled hard from the deaths of her friends. Distraught and directionless, she sequestered herself in the safe house in Munich and refused to see anyone for days, not even Bogart or Otto.

She deliberated on the events again and again, retracing the details, trying to find answers, but she kept coming to the same end: Her friends were dead for no reason except that they had voiced objections to the government.

At one point, she wondered whether August had attempted to help, but she realized he wouldn't have been able to do anything. No one expected the trial to be so fast and the execution to follow immediately.

When a week had gone by without any contact from her, Bogart came to her room, sat on the edge of the bed, and studied her.

"This is a great tragedy," he said. "But you must go on."

She shrugged.

"You cannot bring them back," he said. "You will grieve—you must grieve—but you have work to do."

She took a deep breath. "I was part of their activities," she said, "but now they're gone but I'm still here. Why? How was I spared?"

He brushed her hair back. "Perhaps you have a mission to complete."

"So did they." She turned and faced the wall. "Please leave."

Bogart kissed her head and went into the kitchen to wait.

The next morning, she found him in the library. Her face was a mask of grim, hard resolve. "I know what my mission is. I won't rest until that judge pays for what he's done."

Bogart was glad to see some fire in her again. He nodded. "Let's get to work."

Chapter Sixty-Five

THERE WERE DELAYS ON THE ROAD, AND AUGUST was worried they'd miss the train, between the detours around bombed out passageways and the Gestapo making random checks of the vehicles. But they arrived with time to spare – enough time to make sure his seven students were settled in for their journey.

He followed them onto the train and got them seated. He barely knew them. They were an assignment to him. And yet he found himself hoping desperately that they would escape.

The two women took turns hugging him. They relinquished him, and the men took over: each kissing him on the left cheek, then the right. He bore it all with a grin and motioned for them to sit.

"Remember, you're Abwehr agents," he said. "They aren't that friendly."

They laughed merrily. One of the men took his hand. *"Sheh-Elohim yiyah otcha,"* he said.

The others murmured the same phrase. He gazed at each of them. His Hebrew was rusty, but he understood the sentiment. They were giving him a blessing, not a small thing for these people who had been condemned and persecuted by members of their own country. August smiled and squeezed the man's hand in thanks. He looked at the group once more and exited the train. As he walked down the platform, a smile spread across his face. Suddenly light of heart, he let it form. His step quickened. He was a moment away from whistling a happy tune when he saw the car pull up, swastika flags on the fenders.

Two soldiers erupted from the vehicle and stomped up to the platform. August eyed their insignia. *Gestapo*. His smile faded. He shot a quick glance at the train.

The agents dashed to the conductor, who backed up a few steps, wide-eyed.

The first agent pressed toward the conductor. "The passenger list."

August dawdled. Looking back at the train, he leaned in to overhear the conversation. The conductor handed over the list.

"Anyone in particular?" The conductor's hands moved nervously.

"We're with Monetary and Exchange," the second agent said, quiet but firm. "We're matching bank transfers with travel to certain countries."

Monetary and Exchange Division. They weren't looking for seven Jews. August sighed in relief and strolled away.

Chapter Sixty-Six

AUGUST PULLED UP TO THE CURB AT THE AIRPORT. Canaris and Oster slid in the back seat. As August drove away, he updated the admiral on the people he had left on the train. Canaris smiled. "They were neighbors of mine for years. I felt a duty to protect them," he said.

August nodded. One thing the admiral never needed to explain to him was his loyalty.

They rode in silence for a few minutes. Then August took a deep breath. "Himmler found a replacement for Heydrich. Ernst Kaltenbrunner."

"Not as bad as Heydrich," Canaris nodded. "But still a braying ass."

"I've been reassigned to him," August said, his tone regretful.

"Keep a poker face," Canaris said. "He'll have his own men scrutinizing everyone."

August nodded. "How was Smolensk?" he asked.

Canaris sighed. "We failed. Three plans worked out, none of them succeeded. Dohnanyi is still there cleaning up."

"*Three* plans?" asked August.

"Backups to backups," Canaris said. "One of them was sure to work. We had von Schlabrendorff with us, and he's one of the best."

August was familiar with von Schlabrendorff and knew how fiercely dedicated he was to the Resistance, meticulous with every detail. With both him and Dohnanyi heading the plan, it was assured success.

August studied the admiral's wearied face in the mirror. "What happened?"

"Something went wrong in each case," Canaris said. "The bomb on the plane didn't go off. Two different occasions to shoot him in a crowd went awry."

"That's depressing news," August said. "Almost as bad as what happened with the White Rose group."

"I know," said Canaris.

"There's more news," said Oster.

August looked at him in the mirror. "What now?"

"Gehre was arrested," Oster said. "But he managed to get away. He's on the run now."

"What are his chances?" August asked.

Canaris shook his head. "They'll find him."

Chapter Sixty-Seven

SEVERAL MEN STOOD BEFORE HIMMLER, WHO WAS seated at his desk, fidgeting with pencils and papers on the desk.

He picked up several documents, took his time to review each carefully, then laid them to one side, aligning them with the edges of the desk.

He looked up.

"Heydrich has met a martyr's death at the hands of two Czechs," he said in a calm, deadly voice. "So we will teach all Czechs a lesson."

He looked down at the papers for a moment, then looked up, his face clear and impassive.

"Destroy the town of Lidice. Kill everyone. Level it." The men scurried out to carry out his orders.

~ ~ ~

Inside Abwehr headquarters, Canaris, Bonhoeffer, Dohnanyi, Oster, and August were gathered in Canaris' office. August leaned against the window, teary-eyed.

"About three hundred in all. Ninety of them children," he said, his voice hoarse. "They dynamited the town. Kaltenbrunner laughed at that."

His voice cracked and he stopped. He cleared his throat. "Lidice is gone. To avenge Heydrich."

"Dear God in Heaven," Bonhoeffer whispered.

"They sent a special transport to Auschwitz," August said. "Three thousand. Himmler called it a retaliation measure. Five hundred killed on arrival."

"Transported from where?" Dohnanyi asked.

"Theresienstadt."

"Was your sister among them?" Bonhoeffer asked, his face drawn in pain.

At first August said nothing. Then the rage let loose. "I don't know! I don't know!!" He tore his coat off and ripped the SS insignia on the sleeves and the collar. "I hate this! I hate it!"

Dohnanyi moved toward him. "August! Calm down!"

August ignored him. "My actions caused this! If I'd left Heydrich alive, if I'd left Himmler some hope that he'd recover, this wouldn't have happened."

"Let's try to find your sister and nephew," Dohnanyi said. "They might still be there. The Red Cross just visited—"

"Do you really think the Red Cross visits made a difference?" The look August gave Dohnanyi was wild-eyed and dangerous. "You think they'd find anything if the Nazis want it hidden?"

"Let's just find your sister and nephew," Bonhoeffer said. "Then we can decide what action to take."

August whirled around and lunged toward Bonhoeffer. "Yes! Let's take action against the madmen! Let's wrestle the wheels from them! Do you know how many madmen there are? We're outnumbered!"

"That doesn't mean we do nothing—"

"Don't you get it?? The evil goes so far and wide

we'd have to plan an assassination every day."

He turned to face Canaris. "It's a hydra. A multi-headed beast. We need to stop hacking away at all the heads and aim for the heart." He leaned in, inches away from Canaris. "We need to kill Hitler! It's the only way to kill the beast!" He bolted out the door.

Bonhoeffer picked up his coat and insignia. "I'll go after him."

"Make sure he gets it repaired," Canaris said in a low voice. "I don't want him arrested for being out of uniform."

Chapter Sixty-Eight

BRIGITTE DISCOVERED THAT SHE COULD BE ALMOST anyone. Under Bogart's meticulous direction, she learned how to adopt various mannerisms, specific ways of walking and talking, to stand out or blend into a crowd.

Along with her personas of Traute the nurse and Karin the socialite and Petra the school teacher, she learned to be Margrit and Elke and Heidi and Ursela, and each woman had a distinct personality. Depending on Bogart's need, she became a maid, a florist, a waitress, the wife of an important official who was at the front, and a host of other guises.

She became adept at applying makeup and wigs, and she learned to layer clothes to both disguise her identity and conceal anything she carried.

She refused to settle in any one place but preferred to stay at safe houses in different cities, moving whenever she was called on to treat the ill or injured. She kept a supply of clothes and disguises at each house to avoid having to carry suitcases. She was willing to take on any assignment, no matter the risk, but she was reluctant to kill. All the same, she carried filled needles with her just in case.

The only thing she refused to do was go back to the hospital, and Bogart promised she would never have to go there again. Instead, she was placed in positions to gain information or deliver documents.

After the Scholls were executed, she was often assigned with Otto. He would trail behind her or be just out of sight, but she knew he was there. At first, she resented having him along on her missions, assuming Bogart thought she was weak or didn't trust her to work alone.

That was all dispelled one day when she was almost caught in a search at a train depot.

She was tasked with retrieving some documents from behind the mirror in the women's lavatory. She went to the station, aware that Otto was following her. She tried a few times to lose him, but he ended up getting to the station ahead of her. She ignored him, went into the women's lavatory, found the papers, and tucked them into her girdle. Unfortunately the stack of papers was thick and made her clothes bulky. Her reflection showed an obvious package beneath her garments, even though she had worn loose clothing, and she had to keep her hand pressed against her stomach to hide the bulk. It couldn't be helped. She had to get the papers out of there.

She cracked the door and peered out. Two Gestapo agents stood near the front door. She closed the door.

She stared at her reflection. She couldn't leave the papers. She couldn't stow them in her bag. All she could do was hold her stomach and camouflage the bulk with her bag in front. It looked awkward, but she hoped she could rush out of there without being noticed.

She left the lavatory and strolled to the door, trying to time it to walk out with a group. But there weren't enough people to get lost in the crowd, and it was too late to go in a different direction.

She knew she looked conspicuous. She felt the agents' eyes on her, but she fixed her face into a cool and disinterested expression. They moved toward her with purpose, and her mind raced to come up with a plausible reason for having the documents in her underwear.

Just then a hand clapped her on the shoulder.

"There you are, *Liebchen*!"

She turned. It was Otto in SS uniform. She almost called out his name with relief.

He smiled and took her arm. "You look unwell. Let's get you home so you can lie down."

The Gestapo agents watched them walk down the street, then turned their attention back to others in the station.

He led her several streets over to a waiting car and helped her in. He took off, speeding through the streets, keeping an eye on the rearview mirror.

"Go ahead and take the papers out." He looked out the side window to give her some privacy.

She retrieved the documents from her girdle and replaced her skirt. He was still looking out the window. She cleared her throat.

"Thank you for helping me back there with—"

"I'm there for a reason," he said.

"Because Bogart thinks I need a bodyguard?"

"Because you're one of his most valuable assets." His voice was gruff and perturbed.

"I don't believe that. He's working with several—"

"—hundreds—"

"—okay, hundreds. And you're trying to tell me—"

"—here's what I'm trying to tell you." He pulled over to the curb and twisted his body around to face her. His beady eyes bore into hers. He wasn't angry or threatening. He was simply laying out the facts.

"You have medical skills we need. And you speak several languages. And you're smart. And he doesn't want your safety compromised."

"And I know how to wear wigs and put on makeup," she laughed. He was so earnest and direct that she had to lighten the mood.

It worked. He gave her a weak smile. "Yes, you do."

She nodded. "Okay."

"Don't try to outrun me again."

"I won't. I promise."

He pointed to the house where they were parked.

"Here's where you deliver the documents. Knock twice, count to five, then knock three times. Tell the person who answers the door that Albert sent you. If they say Albert moved last month, give them the documents. If they say okay and ask you to come in, run."

She started to get out of the car, then turned back. "Will you come with me?"

He grinned and followed her to the door.

~ ~ ~

After that she and Otto went on most missions together. She knew almost nothing about his background—they held fast to Bogart's rules about keeping their true identities secret (he still called her Traute; she was certain his true name was not Otto) but as they traveled around, she came to know a lot about his character and ethics.

Before long they were almost inseparable. She knew he was willing to die to free Germany from tyranny and that he would kill anyone who threatened her or Bogart.

He ensured her safety and in turn she nurtured his soul: drawing him into conversations, making him laugh, pointing out what beauty remained in the world.

Because Otto was skilled in a variety of killing methods, Bogart often sent him on assignments to assassinate Nazi officials. Otto called them dispatches. She knew what they were—unmitigated killings—but after working in the euthanasia unit at the hospital, she could appreciate his using a euphemism.

On one occasion she was sent to deliver codes to a Resistance group holed up in the back room of a café in Paris. As usual, Otto went with her. On their return to Munich, he said they must stop in Strasbourg for a dispatch. Brigitte learned it was for a member of a special action team.

They followed the target to a bar. Once inside, they ordered drinks and cased the place. Otto glided around the room discovering the back rooms and exits while Brigitte scrutinized the other patrons. Otto came back to the table and gave her a slight nod.

They watched the target at the bar. He was immersed in the general gaiety of the evening, drinking and telling jokes and having fun with his friends. Otto grew more tense as the evening wore on. Brigitte knew his plan was to catch the target alone—in the lavatory or just outside. But the plan wasn't working. Whenever it seemed the moment was right, someone would approach and mar the scheme. She could tell Otto was becoming more frustrated, and she worried that he would miss the opportunity—or worse, rush into action in a way that would prove dangerous.

He made another recon, searching for an alternate strategy, a diversion that would get the target alone. She had an idea.

While he was gone, Brigitte eased up to the bar. The target had his back to her. She signaled the bartender for a drink, then scanned the circle around her. All clear. She felt inside her pocket and took hold of the needle, slipping the top off with one hand. She glanced around again. No one was paying attention to her. In one swift movement, she pulled out the needle, hid it with the back of her hand, and pressed the plunger, dropping the contents into the mark's drink.

Otto returned and headed toward her. She grabbed his arm and led him out the door.

"It's done," she said.

"What do you mean?"

"I did it. I put serum in his drink."

"What serum?"

"From the needle. T-4. He'll fall asleep and not wake up."

He stopped and turned to her, his face deep red. "You jeopardized the dispatch."

"No, I hurried it along," she reasoned. "It was getting risky to stay in there."

"You were the one taking the risk," he said, agitated. "You could have been caught. You haven't been trained to do this kind of work."

She gave a short bitter laugh. "Really? I have experience with T-4. Believe me. I've given it to innocents. Why are you questioning my training for this kind of work?"

They walked the rest of the way in silence. The car was a few blocks away, but they strolled along to avoid unnecessary attention. By the time they got to the car, Brigitte's anger had dissipated. She fumbled with the door, dropped into the seat, and started shaking.

Otto looked at her with concern. "What's wrong?"

"Oh my God," she whispered. "I just killed someone. On purpose."

Otto nodded. "Yes you did."

"You're right," she said. "I'm not trained for this kind of work. I put poison in his drink. How could I have done that? To just take a life like that."

She was still shaking. Otto took both of her hands into his. "No, no, don't think of it that way," he said. "You saved lives today."

"No, I—"

"—Do you know why Bogart sent me to dispatch that man?" Otto leaned toward her, his voice low. "He's been going throughout the French countryside slaying the women and children. Village to village. Cutting them down. A systematic slaughterhouse."

Brigitte's breath caught in her throat. "Oh no."

"And that's not the worst of it," Otto said. "He actually enjoys it.

Brigitte's eyes filled with tears. Otto lifted her hands and kissed them.

"He was not worthy of life," he said. "You did a great deed."

She exhaled. "Thank you."

He released her hands and started the car. "But let me have the honors from now on. Agreed?"

She nodded.

~ ~ ~

The closest she came to grasping Otto's true character occurred a few weeks later when Bogart sent her to deliver some papers to a home in a Berlin suburb.

"It should be fine, but take Otto," Bogart said. "The house may be watched."

When they arrived, Otto surprised her by bounding ahead and ringing the doorbell. He usually waited in the background. She gave him a curious look.

The door opened to a spate of joyful greetings from an elderly lady.

"Walther! How good to see you! Come in, come in, both of you."

Brigitte looked on in wonder. *Otto's real name is Walther?*

She didn't have time to question him before they were ushered into the library, where two men were waiting. One was Dietrich Bonhoeffer. Otto waved at them both.

Brigitte's lips parted in surprise.

"Pastor Bonhoeffer!" she said. "We haven't formally met, but I did hear you speak at many of Dr. Gerhard's gatherings."

He shook her hand. "I'm delighted to meet you." He turned to the other man. "My brother, Klaus."

Klaus gave her a half-bow, then went into another room with Otto. Bonhoeffer smiled as they left. "They've been close friends since school days."

Brigitte smiled, musing on these revelations of Otto's background.

She handed Bonhoeffer the documents. He glanced through them, nodded, then locked them inside a desk drawer.

The top of the desk was strewn with papers, most with editing marks or handwritten corrections and notations. Curious, she leaned forward to read the notes. She noticed Bonhoeffer watching her.

"Oh!" she said, turning away from the desk. "Forgive me! I saw the editing marks and ... was curious ... I'm so sorry..." She trailed off, flustered and embarrassed.

"It's quite all right," he motioned her back toward the desk. "These pages are destined to be read. Eventually. There is work yet to do on them."

Now with permission, she looked back at the pages. On the far left she saw the title page.

"'Ethics'?" He nodded.

She gave a short laugh. "Apropos the times."

He smiled. "You mentioned the editing marks. Are you an editor?" He waved a hand toward the locked drawer that held the document she had brought, a silent acknowledgment of her work with the Resistance. "In other areas of your life, I mean."

"No, I'm a ..." One of the papers on the desk caught her eye. The heading at the top read: "What Is Meant By 'Telling the Truth'?"

"I was a nurse," she said, looking down at her hands. Hands that put poison into a man's drink. Hands that helped release twenty-seven people before she could escape the evil that was housed on the sixth floor of the hospital. She clasped her hands together. "I used to be a nurse."

"Ah! A healer. What a wonderful gift from God."

She scoffed. "I imagine God regrets giving it to me."

He looked her in the eye, a gaze of knowing and compassion. "The gifts and calling of God are irrevocable."

She looked up at him, a tiny ray of hope on her face. "What?"

"God does not call us one day and dismiss us another day based on our performance," he said. "He calls us. And he gifts us. He does not revoke on a whim or when we are less than perfect. We may fall short at times. In fact, I would say as humans, we *will* fall short. But the gifts and calling are forever. This I know."

A warmth came over her. She had no idea what it meant. But on some level, she felt like she might be whole again one day.

Chapter Sixty-Nine

AT ABWEHR HEADQUARTERS, DOHNANYI PORED OVER a stack of files. Canaris and Oster dropped by his office.

"I'm due for a meeting with General Sack," Canaris said. He glanced around at the files. "Let's get these moved. Himmler's suspicious already."

"Very well." Dohnanyi busied himself with the task. The door opened and Gestapo agents swarmed in.

"We're here for Hans von Dohnanyi and Dietrich Bonhoeffer!" one of them bellowed.

"They're in my division," Canaris said. "What do you want?"

"They're under arrest. Breach of monetary exchange laws."

"Breach of ... what?" Oster asked.

"Giving money to transport Jews to Switzerland."

The agent took two hours to search Dohnanyi's office. Canaris and Oster stayed during the search. At one point, Dohnanyi made eye contact with Oster, motioning toward his key in the safe. Oster gave a slight nod.

The agent pawed over the files and ignored the key, which was attached to a stack of routine files.

When the agent finished the search, he grabbed Dohnanyi's arm. "You can answer at headquarters."

After they left, Oster opened the safe, grabbed the key, and held it up to Canaris. "The Zossen documents."

The key opened the safe in the Zossen Military Headquarters a few miles away. The contents held the entire case they had been building against Hitler—highly incriminating for almost everyone connected to the Resistance.

"Thank God they overlooked that," Canaris said.

~ ~ ~

A few miles away, in his home, Bonhoeffer was engaged in a lively discussion with August about the young lady who had visited him. His heart was warmed as he listened to August talk about her.

When the clock chimed, he looked up in surprise. "Noon already. Hans should have been here by now."

He excused himself and went to the phone to call his sister.

The phone rang again and again at the Dohnanyi home. Bonhoeffer frowned. He knew his sister was home. Why was there no answer? It rang ten, twelve, fifteen times. Just as he was about to hang up, the phone clicked as someone picked up.

"Who is calling?"

It was a strange voice. Bonhoeffer hung up.

He turned to August. "It's over. They'll come for me now. You must go."

"I'll stay with you," August said.

"No. I don't want you to be part of this," Bonhoeffer pleaded. "You still have much to do, so please go now."

He saw August to the door. "God be with you, my friend."

Chapter Seventy

CANARIS BRUSHED PAST THE SECRETARY AND BURST into Himmler's office. Himmler barely looked up.

"Don't bother," he said with a tone of boredom. "They're in custody."

"They're my agents!"

"They broke the law."

"I have plenty of files on people who have broken the law." Himmler's face went red, then he eased back into his chair.

"One day I will find the files you keep on me. Don't forget — we have files too. And your agents will remain in custody."

Canaris turned on his heel and left. Himmler sat back, a satisfied grin on his face.

~ ~ ~

At home that evening, Canaris slumped in a chair and stared at nothing, deep in thought, worry etched on his face. His wife watched, silent.

He got up, weary and broken, and lumbered his way into his study. He eased the door shut and pulled files from his briefcase.

He carried them to a section of his bookshelf and removed several books to reveal a safe. He opened the safe, stashed the files, and replaced the books.

He gave a sharp whistle. The dogs came running. "Come on, time for a walk."

Chapter Seventy-One

THE ABSENCE OF BONHOEFFER AND DOHNANYI WAS A blow to Abwehr headquarters. Even those who didn't know them well were affected, glancing furtively at their office doors in trepidation, wondering if they might be next.

The months between their arrests in April and the end of the year were not kind to the Resistance. Infighting between the Abwehr and the Gestapo grew more treacherous for the Resistance—in direct proportion to the growing paranoia in the Gestapo—with Himmler blocking Canaris at every turn. The result was a near paralysis in the Resistance that grew as the weather turned bitter cold by year's end.

The only compensation was that the months were no kinder to the German Wehrmacht war machine. In May, the Allies sunk forty-one German U-boats over a three-week period.

By July, Italy was in disarray when the Allies invaded Sicily and Mussolini was arrested. Italy surrendered by September. Germany was forced to move men and materiel in place to defend its ally.

The Fall saw the surrender of Smolensk and Kiev to the Russians. The only thing that kept the German high command from total despair was Rommel taking command of the Atlantic wall in the French coast.

~ ~ ~

The holiday decorations were a feeble attempt at gaiety that no one felt: a Christmas tree remained in the corner, and the greenery wound up the stairs and around the doors. A banner on the wall read: "Happy New Year!"

A few people had gathered, bringing as much cheer as they could to dispel the gloom that permeated the house. Having several family members still incarcerated would hardly inspire a verse of "auld lang syne."

August and Karl Bonhoeffer stood apart from the others, drinks in hand. August looked across the room and spotted Paula Bonhoeffer and Brigitte, their hands clasped together, heads bent in close discussion. Brigitte glanced his way and gave him a brief smile. The eyes of both women were shiny and wet. With two sons and a son-in-law still in prison, August could guess the reason for the tears. He was grateful Brigitte had agreed to come.

Karl followed August's gaze. "Your friend has a great deal of compassion."

"A healer at heart," August said, remembering what Bonhoeffer had said. For a moment he was lost in the memory, tracing Bonhoeffer's assertions in his mind. He came back to the present. "How is your wife managing?"

"She knits things for them. Socks, blankets. It keeps her occupied. Action can keep despair at bay."

Brigitte led Paula out of the room and returned several minutes later. She picked up a glass and made her way over to them.

"I talked her into resting for a bit," she said.

Karl grasped her hand in thanks, then turned back to August. "How is Canaris managing?"

August shrugged. "He's distressed, naturally. He spends his days filing complaints."

"Taking action will numb his grief."

"Trust me, not being able to act is more numbing," August said, draining his drink.

Karl studied August's face. "You have to don a mask every day. It is a wearying existence."

August pondered that thought and took a long drink. "It is."

"Did you know," Karl said, leaning forward, "the Greek word for actor is the same root word for hypocrite."

August laughed. "I've been called many things—"

"Do not misunderstand," Karl said, "I happen to think you are quite honorable. I merely observe a psychological truth."

"Which is...?"

"That when a person plays a role for a long time, he either wearies of it or he is consumed by it."

Brigitte smiled and raised her glass. "Here's hoping you choose the lesser of two evils."

August touched his glass to hers.

"Your dilemma is not action versus inaction," Karl said. "It's the lack of honor in what you have to pretend to do."

"And you're robbed of being proud to work for Canaris," said Brigitte.

Karl beamed at her. "Precisely."

August said nothing, but his sagging shoulders acknowledged the truth of her words. Karl refilled their glasses.

August mustered enough energy to make a toast. "To nineteen-forty-four. May it be better than this year was."

They all clinked glasses. Brigitte took a sip and gave August a brief nod. She figured he and Dr. Bonhoeffer had much more to discuss. She moved around the room admiring the decorations.

Christine von Dohnanyi approached and gave Brigitte a warm smile. "I'm glad to meet you, Brigitte. August tells me you're a nurse."

"I...uh, yes, I trained to be nurse," she fumbled. She wasn't sure how much August had told them about her.

"If you will pardon my boldness, I have a favor to ask of you," Christine said, steering her into the parlor. "May we speak in private?"

~ ~ ~

August and Brigitte rode in silence, lost in their own thoughts. August cleared his throat. "Are you staying at a safe house?"

Brigitte looked at him in surprise. "Why do you ask?"

"When I called to ask you to this party, you had me pick you up on a street corner," he said. "I'd like to see you home safely."

She looked out the window. *See me home safely. To the safe house. Is anything in Berlin safe anymore?*

"And by the way, I'm running out of phone booths," he said.

She turned away from the window and faced him. "What?"

"You asked me not to call from the same number twice," he said. "Remember?"

"Yes. It's to—"

"—avoid being traced. I know."

She frowned. "So?"

"So I had to walk five blocks to get to a phone I hadn't used yet to call you."

"So who asked you to call so much?" She turned back to the window and closed her eyes. She hadn't meant to insult him. She was tired.

A curtain of silence descended again.

When August spoke, his voice was light and breezy. "Where shall I—"

"I have to go back to the hospital."

"Tonight?"

"Soon," she said. "I have to get something."

She was rigid, her arms tight against her body. She was struggling for control, he could tell. And he knew what she was afraid of.

"Can they send someone else?"

"They don't know about this."

He pulled over to the curb and turned the car off. He reached for her hand.

"Talk to me," he said gently.

"I can't—"

"I don't care about protocol. I don't care about who we're working for or the rules they enforce so we can remain safe. I just want you to trust me."

She started to shake, and he put his arm around her. She leaned against him.

"Christine asked me to get a diphtheria culture for her."

August's mind raced to fit the puzzle together. *Was Christine planning something? A prison break? Poison the guards and get Dohnanyi out?* "What does she plan to do with it?"

"She's going to use it on her husband."

"Christine would never do that."

"She said her husband asked her to do it," she said through tears. "To make sure he doesn't talk."

August went still. It made sense. Christine might not do it, but he knew Dohnanyi would. Dohnanyi was afraid he would break under torture and reveal more than he should. He squeezed his eyes shut. *Dear God, will this nightmare ever end? Will we ever get the upper hand?*

August took a breath and steeled himself. "What can I do to help you?"

At first she didn't answer. After a while she whispered, "Take me to your place."

He started the car and drove on, still holding her close to him.

Chapter Seventy-Two

AUGUST STROLLED INTO CANARIS' OFFICE. IN THE brief moment before Canaris looked up, he saw the reality of the man's torture—the rounded shoulders, furrowed brow, dark circles under his eyes.

August recalled his conversation with Brigitte and Karl Bonhoeffer.

Your dilemma is not action versus inaction. It's the lack of honor in what you have to pretend to do. ... And you are robbed of being proud to work for Canaris.

The truth of those words pierced his heart. He ached for any kind of action that would bring some hope to Canaris. In fact, that was what had propelled him into the room. August eased himself into a chair.

Canaris looked up, raised his eyebrows. August hesitated. He wanted to ease Canaris' agony without risking embarrassing him.

"I don't think anything will happened to Dietrich and Hans," he said.

Canaris nodded, more of an acknowledgment of August's effort to reassure him—which he was fully aware of—than in agreement. He doubted that they would be safe, but he kept that to himself.

"They're keeping Niemoller alive," August rushed

on with his reasoning. "I think they'll do the same with them. There's a value in keeping them alive. It wouldn't serve any good purpose to harm them."

Affection for August washed over Canaris, and he hid a smile. He knew August was working hard to keep him from despair. He couldn't bear to let him know that it was no use, that he knew exactly what would happen to them. For the moment he pretended for August's sake.

"Maybe you're right."

August smiled and relaxed.

"I need you to make a trip to Spain," Canaris said. "You'll meet with MI-6 and OSS. No papers. Verbal only."

"I understand. What's the message?"

"We have intel on plans for an Allied invasion. We're going to alter the details before we send it to the General Staff."

"And they need to know we did it."

"Yes. To prove we're on the same side. We've got to do something to shorten this miserable war."

Chapter Seventy-Three

TROOP CARRIER SHIPS AND AMPHIBIOUS SHIPS arrived and dumped their cargo of fighters onto the shores of Italy. Flags flapped in the wind, the stars-and-stripes on some, the union jack on others.

Troops swarmed up the countryside on foot, in trucks, any way they could. Tanks blasted away at anything in front of them.

The next day the newspaper headlines told the story of the beginning of Germany's defeat in three words:

Allies Invade Anzio

The Nazis had missed the signs of the impending invasion.

They were meant to. Canaris had seen to that.

Chapter Seventy-Four

STEWART MENZIES HELD HIS EAR TO THE PHONE while an MI agent watched from a chair across from his desk.

"Yes, sir, but all signs show that Canaris deceived the general staff. Absolutely no opposition at Anzio," Menzies said.

The agent whispered across the desk. "Not buying it, is he?"

Menzies shook his head and turned his attention to the phone.

"But Canaris kept his word. And we've achieved quite a bit these past few months due to him." He stopped, listened, took a deep breath. "Very well, Prime Minister."

He hung up and threw the agent a baleful glance.

"He refuses to believe Canaris handed it to us, doesn't he?" the agent asked.

"Exactly."

The agent shrugged. "Pity."

Chapter Seventy-Five

THE CAR SCREECHED TO A HALT OUTSIDE BERGHOF, Hitler's mountain residence in the Bavarian Alps region of Berchtesgaden. August jumped out and strode to the door of the secret compound. He handed over his pistol to the attendant and made his way down the long hallway. At the conference room door he handed the guard a package.

"Intelligence reports."

The guard took it without a word and went inside.

August turned and headed back down the hallway. After a moment the guard came out and yelled to him.

"Wait! The Fuhrer wants to see you."

August made his way down the hallway with some trepidation. The guard opened the door and ushered him inside. August glanced around and saw an array of maps on the wall and in the center, a large oblong table, with all seats filled. August saw a splash of ribbons, medals, and insignia. Upper echelon. He stood erect.

Hitler slapped his hands on the table. "Ah! Wichmann! At last, someone I can trust. You can settle this. Be the tiebreaker in our disagreement."

"With all due respect," the general said, "this is a General Staff meeting and—"

Hitler glared back at him. "Wichmann here has a good logical understanding of strategy. And I say his judgment is as good as yours!"

The general clamped his mouth shut. All eyes turned to August.

"You see, these idiots on my general staff believe the Allied invasion of France will come at Calais," Hitler said. "I believe it will be Normandy. I am not convinced of their argument. What do you say, Wichmann?"

August looked around the room, stalling. "I'm not privy to all the intel." Which was a lie, but one he could make with no effort.

"There is heavy Allied bombardment near Calais," Hitler explained. "I say they want to deceive us into thinking the landing will be there. Eisenhower's sleight-of-hand. But I have them figured out!"

August stole another glance at the generals. He saw their exasperation and impatience. He had bits of information about the Allies' plans for invasion—and even knew that it was code-named Operation Fortitude—but these details had yet to reach this room. His mind raced to find a response that would keep Hitler and the generals guessing wildly off-target.

"It's likely that the Allies have less understanding of strategy than you do," he said. "Calais may be the inferior choice, but if they were not inferior, would they be our enemies?" Then he added in a low voice: "Mein Fuhrer."

The generals relaxed. Some dipped their heads and grinned.

Hitler stared at him. August waited, tense.

"Quite logical. Well said," he said, then turned his attention to the generals. "We will keep the panzer divisions where they are."

Hitler stood and headed to the exit. On the way, he

slapped August on the back. "My astrologer said there would be a late miracle. It was all predicted in the stars." He nodded wildly, giggled, and walked away.

August watched him walk out, stunned. One of the generals leaned in to August.

"Careful," the general said, "or next week you'll end up as field marshal. He loves to promote people who affirm his predictions."

Chapter Seventy-Six

WEEKS OF UNCERTAINTY AND TENSION WERE NOW weighing on Canaris. He leaned forward onto his desk and rubbed his eyes.

A meeting the previous week with Hitler had not gone well. Canaris had been summoned to Berchtesgaden and accused of allowing the Abwehr to "fall to bits," as Hitler put it. Canaris endured an hour of screaming, raging tirades.

When Hitler demanded that he give an account, Canaris made a simple statement: "It's not surprising. We're losing the war."

Hitler threw him out.

Canaris went back to Abwehr headquarters and sat waiting to hear from Sack on whether the other conspirators would be available to meet that evening. There was nothing for him to do but wait. No plans to make, no actions to take.

Thoughts flitted through his head, desperate thoughts, outlandish ideas, bizarre notions—any kind of action to pull him out of the depression that washed over him, the result of months of accomplishing nothing. He would stage a rescue for Dohnanyi and Bonhoeffer. He would fly to England like crazy Rudolph Hess did a few years ago. He would storm communications headquarters, get on the radio and tell everything he knew, giving away as much information as he could before they burst in and shot him.

How well he understood August's desire to take action. But where he was cautious and careful—borne out of years of training, August was young enough to dare all, to jump into the fray and not care about the outcome or his personal safety.

Canaris cared very much about the outcome and August's personal safety. And that was what drove him to counter August's attempts to rush in and do something, anything. It was too high a cost.

He sighed and leaned back in his chair. Then he looked up. Keitel was standing before him.

"I'm here to inform you that the Fuhrer has just signed a decree abolishing the Abwehr," Keitel said. "Your office has been absorbed into the Reich Main Security Office."

"I see."

Keitel grinned, savoring the moment. "Your staff will be managed by Walter Schellenberg."

"What is my position?" Canaris asked the question, dreading the answer.

"You've been reassigned to the Department of Commerce until further notice."

Keitel threw one last smirk and left.

Canaris stared out the window, weary and lost.

Chapter Seventy-Seven

CHURCHILL EASED UP FROM HIS SEAT, PACED FOR A moment, then lifted his head. It was June 6, 1944, and he was about to give the most important speech he would ever give to the House of Commons.

He took a deep breath and began. "The original landing, made on January twenty-second at Anzio, has, in the end, borne good fruit."

Earlier that morning, on the coast of Normandy, the huge twelve-inch guns on the battleships had fired round after round, pounding rock and brick into submission.

"Hitler was induced to send to the south of Rome eight or nine divisions which he may well have need of elsewhere," Churchill said.

At 0630 hours on Utah Beach, troops of the United States VII Corps had clambered down the sides of ships into amphibious boats. Hundreds of them stormed the beach.

"These divisions were repulsed," Churchill continued, "and their teeth broken, by the successful resistance of the Anzio bridgehead forces."

On Sword Beach at 0725 hours, amphibious ships had dumped men, machines, and materiel from the

British 3rd Infantry, 27th Armored Brigade on-shore. The men ran, dodging bullets and shells.

"In the early hours of this morning," Churchill said, "the liberating assault fell upon the coast of France."

At 0745 hours on Juno Beach, men from the 3rd Canadian Infantry, 2nd Armored Brigade had navigated rocks and sand and waded chest-deep, holding rifles and bazookas high overhead.

"An immense armada of upwards of 4,000 ships, together with several thousand smaller craft, crossed the Channel," Churchill said.

The British 50th Infantry, 8th Armored Brigade had traversed mines and barbed wire at Gold Beach at 0753 hours, secured by dive bombers buzzing over their heads.

"Landings on the beaches are proceeding at various points," he said.

On Omaha Beach at 0758 hours, men from the United States 5th Corps had raced across the beach and dropped flat against the sand, some for cover, others in death.

Chapter Seventy-Eight

THE DOGS RAN BACK AND FORTH ACROSS THE PARK, barking happily.

August and Canaris watched from a bench. They were silent for a long time. August heaved a deep sigh and looked at Canaris.

"Kaltenbrunner is sending me to pick up Allied war plans from an agent," he said.

"It won't matter," Canaris said. "The Allies have a toehold in Europe now."

August nodded. He had seen the intelligence reports.

"Bring the plans here when you get back," Canaris said. "We'll alter them before you hand them over."

August said nothing at first, then he sighed again. "I hate this game."

It was Canaris' turn to sigh. He hated that August was forced into playing it.

"I know," he said. "But we need to stay a step ahead of them."

Chapter Seventy-Nine

THERE WAS NO MOON OUT, AND IT WASN'T UNTIL A family of deer walked within a few feet that August realized how dark the night was. The road was deserted, but he waited under the trees anyway. Too much was at stake to throw caution to the wind now.

A car pulled up and the driver got out. It was Barth. August moved into the headlight.

"August! It's good to see you," Barth said. He shook August's hand. "Thanks for taking this to Berlin. I have to get back to Paris." He handed over a packet. "It's from our contact in Lisbon."

August eyed the packet. "Anything interesting?"

Barth held up another packet. "Not as interesting as this one. It's going to reel in a big fish. Former head of the Abwehr."

"Admiral Canaris?"

Barth bobbed his head and grinned. "He's been feeding information to the Allies for years. Did you know that?"

August shook his head. "Have you told anyone else?"

"Not yet. Himmler will be glad to have it. He hates Canaris."

"I'll take it to him." August held out his hand.

"No. I want to be there when Himmler gets the news."

August could feel his stomach knot up. He couldn't let Barth deliver the packet. It would be the end of the admiral. He could feel beads of sweat on his forehead. He tugged at his collar.

He ran through scenarios in his mind. In desperation, he hit on an idea.

"Say, could you give me a ride to my car? It's at the warehouse."

"Sure."

They got in the car. August glanced over and noticed Barth's weapon at his side.

"Is that an Astra 300?"

Barth pulled it out and held it up, showing it off. "Yeah. Got it off the widow of a Luftwaffe ace."

They arrived at the warehouse. Barth pulled to a stop and lay the weapon on the seat. "Where's your car?"

"I always liked you, Barth," August said quietly, looking straight ahead.

Barth looked at him and chuckled. "What?"

August swiveled in the seat and looked Barth in the eye. "But the admiral was right. Trust costs more."

In one swift movement, August grabbed the weapon, brought it to Barth's head, and pulled the trigger, shattering Barth's skull and the driver window at the same time.

August retrieved the packet that held Canaris' information, put the weapon into Barth's hand, and got out. He ran away from the car, stumbled a few feet, then tumbled onto the ground, sobbing uncontrollably.

He breathed in and out a few moments, then pulled himself together. He opened the packet, read the documents, pulled out his lighter, and burned them.

He stood and waited until the flames died down, then tramped down the road.

~ ~ ~

The next morning, August stood at attention before Kaltenbrunner's desk.

"The contact never showed up," he said.

Kaltenbrunner barely glanced up. "Yes, they found him at an old warehouse. Dead. Self-inflicted, apparently."

August stared straight ahead, keeping his face impassive. He wanted nothing more than to get out of there. "Do you need me for anything else?"

"Too bad you weren't here earlier," Kaltenbrunner said. "You just missed a special action."

Chapter Eighty

AUGUST STEPPED INTO THE PHONE BOOTH AND dialed, a mixture of desperate prayer and careful plots running through his head as it rang.

Riiing.

Please let her be there.

Riiing.

What name do I ask for? She told me when it's urgent to ask for Petra.

Riiing.

We can meet at a church. That will be safe enough.

Riii— "Yes?"

He didn't recognize the voice. "Petra, please."

A long pause. "I will get her. Who is calling?"

It was a safe house. They would never say that.

He slammed the phone down and headed back to his office. A chill ran down his back. The safe house was compromised. *Where was Brigitte?*

He caught his reflection in the door glass and sneered at the uniform. He ran inside the building to plan his next move.

Chapter Eighty-One

EXCEPT FOR THE SWASTIKA FLAGS ON BUILDINGS around the city, Paris hadn't changed much since the invasion. German jackboots echoed on the streets and alleyways, but there were still places of stubborn refusal to acquiesce to Nazi rule.

The Passion of our Blessed Lord convent on the *Rue de la Sante* was one such place. It offered shelter to the weary, compassion to the wounded, hope to the lost.

The Mother Superior heard a knock and looked at the clock. Right on schedule. She went to the door and opened. Admiral Canaris stood on the step.

"Your convent is a haven," he said in a low voice. "I have come to pray."

It was the right thing to say.

"*Bonjour, monsieur.* Come in." She led him to a back room where an MI-6 agent was waiting.

Canaris nodded a greeting. "You have an answer?"

"Yes," the agent said. "From Churchill and Roosevelt." He looked away in embarrassment. "They say 'Unconditional surrender.'"

Canaris looked at him for a moment without expression. "Is that all?"

"I'm afraid so."

Canaris' shoulders sagged, and he looked down. He shook his head, then looked up at the agent.

"Thank you." Canaris turned and headed to the door.

The agent called out to him. "Sir?"

Canaris turned back and saw the man's outstretched hand.

"It's been an honor," the agent said. And there were tears in his eyes.

Chapter Eighty-Two

A GUARD PUSHED BONHOEFFER DOWN THE CORRIDOR to the interrogation room. His hands and feet were shackled so the going was slow, but they eventually made it into a room that held only a table and two chairs.

"Another interrogation?" Bonhoeffer asked.

The guard ignored him, walked out, and locked the door. Bonhoeffer moved slowly, the chains dragging on the floor behind him. After a few moments, he heard a click and the door opened to an SS officer. With a start, he saw it was August.

Neither said a word while the guard went out and locked the door.

August held up a finger, telling him to wait. He scanned the room, feeling under the table and the chairs. He nodded to Bonhoeffer.

"Not many places to hide a wire."

"I'm glad to see you, August."

August paced the length of the room—a few steps in either direction. Bonhoeffer peered at him and saw the dark circles under August's eyes, the haunted look.

"What is it? What's happened?" August stopped.

"There was another Special Action. Like Lidice."

"No!"

August resumed pacing. "In Oradour-sur-Glane. Six hundred forty-two people rounded up by the SS. A third of them were children."

Bonhoeffer dropped to the floor, his chains clanking. "How did you find out?"

"Kaltenbrunner. Bragging about how efficient the operation went." He stopped again and looked at Bonhoeffer. "My sister used to live there. I saw the house. What was left of it." He took a deep breath. "I saw the church where my nephew was baptized. It was a pile of rubble. The bishop from Limoges stopped by to see if he could help."

He paced again, faster this time, running from the story.

"And?" Bonhoeffer urged him on.

"He found ..." August stopped, choked on the words, then cleared his throat. "He found ... behind the altar ... fifteen children. All clustered together. Their bodies were charred."

Bonhoeffer's gasp sucked air into his lungs, but he couldn't exhale. He lowered his head, his body shook. He breathed again, clasped his hands together, and bowed his head. "Dear Heavenly Father, receive them into—"

But he couldn't finish the prayer. He buried his head into his hands and sobbed. August eased himself onto the floor beside him, tears running down his face. After a moment he too gave way to the anguish, his shoulders heaving.

A noise in the corridor outside—a reminder that danger was still near—stopped the sounds of their pain, but not their tears. A torrent of grief flooded their faces.

After a while the tears stopped. They sat in silence, spent.

"I didn't go to his baptism," August whispered. "She

begged me to come. But she asked me not to wear my uniform. I told her that dishonored me. I stayed away."

He looked away, fresh tears in his eyes, unable to meet Bonhoeffer's gaze. Bonhoeffer took his hand and gripped it tight.

"That uniform no longer fits you," Bonhoeffer said. "You've become the man your sister knew you were."

August couldn't speak. But he gripped Bonhoeffer's hand in answer.

After a while, he stood. Bonhoeffer stood beside him.

"The next plan ... I don't know if it's worth it," August said.

"What do you mean?"

"If it succeeds, we'll see backlash from those who don't see the evil. If it fails, we're all doomed."

Bonhoeffer smiled at him. "How can success make us arrogant or failure lead us astray when we share the sufferings of God?"

A slow smile crept across August's face. "Always the theologian."

"No. A mere disciple."

August gave Bonhoeffer a serious look. "The odds are against us, you know."

"But hope evens the odds. Those who hope have far more in their favor than those who don't."

August embraced Bonhoeffer. "I hope you're right."

He knocked on the door. Bonhoeffer reached into his shirt and pulled out several papers. "Some things I wrote."

August tucked them into his coat. "Take care."

"God be with you, my friend."

The guard opened the door, and August slipped out.

Chapter Eighty-Three

THE MEETING WAS HELD AT GENERAL BECK'S HOUSE.
Since his resignation from the Army, his Resistance activities had increased tenfold, and he had succeeded in
persuading many notable members of the military to
join.

His influence rippled far and wide among those who
were dissatisfied with the current state of affairs. One
such example was when Field Marshal Erwin Rommel—
the brilliant Wehrmacht leader known as the Desert
Fox—sent a secret memo to several colleagues stating
that he would be part of the Resistance only if it were
guaranteed that Beck would be head of state in the new
government.

People trickled in to the meeting one or two at a
time over the course of a few hours, some going through
a narrow alley to get to the back door. An influx of guests
all at once would have drawn attention, and that was the
last thing the conspirators wanted.

Canaris and August were there, along with several
Resistance members, including Claus von Stauffenberg,
the war hero who had been wounded in Africa. He sported an eye patch, and he was missing one hand and several fingers on the other hand.

The meeting was brief. There was no need for debate or discussion. They were of one mind about what to do. They were there merely to hear the specifics of a plan to kill Hitler.

Stauffenberg showed them a briefcase with a bomb and timer. "How does it work?" August asked.

Stauffenberg held up a pair of pliers and pointed to the bomb. "I'll break this stem and it will set off the timer. I'll place the bomb in the briefcase, and then I'll put the briefcase beside him."

"What are the contingencies?" Canaris asked.

"None. The bunker is concrete," Stauffenberg said. "It will amplify the blast. In all probability everyone in there will die."

"Including you?" August asked.

"My aide will call me out. As soon as we're back here, we'll announce the coup d'etat. It's foolproof."

"Except for the part where you stay and make sure the bomb goes off."

Stauffenberg gave a half smile. "It's not a suicide mission."

"It's not total commitment either."

"We have a commitment to life."

Images flashed through August's mind: Bonhoeffer in chains at Tegel Prison. What was it he had said? ... *we share the sufferings of God.* He knew what it was to be committed. And Brigitte, when he saw her at Heydrich's party. She had dressed the part, complete with a needle to use if she had to. She didn't care if she was caught and killed. *If I had to use it, I would have rid the world of a great evil. Sometimes it takes a great risk to accomplish a greater good.*

They both had a commitment to life, and their commitments went beyond saving their own skin.

He slammed his fist on the table. "What are we *talking* about? If the bomb doesn't go off, you pull out a gun and you *finish* him!"

"We aren't going to—"

August drained his glass and slammed it down with a clunk. "Fine. I'll stay behind. I'll make sure the bomb goes off."

"No!" Canaris yelled.

Everyone turned to him in surprise.

"No??" August stared Canaris down, then looked around at the others. "You know what the problem is here? There's no follow-through. No one is committed enough! Well, I am!"

"Your presence will be questioned. It's too risky." Canaris was quiet and calm, but he gave August a hard look.

August knew that look. It meant Canaris' word was final. August turned on his heel, walked to the door, and slammed it behind him.

Chapter Eighty-Four

ENGLAND'S SECRET INTELLIGENCE SERVICE HAD never been busier. With the Allied invasion in full swing, the halls of the SIS Building on St. James Street were crowded, agents dashing to and fro with orders, interceptions, requests, and tidbits of anything and everything having to do with the war.

And so it happened that they were among the first to get the news about the assassination attempt and the deadly outcome for the conspirators.

An agent saw Menzies down the hall and rushed to greet him. "You get the scuttlebutt? They tried to do in Hitler. Bomb in a bunker."

"Who?"

"Some of their upper-crust guys. We got word he was dead, but then there he is on the wireless raving like the daft bugger he is."

"I wonder if Canaris is compromised."

"Whether he is or not, bloody shame they didn't finish the job, what?"

Chapter Eighty-Five

CANARIS WAS IN THE BACKYARD WALKING ACROSS THE grounds with his dogs when August arrived. Canaris eased onto a bench.

"What went wrong?" he asked.

August sat next to him and took a deep breath. "You want the full list? It wasn't in a concrete bunker, so it didn't amplify. The blast wasn't large enough to kill everyone."

Canaris leaned forward and shook his head. "How can mere mortals be so damned difficult to get rid of?"

"They didn't wait for confirmation," August said. "They should've confirmed the kill."

"I know."

"Stauffenberg and his aide have already been executed. So much for a commitment to life." He recounted all the news he'd been able to cobble together, along with the names of those who'd already been executed or forced to commit suicide. "Beck's dead too."

Canaris closed his eyes.

"They'll come for us," August said. "Won't they?"

Canaris opened his eyes and focused on the dogs running across the yard. "Almost certainly for me. Probably not for you. They still think you're SS to the core."

"What will you do?"

"Update my will. And wait for the last card to be played."

"What do you want me to do?"

"Stay alive."

August gazed into the distance, thinking hard. "I'm going to kill Hitler. I have access to him now and then. If I hide my weapon at the checkpoint, all it would take would be—"

"No. You'd be killed. And it's not an even trade, your life for his."

"I'm not afraid to die." He was quiet and matter-of-fact. "It would be a meaningful death."

Canaris stood, his usual melancholy suddenly replaced with a surge of passionate anger. "Commitment to life is not a weakness, August! Anyone can die. Plenty of fools do it every day. It takes more courage to live. And for those who continue to live when all around them grows dark, it's more than courage. It's victory!"

August grinned at him. "You sound like Dietrich."

Canaris' eyes unexpectedly filled with tears, and August regretted mentioning their friend. Canaris looked away. He whistled for his dogs.

"No," he said, his voice thick with emotion. "Dietrich would search until he found out where God is in all this."

Chapter Eighty-Six

CANARIS' WORDS WERE STILL ECHOING IN AUGUST'S ears weeks later. *Dietrich would search until he found out where God is in all this.*

"I have no doubt he'll find the answer eventually," Karl Bonhoeffer said.

August looked at him in surprise, then realized he had spoken the words out loud.

They were in the Bonhoeffer living room, drinks in hand. August had dropped by to give him some letters from Bonhoeffer. He had gotten them from a guard at the concentration camp, a man who had come to admire and respect Bonhoeffer a great deal.

It was no surprise that Bonhoeffer was able to influence the people around him, even in such dire circumstances. Nevertheless, August grinned at the thought of what Bonhoeffer was probably telling them.

"Any news about Dohnanyi?" August asked.

"He's still in Sachsenhausen," Karl said. "They told us he had contracted diphtheria. He's partially paralyzed. He might never walk again."

August looked down. It wasn't news to him. He had driven Brigitte to the hospital to get the cultures, then had delivered it to Christine. "I hate to hear that."

They both looked off into the distance, a silent tribute to the man whose intellect had held the Resistance together for so many years.

Karl poured another drink. "I appreciate your bringing Dietrich's letters to us. He seems hopeful."

"He told me those who hope have an advantage over those who don't."

"Yes. A solid concept. Both theologically and psychologically."

"Do you have hope that we'll win?"

The drink in Karl's hand stopped midway to his lips. He lowered the glass and thought for a moment. "I'm not as spiritual-minded as my son. I've always put my faith in science and reason. But I see so little reason now." He looked at August with a faint smile. "I don't know if we'll win. But I trust in Dietrich's hope that we will."

"So do I," August said, and he returned the faint smile. "And I'm not spiritual-minded either."

"Where do you place your trust?"

It was August's turn to ponder. "I suppose in my ability to take action."

"That takes commitment of purpose."

"Unlike the failed attempt." They had already discussed the July 20 attempt, and August had released all his frustration at the situation. "If they'd been more committed, more willing to die—"

"Perhaps they had too much to live for," Karl shrugged, "things they find valuable in this life."

"I offered to be the sacrifice. Canaris denied me the task."

"Ah. You discovered what he values." And he raised his glass to August.

Chapter Eighty-Seven

BOGART HAD A HECTIC WEEK MANAGING RESCUES and hideouts for the conspirators and their families, but he still took time to track down Brigitte.

He found her at the safe house in Berlin. She had already heard the news—that is, Goebbels' propaganda —about the failed assassination attempt, but he was able to give her the inside details.

She listened to his summary without saying a word. The only sound she made was a quiet sniffling as tears rolled down her cheeks.

Bogart wound down his recitation. "And I heard that they will hold trials, but we know what those will be like."

She stared into space, taking in all the information. Then she focused on Bogart.

"Who is the judge?"

Because he knew how she would react, he hesitated to say the name. He would have withheld it forever to spare the grief he knew was coming, but he also knew she would find out soon enough. It might as well be from him.

"Freisler."

But she didn't get angry or cry or yell, as he expected. She merely wiped her eyes and stood up. Without a word she leaned over the table, kissed his cheek, and walked out the door.

Chapter Eighty-Eight

CANARIS WAS IN HIS STUDY WHEN THE KNOCK CAME. Ordinarily the dogs barked at the sound of a knock, but in this case, one of them lowered her ears and the other let out a low growl.

And that was how he knew, before he even went to the door, that all was lost.

Canaris opened the door to find Walter Schellenberg, who had taken over several divisions of the Reich Main Security Office, on his doorstep, flanked by armed guards.

"Somehow I felt it would be you," Canaris said.

Schellenberg had not been part of the Resistance, but there was a mutual respect between the two men. At the very least, he knew Schellenberg wasn't among those braying for his blood.

Before the formalities, Canaris had one question. "Have they found anything in writing?"

With a quick glance, Schellenberg dismissed the guards so he could talk freely.

"Hanson's notebook," he said. Colonel Georg Hanson had taken over most of Canaris' duties. He was not active in the Resistance, but he did know of its existence. "Among other things, it had a list of those who were to be killed. But nothing about you."

Canaris shook his head. "The general staff and their scribblings. It'll be the undoing of us."

Schellenberg told him how sorry he was that he'd been given the assignment to arrest him.

Canaris accepted the apology. "I hate that this is how we have to say goodbye," he said, then mustered a dose of optimism. "But all will be well in the end."

He had only one request: that Schellenberg promise to get him an audience with Himmler soon. "I must talk to him directly. Kaltenbrunner and all of those in Gestapo – they're nothing but filthy butchers."

Schellenberg agreed. He looked around, stalling. "If you need some time to be with your family..."

"Thank you." Canaris turned to his wife, who was standing nearby, her face white and strained.

"Willi?" she said, her voice high and terror-stricken.

He shook his head, went to her, and embraced her. He slipped a folded paper into her hands, making sure no one saw, then kissed her gently.

He walked out the door, his face impassive and calm, and joined Schellenberg in the car.

His dogs chased the car down the road after him, howling and barking.

Part 5

Christians stand by God in His hour of grieving.

~ Dietrich Bonhoeffer

Chapter Eighty-Nine

AUGUST AMBLED AROUND IN THE BUTCHER SHOP waiting for it to be empty. As the last customer left, he made his way to the counter.

The butcher reached under the counter and brought up a British newspaper.

The dateline was August 25, 1944. A photo of the Eiffel Tower took up almost the entire page. The headline was in large bold type:

"PARIS IS LIBERATED!"

"I thought you might want to see the true story," the butcher said. "German propaganda will never let the people know about this."

"So Paris is free again." He took the paper and gazed at the Eiffel Tower. "I wish I'd been there."

He folded the paper and handed it back to him.

"Have you seen Canaris yet?" the butcher asked.

"No. It would arouse suspicion. But I told Himmler I'd help interrogate."

The butcher smiled. "Good. When you see him, tell him my shop is still open."

August nodded and turned to leave.

"Wait, I have another message for you." The butcher held out a note. August opened it.

Volkspark Friedrichshain. Noon. BB

BB. Brigitte Bauer. August heart leapt. The park was a short walk from his apartment. He wanted to ask the butcher how he knew her or how she knew that he knew the butcher, but what did it matter? He had connected with her.

"She said she'd go there at that time on Mondays and Fridays," the butcher said.

August held up the note and nodded his thanks.

"Oh, one more thing," the butcher called out before he opened the door. "She said you'd find her as Elke."

Chapter Ninety

CANARIS WAS SEATED, WITH SHACKLES ON HIS HANDS and feet, while Himmler stood above him gloating.

For August it was the most disgraceful moment of his life. He started to shake. *Play the part, play the part.* He gradually assumed a stone-faced stance.

"Tell me where the documents are," Himmler said. "I can make things easier for you."

Canaris gave no answer.

Himmler turned to August. "Did you get any information from the others?"

August had been allowed to "interrogate" Oster and Sack. In reality he had spent the time transferring information back and forth. He was waiting for the right moment to give the admiral word of their situation.

"They don't know anything," August said, deadpanned. "From what they said, he didn't trust anyone besides his dogs."

Canaris managed a weak smile, then went straight-faced. Himmler twisted his face into a smirk. He leaned down into Canaris' face. "I know you too well to buy your innocent act."

Canaris spoke for the first time since they'd entered the room. "If you did know me, you'd know I'm too wise to try to sell it to you."

August wanted to laugh. Canaris was a master at interrogations. There was no way Himmler was going to break him.

Himmler's eyes bore into Canaris. "The documents."

Canaris gave him an innocent look. "What documents?"

Himmler's face was open rage. He went to the door and knocked.

August took the moment to lean toward Canaris and whisper. "Oster and Sack send regards. Tight ship." This was the code Oster said to give to Canaris, letting him know they had not revealed any secrets.

Canaris nodded.

A guard opened the door. Himmler looked back at Canaris, his face taut with malice and rage. "I will find them. And you will hang."

Chapter Ninety-One

AUGUST AND BRIGITTE, BOTH CLOAKED IN A DRAB AND nondescript persona, strolled around the park far from earshot of others. They both glanced around constantly as they talked.

"Do you think Himmler is serious about hanging him?" she asked.

"It won't get that far. There's not enough evidence."

"As if that would stop them. Look what happened to my friends. And countless others the judge killed."

"More summary executions?"

She grimaced. "Every week. The latest was Otto's best friend. And he's gutted over it."

"Will this nightmare never end?"

They walked for a while in silence.

Brigitte leaned toward him. "It must have been difficult to pretend to interview Canaris." Her voice was almost a whisper.

"Worse than pretending to be Heydrich's rising star."

"What are you going to do now?"

"Kill Hitler," he said. "There's no one to tell me 'no' anymore. What about you?"

"I'm going to kill the judge," she said. "There's no

one to tell me 'no' either. Not even you. So don't say anything."

He stopped and turned her toward him. "Everything I want to say is what Canaris told me: That you need to stay alive, that it's not an even trade, your life for his. But I'm a hypocrite if I do."

She took his hand. "Then let's just wish each other luck."

They strolled on, hand in hand.

Chapter Ninety-Two

AUGUST ACCOMPANIED KALTENBRUNNER TO Berghof, Hitler's home in the Bavarian Alps, and found the compound even more secretive than ever. They handed over their pistols to the attendant and were frisked before they could tread the long hallway to the conference room.

August had no idea why he was there, except to be an errand boy. The upper echelon tried to outdo each other in number of personal assistants. Ordinarily August would have openly scorned such practice and found a way to be absent so he wouldn't have to participate, but he was looking for opportunities to gather information on Hitler's whereabouts. Other attempts had failed, but he still hoped to one day deliver the coup de grâce for his country.

Several officers were already milling around before the meeting started. August paced around the room and listened in on conversations.

"—since Operation Wacht em Rhein in December. Four months of his crazy—"

"Did you hear what they're calling it in America? 'Battle of the Bulge.' Isn't that just—"

"Our supplies are almost depleted."

"Ha! As depleted as our leadership these days, thanks to the scaffold—"

"You think that's funny? How would—"

Hitler entered, and all heads turned, all conversation stopped. He greeted them with a slight wave and headed to his seat. He spied August and made a detour to him.

"Ah, Wichmann. About the admiral." He looked August up and down. "Do we show mercy? Or make an example?"

All eyes turned to August. August looked around at the room—*remember, you're a loyal German, a faithful member of the Nazi party*—then he locked eyes with Hitler. He swallowed hard before answering.

"Admiral Canaris possesses a great deal of knowledge," he said simply and logically. "We wouldn't want to lose that."

Hitler nodded briefly and went to his seat. August took a seat against the wall.

From across the table, Himmler glared at him.

August turned away. If he was able to influence Hitler to release Canaris, Himmler's opinion of him wouldn't matter.

He allowed a glimmer of hope to grow.

Chapter Ninety-Three

GESTAPO AGENTS STOOD OUTSIDE CANARIS' STUDY.
The room was in disarray, books knocked off shelves,
end tables turned over.

Documents were laid out on the table, among them
diaries and files on Himmler, Goering, Goebbels, and
several others.

Himmler walked in, picked them up, and breathed
a sigh of relief.

~ ~ ~

Himmler strutted into Hitler's office in triumph and
spread the documents out on the table. "I told you he
could not be trusted."

Hitler looked at the documents wild-eyed. "Then
you told me too late!" he screamed. "That traitorous rat!
They're all rats!"

He swept his hand across the desk, casting the documents across the room, away from his sight.

"What shall we do with them?" Himmler asked.

"The death sentence," Hitler yelled. "For all of them!
Do you hear me? I want them dead! I want them strung
up with piano wires!"

Himmler endured the frenzy of Hitler's rage with a secret smile on his face. It was checkmate. He couldn't wait to deliver the orders.

Chapter Ninety-Four

BRIGETTE NEEDED TO BE NEAR THE FRONT OF THE courtroom, close enough to rush to the judge and jam a needle into his neck. She mentally flipped through her personas to come up with one that could get through the security guards and gain a front-row seat.

Petra was her stern schoolteacher, but she would also serve as a stenographer. She dressed the part with a smart tailored suit, glasses, hair pulled back into a bun, holding a notepad and pen. She was afraid she might be verging on caricature, but there was no time for layering subtleties or battling stereotypes. She had to get in. She was on a mission.

She hadn't planned to attend until Otto stopped by the night before to tell her about the day's proceedings at the People's Court. He had been attending all of the trials of the July 20 conspirators in something akin to a fevered obsession.

Brigitte had gone with him to the Great Hall once last summer and had seen what a farce the trials were. The accused were brought out in ragged, ill-fitting clothes, some without belts or shoes, and Roland Freisler had humiliated them before the entire court. It was a mockery of the judicial system. Watching them, she was reminded of Sophie and Hans, and she fled the room, bursting through the doors and sobbing on the sidewalk.

She hadn't seen Otto in several months, and she was shocked at how thin and brittle he had become. Sitting stiff and upright on the sofa, he recounted the day's activities in a subdued voice, almost monotone, staring straight ahead.

He showed emotion only once, when he told her that Klaus Bonhoeffer, Dietrich's brother, had been sentenced to death. Tears rolled down his cheeks, and he turned away. She went to him and hugged him, but he was so spent, he couldn't return the gesture, and his arms lay limp at his sides.

She spent a restless night and awoke with one thought: Freisler had to die. She was done with waiting for him to taste the same justice he dished out to innocent people. She would have to take matters into her own hands.

Dressing for the part was easy. She made sure to coordinate her outfit with the coat that had secret pockets in the lining for the needles.

Not so easy was figuring out what to tell the guards about who had sent her. Not long ago she could have said the Abwehr had asked her to take notes, and no one would have questioned it. But now, primarily because of the July 20 plot—the very reason for the court session today, in fact—the Abwehr was disbanded, and many of the longtime agents were under arrest, or at least under scrutiny. She mentally sifted some possibilities. The latest assassination attempt had decimated her list of military connections high enough to quell suspicion.

She grabbed her satchel bag and tossed the notepad and pen into it, then studied her reflection in the mirror, appraising her look. Stern. Serious. Efficient.

"I am stenographer," she said to the mirror. *Believable enough.* "I am here to take notes of the court proceedings on behalf of—" She stopped, searching for a name. Who would request notes before the court released its judgments? Someone important enough that she wouldn't be stopped. Someone who would want the information early.

The clock chimed. Time to go. She'd have to solve the dilemma on the way.

~ ~ ~

The People's Court was holding a special session on a Saturday, but it still brought out a crowd. The line stretched down the hall, and the guards were searching everyone. When it was her turn, Brigitte was glad she remembered to grab the satchel. She hoped it would divert attention from the hidden needle. She held out the satchel.

"I am a stenographer," she said, her voice clear and bold.

"The stenographer has already arrived," the guard said, harsh eyes probing her.

"I'm not appointed by the court," she said, holding her head high. "I'm here to take notes and deliver them personally—" she steadied herself and pressed on "—to the Fuhrer."

She held her breath. *I can't believe I just said that.* But it was too late to back down.

The guard looked her up and down, then studied her face. She did the same, matching his gaze. At last he handed the satchel back to her and saluted.

"Heil Hitler!"

She tossed him a cool glance and nodded. She started into the courtroom, but he took her arm and led her inside.

Her heart started to race. *Oh no, please, no scene. Please don't make an announcement. I can't have any attention on me. Please.* But the guard merely escorted her to the stenographer's table, gave a curt bow, and left. Brigitte exhaled, clenching her hands together to stop them from shaking. She pulled the pad and pen from the satchel.

The stenographer sat rigid, hands poised over the steno machine. She grinned at Brigitte's pad and pen. "I hope you can keep up. He's fast talker."

Brigitte flashed a brief smile and ignored her.

Several prisoners were brought in, disheveled and dirty—like those she saw in the summer. It made her hate Freisler all the more.

He entered the room to fanfare. It took all of Brigitte's energy to not sneer at him. She wanted to rush at him with the needle, stab him in the arm, and pump his veins full of the poisons that had killed her patients at the hospital. The urge was so strong she had to steel herself and take deep breaths to calm down.

It was a vulgar display, abuse of power at its finest. She waited through two hearings, trying not to listen to Freisler's pompous tirades at the men he was judging, but having to pay attention just enough to pretend to take notes.

She held back her tears and could feel a headache coming on. She wanted to scream out at him, to humiliate him, but she knew that if she did, she would lose the opportunity to destroy him. And it would probably be the last chance she ever had.

He finished up a case and held out his hand for the next. Her headache grew worse. She had hoped for a recess so she could take a break from the endless stream of abuses. Would this tyrant ever shut up? She stole a glance at her watch. A few minutes after 11:00. She had to get out of there. She shoved the notepad and pen in her satchel.

"Fabian von Schlabrendorff!" the court clerk called out.

And right at that moment, the shriek of the air raid siren tore through the room.

Freisler jumped to his feet. "Adjourn! Adjourn! Take the prisoners to the shelter!"

The guards grabbed the prisoners and swept them away. In a mad rush of scraping chairs, shuffling feet, and babbling voices, everyone headed for the exit.

Except Brigitte. She headed for Freisler.

She saw him grab a stack of folders. She glanced around and saw that they were alone. In one swift movement, she ripped the lining of her coat and pulled out the needle. Freisler's back was still to her as she made her way to him, close enough to see the name on the top folder: Schlabrendorff.

Freisler whirled around and almost bumped into Brigitte. His surprise gave way to irritation.

"What are you doing in here? There's an air raid. Get to the shelter."

She said nothing.

He flicked his hand, dismissing her. "Did you hear me? Get out of here!" He bared his teeth and yelled. "Get out! Get out of my way! Do you know who I am? You're obstructing justice! I'll have you arrested!" He was using his courtroom voice, the one that belittled and humiliated those on trial.

But now she caught an undertone of fear. The sounds from outside were growing louder—planes overhead with occasional explosions, each one closer than the last.

She held up the needle so he could see it. "Time for you to leave," she whispered.

"Wh—what is that?" And now his voice was transformed to a quiver.

She pulled the cover off the needle and moved toward him. Just then a deafening blow shook the building, blasting pieces of plaster and wood through the room. Brigitte was thrown off her feet, and a cluster of splinters lodged into her cheek just below her eye socket. She ignored them and pulled herself up, looking around for Freisler. The smoke and dust were thick, and for a moment she was afraid he had escaped. But then she heard a phlegmy cough and spotted him a few feet away. The explosion had knocked him back against his desk. He brushed himself off and looked around for the door.

The needle was still in her hand. *Now! Do it now!* She gripped the needle tighter.

"You're not going anywhere," she said.

"I said let—" he started to say, but his voice was drowned out by a loud *KER-ACK*, like a great tree being felled, but amplified to a terrifying volume. They both looked up and saw the central beam in the ceiling splintering. Brigitte threw herself under a desk. Freisler, still clutching the stack of folders, was barely able to turn around before the beam crashed down on top of him.

Brigitte crawled out from under the desk and made her way over to the beam. Freisler lay under it, crushed but still conscious, blood streaming from the side of his mouth. He looked up at her, agony and panic in his eyes in equal measure.

"Help me," he whispered. "Please. The pain—"

He was dying. There was no help to give, nothing

she could do. She sat down on the floor beside the beam, took a deep breath, and exhaled. He would no longer be able to harm or destroy.

"Please do something," he cried. "It hurts."

She could put him out of his misery. It would be a kindness, a testament to her training. She was taught to heal regardless of her feelings about the individual. She looked down at the needle, then back at him. She saw the pleading in his eyes, begging her to end the pain. She leaned toward him.

"You're not worth it," she said.

She put the needle in her pocket, turned away from him, and leaned against the beam to wait it out.

It didn't take long. When his whimpering stopped, she counted out five minutes in perfect calm and quiet. She checked his pulse—making sure the release was complete, as she had been taught at the hospital—and when she could detect no beat, she walked out of the building.

She strolled down the street, ignoring the frantic crowds, the fires, the broken buildings. The deed was done, and she was at peace.

She ambled along, her thoughts coming in random order. *It's time for lunch.* She looked into the shop windows she passed and saw the splinters still stuck in her cheek. She pulled them out, ignoring the sting. *Otto will be pleased to hear he's dead. Is there a deli still standing in this town?* She glanced up with idle curiosity as a fire truck raced past, sirens blaring. *Wonder where I can find August. I can make lunch at his apartment. I wonder if it was damaged in the bombing.*

"Papers!"

Brigitte looked up to see two Gestapo agents barring her way.

One of them held out his hand.

"I don't have them. My bag is in there," she pointed back in a vague direction toward the courthouse, now a broken shell of a building. As she turned, she saw the car with the Gestapo insignia on the front. She had been so distracted she hadn't seen it.

The first agent nodded to the other, who patted her down until he found the lump in her pocket. He reached into her pocket and pulled out the needle.

"What is this?"

Brigitte said nothing.

The first agent took her arm and pushed her into the car. "Don't worry, we have ways of finding out."

Brigitte remained silent all the way to Gestapo headquarters. She knew what would happen now. She said a prayer of thanks that she wouldn't have to stand trial in Freisler's court.

Chapter Ninety-Five

A GUARD STRODE THE LONG CORRIDOR INSIDE THE Flossenberg Concentration Camp until he reached cell 43. He unlocked the door and looked with contempt on the grey-haired man, once a figure of strength and position, now a gaunt, withered shell of a man.

"Strip," the guard barked out.

Canaris stood and took off his clothes without a word. The old man's calm demeanor infuriated the guard, and he shoved the rifle into Canaris' back, pushing him into the corridor.

Canaris knew his show of dignity irritated the guard, so he walked with a regal bearing, ignoring the weapon slamming into his back.

Moments later Canaris entered the courtyard and joined Bonhoeffer, Oster, Sack, and Gehre—all of them naked. They nodded to each another with knowing and acceptance.

They were ordered to stand for sentencing, and the death sentence was pronounced for each of them. A makeshift scaffold was in the center of the courtyard with looped piano wires hanging from meat hooks.

There were no eulogies, no last rites. He stood beside Bonhoeffer and listened to him praying. He looked up to the heavens and smiled. *What an honor to die with this man.*

Canaris was the first to go. As the wire was fitted around his neck, he caught the eye of a man in the corner, recording every word, every movement. He knew the report would make its way to the Reich Main Security Office.

Dear God, he prayed, *if ever I deserved a moment of grace, let it be now in this one request—that you comfort August when he reads of this.*

He took a deep breath and gave a half smile, as he always did when a difficult task was completed with satisfaction.

~ ~ ~

The report reached August a few days later. He read it carefully, then put it face-down on his desk. He stared into the distance, his eyes brimming over. He reached into his secret pocket and pulled out a folded paper that Bonhoeffer had given him months ago.

Men go to God when he is sore bested
Find him poor and scorned, without shelter or
    bread
Whelmed under weight of the wicked, the
    weak, the dead
Christians stand by God in his hour of grieving

August soaked up the words, his hands trembling.

"The Fuhrer needs this report at once!"

August looked up, startled. Kaltenbrunner dropped a folder on his desk.

August took it, stashing the paper under some documents on his desk while he rubbed his eyes, feigning fatigue.

"Right away."

He stowed away Bonhoeffer's poem, picked up the folder, and headed out. An agent caught up with him and held out a slip of paper.

"The weather report you requested, sir."

August glanced at it. *The butcher*.

~ ~ ~

The shop was empty when August walked in. The butcher nodded a greeting.

"Cold front moving in?" August asked.

"I wondered if you'd get word. Kaltenbrunner's men are asses."

Even though no one was within earshot, the butcher leaned across the counter and spoke quietly. "She went to Auschwitz. She was alive a few months ago. They don't have any recent reports coming out of there."

August's heart sank but he kept his face impassive. "What about my nephew?"

The butcher shrugged. "They say some kids were smuggled out and sent to homes in Poland." He looked at August with kindness, but his voice was firm. "The odds are against finding them."

August nodded, close to defeat. He opened his mouth a few times, but closed it, afraid he would break down. When he found his voice, it was subdued.

"I know. But hope evens the odds." He turned to the door. "So I've been told."

Chapter Ninety-Six

THE CAR INCHED TOWARD HITLER'S BUNKER. RUBBLE blocked most of the way, but August steered through the devastation, lost in thought. His mind went back to the last time he saw his sister.

~ ~ ~

They had been in the living room at Helga's house in Oradour-sur-Glane one afternoon when Kurt was on call at the hospital. August rocked his nephew while Helga lounged on the sofa.

"I know what we look like to you. Like we ran away. Like cowards." Her voice was quiet and sad.

"I didn't say you were cowards—"

"You didn't have to. I know you. You never walked away from a fight, never shirked responsibility, not even the burden of raising me."

"It was no burden. I took—"

"Yes, you took action, August. It's what you do. And I love you for it." She shot up, her face animated the way he used to see it, when she was gearing up for a fight. "But for God's sake, August, we chose life! Isn't that action enough?"

"Okay. Yes." He mustered up his best debate stance. "But isn't there honor in being willing to die for a cause?"

The fire in her mellowed, and she started to cry. "Only if the cause is worth more than you are. I couldn't bear to lose you over something trivial."

He had let the argument go, not wanting to upset her further. He figured he could make his point another day, in another debate.

But there was no other day, no other debate. He never saw her again.

~ ~ ~

August drove on. Half-standing houses, piles of brick, and smoking heaps were all gliding by, but he paid no attention. When he arrived at the building, he pulled out his pistol and put it in the briefcase. *I'm going to do it. There's no one left to tell me no.*

He dashed into the building and strolled through the outer office. It was empty except for a few people sitting idle at their desks, tense and worried. Bombs hit the ground above, shaking the bunker and showering them with fine sprays of mortar and dust.

August ignored it all. He stopped at the door to Hitler's office. An aide looked up.

"Reports from the Security Office," August said in a formal tone.

The aide stood and held out his hand. "Your weapon."

"I left it at the entrance."

The aide reached for the briefcase. August pulled it back. "For the Fuhrer's eyes only," he said, his voice raised in a vague threat.

The aide started to challenge him, but just then the

door to Hitler's office opened.

A small blonde woman eased out and pulled the door closed behind her. Eva Braun, Hitler's longtime mistress and constant companion. She glided past them, quiet and unpretentious, and glanced up once with a quick smile.

August watched her for a moment then turned back to the aide, ready to press him for a private audience.

But he didn't have to. A bomb hit the building above them, rattling the chamber. The aide shrugged and led August into Hitler's office.

Hitler was slumped in his chair: small, bewildered, weary. And alone.

The aide left them together, closing the door behind him. August opened the briefcase and gazed at the pistol. Hitler looked up at him, curious.

"I'm glad you're here, Wichmann. I want your thoughts about the—"

"You want my thoughts? Fine." He started out quiet and agreeable, but then he stared at Hitler with contempt and his voice turned bitter. "I think I'm tired of all the lies, the deception, the subterfuge."

"What is the meaning of this—"

August walked around the desk and leaned in. "'Whelmed under weight of the wicked, the weak, the dead.' Those are Dietrich Bonhoeffer's words. Prophetic, aren't they? *You* did that to Germany."

"I think you are—"

"I don't *care* what you think. And neither does anyone else," he said in a deadly tone. "No, I'm not going to listen to what you think. I'm going to tell you what *I* think."

August grabbed the weapon and pressed it against Hitler's temple. Hitler looked sidelong at him, wild-eyed.

"I think I could put this bullet through your brain and not blink," August said. "I think a handful of people would mourn. That idiot Goebbels might make use of the moment, but everyone else—including the military —would cheer."

"Wichmann, you're going to—"

August gripped Hitler's collar and pulled it so tight that Hitler could barely breathe. August pressed the pistol harder against his temple.

"I'm not finished!" he roared. "You're weak and pathetic. Sending armies you don't even have to the front. Ordering atomic missiles to England that haven't been manufactured. What a clown you are. An imbecile."

A huge explosion from above shook the room. August saw the terror in Hitler's eyes.

"Hear that? That's the sound of your defeat. The Allies are outside of Berlin. They're coming for you. And what a shining example they'll make of you. 'Unconditional surrender.' You know what that means? It means they'll make you dance around like a monkey when they capture you."

He yanked Hitler's face closer. "Unless I finish you first. And believe me, it will be a pleasure, even if it costs me my life. A crowning achievement. The world will praise me for it."

The intercom burst into life. The aide's voice came through.

"Mein Fuhrer? The doctor is here."

August lowered the pistol and released his grip on Hitler's collar. His breath, at first short and agitated, calmed down. He stared Hitler down. When he spoke, his voice was low and deadly.

"Know what else I think? Canaris was right. It's not an even trade. Your death is not worth my life."

Hitler cowered and squinted, and his body shook. Specks of foam rolled down the side of his mouth.

August put the pistol back, picked up papers from the briefcase, and dumped them on the desk. He closed the briefcase just as a louder explosion from above rattled the bunker. Hitler looked up in alarm, shaking uncontrollably. August turned on his heel and walked out the door into the outer office.

The doctor was waiting, bag in hand. "How is he?" the doctor asked.

"He seems paranoid and delusional," August said. "A lot of incoherent babbling."

The doctor sighed. "Again?"

Chapter Ninety-Seven

IT WAS LATE WHEN AUGUST DRAGGED HIMSELF INTO his apartment. He dropped onto the sofa and put his head in his hands. He chased the questions around in his mind. *I had him. I could have done it. Why didn't I?*

He heard the bed creak, then soft footsteps. He grabbed his weapon and was on his feet, holding aim at the door, waiting for the intruder to emerge.

A vision in white crept around the corner: snowy attire, translucent skin. He inched over, still holding the weapon—and saw that it was Brigitte. Or a shadow of her.

The white vision fused into the reality of his t-shirt over a gaunt frame. Her hair was cropped above her ears, and dark circles rimmed bony cheeks. He put down his gun and dashed over to her.

He wrapped his arm around her shoulders. "Thank God you're alive," he whispered. She clung to him and nodded.

She reminded him of Dina, the girl who had to dig herself out of a mass grave. *Dear God, what has she been through?* He needed to know what had happened, but he dreaded hearing the truth.

He led her to the sofa and wrapped both arms

around her, enveloping her in warmth and safety.

"Where were you? How did you get here?"

"Dachau," she whispered. "The American Army liberated it yesterday. One of the soldiers gave me a ride to Berlin."

They stayed that way for some time—minutes? hours? days? He couldn't tell—until she spoke again.

"I didn't kill him," she said in a low voice, strained with a mixture of relief and regret. "The judge. Freisler. I was there when the building collapsed. He was dying. There was nothing I could do. And he begged me to finish it for him. He saw the needle. I had one of my needles there. I know you said I shouldn't carry them. That I'd get caught. And you were right."

She was talking fast, edgy and high-strung, purging the story from her soul. "That's what they got me on, did you know that? Everything I did, and they put me in a concentration camp because I was carrying a needle with T-4 in it. After all I did, that's what got me arrested."

She let out an incoherent giggle. After a few moments, her giggle softened into a few sniffles and then a slow steady weeping.

"You were right, August. You said I'd be caught. And you were right."

He held her tight and kissed the top of her head. "Shhh. It's okay."

"They questioned me for three days. The same questions over and over. And I had the same answers. They learned nothing from me. Bogart was a good teacher."

She leaned against him. He felt her tears soaking his shirt.

"I don't know what happened to Bogart," she said in a soft, wondering tone. "Or Otto. I hope they're alive."

She went silent for a while, then started up again.

"I saw Frau Gerhard there. At the camp. You never met her, did you? Such a sweet lady. She didn't make it. They sent her to the gas. A couple of days before it was liberated. I wish she could have made it. She asked me once if I knew where her husband went. I didn't know, but I told her I heard he escaped. It was a lie, but it made her happy. Sometimes the lie isn't bad. Not when it gives hope."

"You did the right thing," August said.

She shrugged. "That's what Pastor Niemoller said."

"You saw him?"

She nodded. "I talked to him a few times. I told him about the judge. The reason why I didn't kill him."

"You were trained to heal. That's why you didn't do it."

She wrenched around to face him. "That's not it, though. I didn't *want* to heal him. I didn't *want* him to have a mercy killing. I wanted him to suffer."

"It's okay," he soothed.

"It's not okay." She wiped her tears with the back of her hand, then moved to a chair on the other side of the room. "My whole life I've wanted to ease the pain others feel. I told Bogart if I had to kill, I wanted it to be painless. That's why I carried the needles."

She broke into sobs again, so hard she couldn't talk. Several times she opened her mouth, but the words wouldn't form. After a few moments, it rose up out of her in a high-pitched wailing: raw, unmitigated truth.

"August, I sat there and waited for him to die. And I wanted it to take a long time. He was gone anyway. I could have ended his suffering. But I didn't, not even when he begged. What kind of healer would do that?" She held out her hands palms up, pleading. "He won in the end, didn't he? All that was good in me was stripped away."

August went over, knelt in front of her, and looked into her eyes. "No, no! He didn't win, you did! You're alive."

He took her hands and kissed them. "Dietrich told me that you have the heart of a healer. And he's right. No one could strip that away."

She looked off into the distance. "He told me something like that too. He said healing was a gift from God and that the gifts and calling of God are irrevocable." She smiled at the memory.

She looked back at August. "Is he still in prison?"

August looked down and shook his head.

And she saw his pain.

She took his hand and led him to the bedroom. She helped him out of his uniform and tossed it ruthlessly onto the floor. She lay next to him, facing away, but she snuggled against him so they were spooning. She pulled his arm over her side and clasped his hand.

Now calmer—the memory of Bonhoeffer's words had washed over her, easing some of her doubts and fears—she talked about the two months she'd spent at Dachau. The back-breaking work. The hunger. The daily threat of the gas chambers and incinerators. She insisted she was better off than many who had been there for years. August listened in silence, with an occasional kiss on her head or caress of her arm.

She spoke softly, a light melodious melancholy, but she grew animated when she described the moment the Allies liberated the camp.

"The United States Seventh Army's 45th Infantry Division, those are my heroes," she said. "That American flag was the most beautiful thing I've ever seen. And the soldiers were magnificent. So kind. And so brave. I wanted to help them, so I told the soldier who gave me a ride where he could find a stockpile of supplies," she said.

"An excellent payback," he said, kissing her neck.

She turned around to face him. "Tell me about what happened to Dietrich."

He was silent at first, searching for the right words, wanting to spare her any grief. But she was owed the truth, honest and unvarnished.

"He was executed." His voice was quiet, solemn. "So were Oster, Dohnanyi, several others. The admiral too. Implicated in the assassination plot. Death by hanging. I heard that Hitler filmed a lot of the executions so he could watch them over and over."

She caressed his cheek, his forehead, his brow. A tear rolled down from the corner of his eye, and she wiped it away.

"I went to Hitler's bunker today," he said. "I was going to kill him. I even had my gun pressed against his temple at one point."

"Why didn't you do it?"

He shook his head. "I–I don't–" He stopped and thought for a moment. "Something came to me in the middle of it all. The admiral had said something to me a few months ago about it not being worth it. That Hitler's death was not worth my life. So I hesitated. I wish I had just done it. I probably won't have that chance again."

She laced her hands behind his head, pulled him close, and kissed him. "Don't second-guess it," she said. "Canaris was right."

He closed his eyes and nodded. "The admiral was always right."

Chapter Ninety-Eight

AUGUST HADN'T PLANNED TO GO TO WORK. IN FACT, he never wanted to set foot in the building again, no matter the consequences. But Brigitte convinced him it was a good idea to find out what was happening.

The following morning, he made his way to the Reich Main Security Office, intending to keep a low profile.

Everything was in an uproar. People huddled together in small groups, whispering together, shaking their heads in disbelief. The room was rife with contained panic.

August glanced around on his way into Kaltenbrunner's office. He tossed his thumb over his shoulder, motioning to the others.

"What's going on?"

"We just got word," Kaltenbrunner said, his voice somber, a touch on edge. "Hitler committed suicide last night. He and Eva Braun."

"Is that so?"

"The Goebbels family too," he said, near tears. "It's a disaster."

August left Kaltenbrunner staring into the distance, lost and bereft. He went back to his desk and watched the chaos in the office without expression.

"I'd call it trivial," he said to himself.

He stared off into the distance, forming an image in his mind of the statue of Hitler that stood in the public square. In his mind's eye, he saw the statue teeter, begin a slow descent, and then crash to the ground, shattering into a million pieces.

The phone rang, bringing him back to the present. He picked it up.

"Wichmann." He listened for a moment, his face lighting up. "Of course. I'll be right there."

~ ~ ~

August dashed to the café, his walk brisk and eager. He found Frau Canaris at a bistro table outside. He sat across from her.

"I'm sorry that ..." he began. He wasn't sure exactly what to say or what he could offer. He was just pleased that she had called him.

But she hadn't come for his care and compassion. She interrupted him, brushing away his awkward attempts at comfort.

"Just before he was led away, Willi asked me to give you this." She held out a folded note to August.

He flipped it over but didn't unfold it. "What is it?"

"Something Dietrich wrote. Willi carried it around for some time. He handed it to me when they came to arrest him," she said.

August looked at the paper and nodded, loath to speak for fear his voice would break.

She pulled several papers out of her bag. "And he updated his will." She handed them over to August.

He scanned them and looked up.

"You're sure?" he asked.

She gave him a brief smile, then walked to the edge of the building and tugged gently on two leashes. She led the dogs around the table. They sat before August and looked up expectantly.

She bent down to pet them. "I'm sure." She looked up at him and smiled. "He trusted you."

She petted the dogs once more, then stood and walked away. August gripped the leashes firmly and watched her shuffle down the street.

Chapter Ninety-Nine

AUGUST LED THE DOGS INTO THE APARTMENT. THEY sniffed, looked around, alert, then broke away from him and bounded into the living room.

"Kaspar! Sabine!"

Brigitte's joyful greeting reached him, and he sagged with relief. *She's still here. Thank God.*

He found some meat in the refrigerator, put it on plates on the floor, and whistled. They came running.

He went into the living room and collapsed onto the sofa.

"They have great memories," he said. "They still remember you.

She smiled. "Kaspar and Sabine are old friends of mine."

He pulled out the note and unfolded it. Brigitte curled up next to him.

August read out loud the words that gave life once more to Bonhoeffer's voice of faith.

"I believe that God can and will bring good out of evil, even out of the greatest evil. For that purpose, he needs men who make the best use of everything."

His voice started to shake. "I believe that even our mistakes and shortcomings are turned to good account, and that it is no harder for God to deal with them than with our supposedly good deeds."

He paused and took a deep breath. *Bonhoeffer. What insights he'd had, what vision into men's souls. What a loss to the world.*

He pressed on. "We have been silent witnesses of evil deeds; we have been drenched by many storms; we have learnt the art of equivocation and pretenses; experiences have made us suspicious of others."

His voice cracked, and he couldn't go on. He put the paper down.

Brigitte picked it up and read aloud. "Will our inward power of resistance be strong enough, and our honesty with ourselves remorseless enough, for us to find our way back?"

She pointed to a note in the margin. "What's this?"

August studied it. "That's the admiral's handwriting."

"August is the only one who can do this," Brigitte read.

August looked into the distance. His heart ached to see the old man again, to banter with him, to share his hopes and fears. *August is the only one...*

The admiral had trusted him, had believed in him—and that was a rare gift.

He folded the note with care and tucked it into the secret pocket. He looked at Brigitte. The admiral had trusted her too. He took her hand and kissed it. "I'm so glad you're here."

The dogs trotted into the living room and sat in front of them, looking back and forth from August to Brigitte.

"They look ready for an adventure," she said, then regarded his uniform. "Why don't you get changed?"

He squeezed her hand and went into the bedroom.

She called to him, "And bring me your uniform."

He came back in civilian clothes and handed her the uniform.

She held up a pair of scissors and smiled. "Never again."

Within a few minutes his uniform lay shredded in pieces on the floor.

"Niemoller would be proud," he said.

"When we find him, we'll tell him," she said.

He surveyed her handiwork. "It'll be the only clue when the Gestapo comes looking for me.

"Think they'll find us?" she asked.

"Not a chance. They won't be looking for a farmer and milkmaid bringing crops to market."

"Or an inspector with his assistant."

"Or a civil servant on holiday with his wife."

"We can be anyone, can't we?"

They laughed, embraced, and kissed. The dogs jumped up between them.

August petted them. "You can keep a secret, can't you?" he said to the dogs. "I have it on good authority that the Allies are on their way."

He attached the leashes and stood up.

"And Auschwitz is liberated," Brigitte said, taking his arm. "Let's go find them."

The dogs gave a happy bark and pulled them out the door.

Afterword

Executed together at Flossenberg
on April 9, 1945, were:

Admiral Wilhelm Canaris
Pastor Dietrich Bonhoeffer
Major General Has Oster
Judge Advocate General Karl Sack
Captain Ludwig Gehre

On the same day they were executed,
Hans von Dohnanyi
was hanged at Sachsenhausen.

Two weeks after their executions,
the concentration camps at
Flossenberg, Sachsenhausen, and Dachau
were liberated by the Allies.

Martin Niemoller, who had spent time
in both Sachsenhausen and Dachau,
was among those freed.

Three weeks after their executions, Hitler committed suicide.

One month after their executions, the Germans surrendered to the Allies.

Four months after their executions, Japan surrendered to the Allies. The war was officially over.

What followed were moments—days, weeks, years—of anguish as the world became aware of the barbarism committed by the Nazis.

The Nuremberg War Crimes Trial revealed Canaris' strenuous efforts in trying to put a stop to the crimes of war and genocide. Reports from witnesses of how honorably he had sought to end both the war and the war crimes gave him the eulogy he deserved.

Today, Bonhoeffer's "Letters and Papers from Prison" and his other writings tell part of his story and give the world a model of the full meaning and cost of discipleship.